Also by Caridad Piñeiro

At the Shore Series
One Summer Night
What Happens in Summer

The

FAMILY SHE NEVER MET

CARIDAD PIÑEIRO

sourcebooks
casablanca

Published by Sourcebooks Casablanca, an imprint of Sourcebooks
P.O. Box 4410, Naperville, Illinois 60567-4410
(630) 961-3900
sourcebooks.com

Cataloging-in-Publication Data is on file with the Library of Congress.

Printed and bound in Canada.
MBP 10 9 8 7 6 5 4 3 2 1

This book is dedicated to those who dared to dream:

Antonio and Nieves Gonzalez, Celsina and Salvatore Scordato,
and Elizabeth and Vincent Yervasi;
My mother, Carmen Piñeiro, who sacrificed so much
for her family and for a free Cuba; and
the United States of America and its wonderful people, who have made
it possible for so many of us to achieve the American Dream.

Chapter One

"I KNOW YOU THINK I'm crazy to ask this of you, *mi'jo*."

Luis Torres examined the features of the elegant woman seated across from him in the shade of the large market umbrella. While outwardly calm, he couldn't fail to see the slight lines of tension on skin that was surprisingly smooth for an eighty-three-year-old. He also knew that she was anything but crazy. Stubborn, intelligent, determined, and loving—but never ever crazy.

"I appreciate how important this is for you, Carmen," he began, but she cut him off with an imperious slash of a bejeweled hand. Gold bangles danced musically on her thin wrist with the movement.

"I don't think you do, Luis," she said with a determined tilt of her head, her green-eyed gaze pure steel as it locked with his.

In the years that he had known the older woman, he had carried out many assignments for her, but he sensed none were as important as this one. Sadly, he also recognized that whether he succeeded or failed, there was the possibility that Carmen would pay for it with incredible pain. He loved her too much to allow that to occur.

"*Viejita*," he began with affection and covered her hand with his as it rested on the wrought iron table before him. "Have you thought about what will happen if she comes and it turns into—"

"A hot mess? Is that what you would call it?" she said with an indulgent smile and playfully smacked his hand to try to alleviate his concern. "It's a risk I'm willing to take," she added in a tone which brooked no disagreement.

But am I willing to take that risk? Luis thought. He remained silent as Carmen's majordomo approached the patio table, wheeling a tray with covered dishes, crystal wineglasses, and a pitcher of white sangria swimming with slices of citrus and berries.

"I hope you don't mind that I asked Manny to prepare lunch for us. *Gracias*, Manny," Carmen said and peered at Luis, almost daring him to refuse with a pointed lift of a perfectly shaped brow. He was beyond tempted to refuse. Lunch was just a ploy for Carmen to continue pressing him to undertake what he thought was a fool's errand.

He wasn't wrong. As soon as Manny had finished serving them a delicately prepared lobster salad and filled their glasses to the brim with sangria, Carmen resumed their earlier discussion.

"I'm asking you to do this as a personal favor. I have my reasons," she began as she speared some of the lobster.

"You're okay, *verdad?*" he asked, worried she was keeping something important from him, like a health scare.

"I'm fine. *No te preocupes*," she said and met his gaze directly, relieving some of his worry.

Luis stared past her and the carefully manicured lawn to the waters beyond Star Island and the skyline of South Beach in the distance. Sun shimmered on the calm waters of Biscayne Bay while a soft breeze teased the fronds of the palm trees along the edges of the multimillion-dollar property, a testament to Carmen's fortitude and her belief in the American Dream. A dream she had selflessly shared with others like him and his family. It was what made it so hard for him to refuse her request.

Peering back in her direction, he couldn't deny that, as vibrant and dynamic as she still was, Carmen was no longer the woman he remembered meeting as a young boy. Her luscious, thick black hair was now a shock of carefully coiffed white. What had once been voluptuous Cuban curves had thinned with age, and that indomitable energy that had so captured his attention had ebbed somewhat. It was part of the reason why, over the years, she had turned over more and more of her duties to her daughters, grandchildren, and him, of course. As president of Guerreiro Enterprises, she had come to rely on him for so much, but this request…

"What if I go and she says no?" It was a very real possibility, considering that they'd had no contact with that part of the family in over thirty years.

Carmen chided him with a shake of her head and chuckled softly. "*Mi'jo, por favor.* I know how persuasive you can be."

He couldn't refute that. But his logical side told him to rebuff Carmen's request. If it did become an epic fail it could only bring her a world of hurt. His emotional side, however, understood only too well what it was like to be missing a piece of yourself. Since the day his family had fled Cuba during the Mariel boatlift, they'd longed for the island they'd left behind. Like so many exiled Cubans, they'd passed that yearning on to their children, but it was a hopeless dream, unlike Carmen's very real wish. A wish that he could help fulfill for a woman who'd given so many so much.

Picking up his glass of white sangria, he raised it in a toast and said, "Here's to being persuasive."

Carmen smiled, raised her glass, and clinked it against his. "I knew you would do it."

A sharp laugh burst from him, and he dipped his head in acknowledgment. "Of course you did, *viejita.* You were the one who taught me, after all."

Jessica Russo closed her eyes and ran her hand across the surface of the tabletop. She had spent the better part of the morning cleaning and sanding off nearly a century of grime and varnish to reveal the beauty of the wood. The oak was smooth beneath her fingers, and she imagined how many hands might have touched the table over the years. The families who might have shared a meal on its surface or hung out playing a game of cards or doing a puzzle. Families like her own big, boisterous, and loving Italian family.

It was one of the reasons she treasured what she did so much: because the pieces spoke to her about the past and the lives they had touched. Bringing the pieces new life was not only emotionally rewarding, it had let her make a nice life for herself and others.

Opening her eyes, she cleaned off the last of the sanding dust from the top and legs of the folding table. The piece had called to her as soon as Jessica had spotted it at an upstate flea market because it was perfect for the New York City millennials and hipsters who frequented her Brooklyn-based shop. With its simple folding legs, the table would fit in a closet or under a bed for those who had smaller apartments and couldn't give up the space to a permanent dining table.

Jessica grabbed a can of dark espresso stain from a shelf and a rag to spread the liquid over the surface of the piece. She eased on nitrile gloves and lovingly worked the stain into the oak, running with the grain and removing any excess to make sure the color was even. She had just finished the first application when Sandy, one of the local moms who worked the storefront for her part-time, hurried into her workshop.

Sandy seemed a little agitated as she jerked a finger in the direction of the customer area. "There's a man here to see you."

Puzzled, Jessica tried to remember if she'd scheduled any appointments for that afternoon, but as far as she knew, she hadn't. "Did you get his name?" she asked.

Sandy fidgeted from one foot to the next and wrung her hands together. "He wouldn't give it. He just insisted that I get you. 'For a private matter,'" Sandy advised, emphasizing the man's words with air quotes.

Weird, Jessica thought. She kept private things to her small circle of close friends and her immense Italian family. Of course, once family got involved, there was no such thing as private.

"Does he seem like trouble?" Jessica asked as she yanked off the nitrile gloves with a snap, grabbed her phone, and opened the security camera app for a glimpse of the unexpected visitor. Flipping to the view of the storefront, she shifted the camera until she could get a good look at him.

Trouble, all right, but not in a criminal kind of way. He had the kind of looks and confidence that said he could be difficult.

Her visitor was dressed in a light-colored suit that hugged broad shoulders and lean hips. Dark hair topped a handsome face and he looked none too pleased at having to wait. He moved with nervous energy from one piece of furniture to the next, skimming his fingers across the surfaces before he whirled, stared straight at the camera, and jammed his hands in his pockets.

With a chuckle, Jessica said, "No worries. I can handle him." After all, she was used to dealing with the high-powered and sometimes egotistical financial types that came into her shop.

She slipped the smartphone into the front pocket of her overalls and hurried into the store, annoyed that her work had been interrupted and feeling decidedly grungy in her paint- and stain-splattered overalls and ripped T-shirt. She liked to be at her best when seeing prospective customers, and this man had placed her at a decided disadvantage. He was well-heeled and clearly well-off.

The linen suit was obviously bespoke and perfectly fitted to his lean body, but lightweight for a chilly New York City spring day. A hint of a shirt in pastel pink peeked out from beneath the collar. Gold glinted on one wrist and a big and expensive wristwatch wrapped around his other.

"How can I help you?" she said as she approached him. He stood staring at a combo bar/console against one wall of her store's showroom.

He turned and met her gaze full-on. His eyes were a dark hazel shot through with strands of green and gold in a face far more handsome than it had looked on her smartphone screen. Sharply chiseled features were softened by full lips and long, thick lashes. His dark hair was closer to black than brown with bed-tousled waves.

"Jessica Russo, I presume?" It was impossible to miss the hint of annoyance in his tone as well as a slight singsong that said he wasn't a New Yorker.

"I am. How can I help you?" she repeated, eager to get back to work.

He stepped closer, forcing her to look up, thanks to his much greater height. He had nearly a foot on her and the proximity to so much masculinity was surprisingly disconcerting.

She gave him props for sensing that she was uncomfortable and taking a step away. "I came to speak to you about your grandmother."

Fear replaced her earlier emotions. She laid a hand across her stomach to quell the distress and also her confusion. Her grandmother Russo was relatively young, so he had to be referring to her ninety-three-year-old great-grandmother, who insisted on living alone in her own home. But nothing about this man said "cop," so she tempered her concerns that he might be there with bad news. "Is *Bisnonna* Russo okay? Nothing's happened, right?" she asked.

His full lips thinned into a knife-sharp line, and irritation blossomed in his eyes. "I'm here about your *abuela* Gonzalez and to ask for a favor."

The fright she had experienced just moments earlier fled and a maelstrom of emotions filled that vacuum. They swirled together as powerfully as a Category 5 hurricane.

"My mother's mother?" she asked, confusion and surprise taking control of her emotions.

He dipped his head regally. "Yes, your Gonzalez grandmother.

And as I said, I'm here to ask a favor," he explained in calm tones, but Jessica was feeling anything but calm.

"For yourself or for her?" she challenged, a growing spiral of anger twisting into the emotional storm within her. Whenever she had asked about her maternal grandparents, her mother's gaze would cloud with pain, warning her that it was a topic not to be discussed.

"For her and hopefully for you as well," he urged, his tone persuasive but unconvincing.

"I think I've been doing just fine for myself the last twenty-eight years," she shot back. Her mother's Miami family had never been a part of her life, and as far as she was concerned, it could stay that way. Giving in to the request was bound to cause hurt for everyone involved.

He seemed chastened by her statement and tried a different tack. "Your grandmother loves you and your mother very much. It's why she sent me here to ask you to visit with her."

She crossed her arms and tilted her head up a determined inch. "Funny way to show her love, considering she hasn't been around for all of my life. And I'm too busy to leave the shop right now."

He peered around the empty store in obvious disbelief. "Doesn't seem too busy to me."

"It's a weekday and the middle of the afternoon," she said and then shook her head. "You know, I don't need to explain anything to you. And who are you, anyway?"

He reached into his inside jacket pocket and took out a business card that he presented to her. The cardstock weight was heavy, and the card had his name embossed in bold gold. Not a cheap online business card by any means. "I'm Luis Torres, President of Guerreiro Enterprises, but more important, I'm a man who owes a great deal to a woman who wants to meet her granddaughter before...let's just say it's time to set things to rights."

He hadn't said it, but the reason for the request hung there like a great big softball waiting to be hit out of the park. *It's time to set things to rights before time runs out and she dies.*

Before Jessica could say anything, he reached out and laid a hand over hers, the gesture meant to reassure. He squeezed her hand gently and said, "I know this has probably come as a shock—"

"Says the Master of Understatement," she parried, but without sting because she sensed the sincerity in his request.

With a dip of his head, he continued. "I understand. All I'm asking is that you think about it. For an old woman who doesn't want to end her life without knowing her granddaughter. *Por favor*," he said, his gaze teeming with emotion. The tone of his voice was filled with concern and not just for the grandmother she had never met.

Somehow, she sensed that he wasn't the kind of man used to asking, and that made his request all the more powerful. But it wasn't enough to alleviate the worry she had about meeting a woman who had apparently driven her daughter from her Miami home and never made any effort to end the rift between them.

"I appreciate how important this is to you," she said.

"*To her*, Jessica. This is very important *to her*. To *you* as well. Before it's too late to make things right," he said, once again strumming her heart strings and rousing compassion. But she had to protect her own heart and her mother's as well.

Because of that, all she could say was "I'll think about it, Mr. Torres."

He squeezed her hand gently again and said, "Luis, *por favor.* And thank you. I know this can't be an easy decision for you to make."

"It isn't…Luis." She held up his business card and said, "Can I reach you at this number?"

He nodded. "I'll be at the Mandarin Oriental all week."

"Try the veal," she quipped, but he just stared at her as if he didn't understand the old joke, so she charged on. "I'll call as soon as I can."

"I'd appreciate that," he said, leaned down, and brushed a quick kiss across her cheek.

Before she could protest the gesture, he turned and hurried from her shop, leaving her to ponder what to do about his request.

At a slight noise behind her, she whirled to find Sandy returning to the showroom. "I guess he wasn't trouble after all," Sandy said with a smirk.

Jessica blew out a harsh breath and shook her head. "That remains to be seen," she replied and headed back toward her workroom. Work always made her feel better and let her clear her mind of anything that bothered her. Luis Torres and his request definitely bothered her, only she wasn't sure she had enough projects to work on to restore peace to her world.

Chapter Two

FOR SO LONG, LARA had forced any memories of her mother and Cuba from her mind—they were just too painful. And now her daughter sat before her, asking for those memories. Wanting to resurrect them and bring her mother, Carmen, back into their lives.

"I don't want to talk about this, Jessica," she said and looked away from her daughter. Jessica was so much like Carmen at times, both in looks and temperament, that it almost hurt to see her. Much like it hurt to look in the mirror and see her own face, since she favored her mother strongly also. As Lara aged, she looked more and more like the woman she had left in Miami thirty years earlier.

Her husband, Salvatore, laid a hand on her shoulder, the gesture reassuring. "Maybe it's time, Lara," he said, the tone of his voice soft. Soothing. Ever the mediator.

Lara shook her head. "I don't know if it could ever be time for this discussion."

"Mom, *please*. I love you and I don't want to hurt you, but I need to understand," Jessica said, her tone pleading. Insistent. Like Lara's mother, Carmen, when Jessica wanted something, she didn't let go.

Lara sucked in a deep breath, bracing herself. *Where to begin?* she wondered. *Which hurt should I pull the bandage from, exposing the still unhealed wound to my daughter?*

She faced Jessica and her daughter's green-eyed gaze locked on hers, demanding an answer.

Maybe it is time, she thought and began. "I was four when she left Cuba."

———————————

Havana, April 1959

The dirty black boots stomped across the floor, leaving footprints and clods of soil on Abuela's freshly mopped tiles.

Clomp. Clomp. Clomp. The force of the footfalls shook the terracotta beneath her body. The vibrations grew stronger the closer the soldiers got to the bed. The toe of a worn black boot, caked with mud, skimmed the bottom edge of the pale pink bed skirt.

Lara huddled into an even tighter ball and hugged the wall closest to the headboard. She had learned to make herself so small in that darkest bit of space that the soldiers never ever saw her when they came. And they came quite often.

As had happened dozens of times before, a dirt-smudged hand lifted the bed skirt. Higher and higher until a young soldier with a face covered in a scraggly beard peered beneath the bed, searching for her. Squinting his eyes as if to see better. She shrank even smaller as he sought her out. She might have only been four, but she knew this was no game of hide and seek.

"*Vamos, viejita. Donde esta la niña?*" asked the soldier who was barely out of his teens.

They always want to find me, but I'm so good at hiding, Lara thought and hugged her little baby doll tighter.

Her *abuela* huffed out a reply. "*Donde debe estar. Con su mama,*" she answered, only Lara wasn't with her mother.

Her *mami* had left her, and even though Abuelita said they would be together soon, it hadn't happened. Months and months of waiting. Of phone calls and letters and her *mami* was still gone.

Her *mami* had left her, and Lara was afraid she'd never come back.

"She left you?" Jessica said, eyes wide with surprise. "Like, left you in Cuba when she came here?"

Lara nodded and looked away from that green-eyed gaze again, pain twisting her gut into a knot. "The secret police were after her and other former members of the Civic Resistance who had banded together after *la Revolución* became something they didn't want. She had to leave to avoid jail...or worse."

"Worse?" Jessica squeaked out.

"Torture. Death. For months, Castro and his friend Che were busy eliminating anyone who might pose a threat to their vision for a new Cuba," Lara explained. Not that she had known that at the time. All she'd known was that she was alone with her grandparents, wondering where Mami had gone and why the soldiers came so often to spread their fear. Papi had left months earlier, already in danger since he'd been a police officer under Batista. The fact that he had worked with the Resistance to help Castro might not have been enough to save him from Che's firing squads.

"So she had a good reason for leaving?" Jessica said, and even though it was true, Lara hated that Jessica was defending her mother's abandonment. Lara would never have left her baby alone. Never. And that had only been the beginning of Carmen's abandonment.

She whipped her head around and nailed Jessica with her gaze. "Maybe she did, but what reason did she have to ignore me when I finally got to Miami? She was always working or out of the house at one meeting or another. And she was having another baby! I know it's irrational, but all I could wonder was if she was replacing me."

"Mom, I know you don't believe that. That she was replacing you," Jessica pressed, but Lara was too far gone for reason and forged ahead, revealing the wounds she'd kept hidden for decades.

"She spent most of her free time with other exiles, plotting a return to Cuba. *Volveremos*, they'd say and sing their sad songs about leaving and going back. Only they never did go back, did they?" Her voice rose with each word until she was almost yelling. Her body shook with the anger she had kept bottled up for so long, and it was all she could do to maintain control.

"No, Mom, they didn't. That must have been hard for them," Jessica said, and her daughter's defense was too much for Lara. Too much to keep the pressure of that roiling anger from erupting like a volcano spewing lava, her hurt gushing from her soul as she bolted to her feet and wrapped her arms around herself.

"What about me, Jess? How hard was it for me not to have a mother who cared about me? A father as well, since he kept on leaving until one day when he didn't come back," she said, jabbing a finger in her chest.

"I understand, Mom. You were always there for me. Dad too. I can't imagine what it would be like not to have that," Jessica said, hands splayed on the table before her as if to steady herself. Salvatore went to Jessica's side and wrapped an arm around their daughter but peered at Lara, his warm, brown gaze offering reassurance.

With a shrug and a nod, Lara swiped away tears from her cheeks and said, "For years I tried to understand, but then I just gave up. I had my sisters and my friends and that was enough, until I went off to college and met your father." She held her hand out to her husband who moved from beside Jessica and took hold of Lara's hand. He smiled at her, and in that moment, the years of hurt faded and she was whole again.

Her gaze wed to her husband's, Lara said, "Carmen finally woke up to the fact I was alive when I said we were getting married and I was staying in New York. She wanted me to return to Miami and join the family business."

"But you left and never went back? Not even to see your sisters?" Jessica asked, brows knitted together as she considered Lara's words.

"My sisters sided with her. They wanted me in Miami as well and worried that Sal was only interested in me for our money."

"Your money?" Jessica asked, obviously puzzled.

Lara shared a look with Sal, and after he nodded, she finally answered. "My family's business had become quite successful."

"And I was just the son of a plumber from Brooklyn. First ever to graduate college in my family," Sal said with a dimpled grin that made him look years younger. Almost like when she had first met him at a freshman-orientation mixer. Except for the salt and pepper in his now-thinning hair and the tire slowly inflating around his middle.

"But you have your own successful business," Jessica said in her father's defense.

He does, and since there is little else to say, it's time to end this discussion, Lara thought.

"None of that mattered to my mother. *Nothing* I wanted *ever* mattered to her. And she didn't give up even after we were married. She kept on reaching out to me for years, pushing for me to come back to Miami. She was selfish then and she's selfish now," Lara said, brooking no disagreement, but as she glanced at her daughter, she sensed that none of this had been enough to dissuade Jessica.

"Mom, I get that she's hurt you. But to never talk to her or your sisters? You and Dad...you're always the ones to say family comes first," Jessica said.

"Family does come first, Jess," her father repeated and shot a worried look between Lara and his daughter.

With a determined nod and lift of her dimpled chin, Jessica said, "Then I guess you understand why I have to go. Why I have to know more about them."

It was more than Lara could take. She slammed her hands on the kitchen table and leaned toward her daughter. "You are not going to Miami."

Jessica stood and came closer until they were almost nose to nose. "I *am* going, Mom. I need to make my own decisions about this."

"This?" Lara screamed and reared back from the table. She wrapped her arms around herself again and walked around in a circle, trying to find her footing, before whirling to face her daughter. "What is there to decide, Jessica? If I'm to blame for our estrangement? Is that it?"

In truth, Lara had asked herself that time and time again over the years. Was she being selfish not to understand her mother had had important things to do? Was she lacking somehow? Was that the reason her mother had only had time for her sisters? For her business? For strangers even?

Jessica's gentle touch on her arm brought her back from those self-hating thoughts. "You're not to blame, Mom, but I need to know the why of this. Why this happened. Maybe even how to make it right," she said.

Lara blew out a breath, tears shimmering in her gaze. "Make it right? It can never be right," she said, shaking her head, but she knew Jessica would not leave it alone.

"I'm going. Nothing you or Dad can say right now will stop me," Jessica said, and before either she or Sal could utter another word, Jessica rushed from the room.

Sal's touch came on her shoulder again, and he drew her close, wrapping his arms around her. "It'll be fine, Lara. She'll go, meet her, and then be home before you know it. Her life is here. With us."

Lara burrowed her head against his shoulder, as if by doing so she could blot out the world around her. How she wished she could be as certain as her husband, but inside she was still that scared little four-year-old hiding under the bed. Hiding from the monster just beyond the bed skirt, waiting to devour her. Waiting for a mother's love that never came.

"I hope so, Sal. I don't want to lose her too," she said. She'd already lost too much in her life. A Cuba she barely remembered. Her mother and sisters. The Miami of her youth.

She couldn't bear the thought of losing her daughter as well.

Like your mother lost you? the little voice in her head chided, but Lara beat it back.

For over thirty years she'd survived just fine, and she'd get through this as well.

———————————— ⬥ ————————————

Carmen had sent him to do a difficult task, but Luis was determined not to fail, even if he thought it might cause hurt for everyone involved. It was the reason why he'd agreed to join Jessica for dinner once she had called the day after their short meeting.

She'd suggested a restaurant not far from her shop in Williamsburg, a ploy he recognized well from his many years in business. On her turf, she'd have more control of the situation, but he'd acquiesced because the stakes were high, and a familiar place might make her more receptive to his plea.

As he walked in and was led to a table where Jessica sat, he took note of the ambiance of the small restaurant. In some ways it struck him as being a lot like the woman waiting for him. A little edgy, with its industrial-style black-steel-pipe tables with wood tops, but also soaked in history, from the original brick walls to the distressed horseshoe-shaped wooden bar from another era.

She barely rose as he came to the table. He got it—she was calling the shots—but he wanted her to know he still had some say, and instead of sitting across from her, he took the closer spot next to her.

"Thank you for agreeing to meet with me, Jessica," he said as he took off his leather jacket and sat. The table was narrow, and beneath the surface, their knees bumped and prompted him to shift back slightly to give her space.

"I have to confess that I'm not sure what I'm doing here," she said, and her upset was apparent on her face. Her green eyes were emerald-dark, clearly troubled. The features of her face, pretty but not in a classic way, were tight and filled with anguish.

"I understand. To be honest, I had my concerns when Carmen— your *abuela*—asked me to do this," he admitted. Guilt filled him at the pain his request had likely caused, but he reminded himself he was only the messenger, and the pain...the pain had already been there for over a generation.

The waiter popped over at that moment, and Jessica said, "They have a great selection of their own microbrews. Burgers as well."

"*Por favor*, choose whatever you'd like," he said and held out a hand toward the menu in her hands.

She quickly placed an order for a pitcher of the house IPA and a cheeseburger, and he said, "I'll have a cheeseburger as well. Medium, please."

As the waiter stepped away, Jessica shook her head and chuckled. When he arched a brow in question, she said, "You don't strike me as the burger type."

"Burger's just chopped steak, right? I'm a steak kind of guy," he said with a shrug and a smile, trying to put her at ease.

A steak kind of guy sporting a very expensive leather jacket that he had tossed carelessly over his chair back. He was clearly successful and, as his business card had said, well-placed at the Guerreiro family business. Since their discussion yesterday, she'd wondered why he'd been the one chosen to deliver the very personal request. She reminded herself not to hate the messenger, since he was only doing as he'd been asked.

She leaned closer to examine him as she asked, "Why you?"

At his puzzled look, she clarified her question.

"Why didn't my grandmother reach out to me directly?"

His brow furrowed and he looked down, clearly pondering what to say, which only roused that storm of emotions from the day before. When he finally looked up, his hazel gaze was direct and straightforward. "You asked why Carmen sent me and that's simple: She trusts me to get things done because I owe her a great deal."

Wanting to know more, she gestured for him to continue, and he did.

"My family escaped Cuba during the Mariel boatlift in 1980. Over a hundred thousand refugees flooded Miami in just six months and they weren't welcomed by many. Your grandmother was one of the few people who was willing to give my family a chance, and that changed our lives forever."

She had no doubt he was sincere. It was there in his tone and in the way his gaze softened as he spoke. But it did little to appease the growing discontent she was beginning to feel once again. "You'll forgive me if I find it funny that she's willing to do so much for strangers and so little for her daughter."

He nodded in understanding but remained silent as the waiter placed glasses in front of them and filled them with beer from a pitcher. After he set the pitcher on the table and left, Luis raised his glass and said, "To what I hope is a new friendship."

Jessica eyed him intently, not sure if she could be friends with this man. Certain that if they got past the issues raised by her family's history, there might be other hurdles between them. Other challenges like the fact that a furniture flipper wasn't the kind of person wealthy CEOs had as friends. But for now, she'd go with it to keep the peace. "To new friends," she said and clinked her pint glass against his.

After taking a sip of the beer and offering an appreciative murmur, Luis continued with their earlier discussion. "I can't speak as to what your mother and grandmother have said to each other. That's not my story to share, but I can tell you that it would mean a lot to an old woman to be able to meet her grandchild."

She suspected that he did know what had been said but admired that he was willing to maintain the confidentiality of that discussion. She had already heard her mother's side of the story, but instead of clearing things up, it had only added to her confusion about the situation. Before she could say anything else, he said, "Didn't you ever wonder about your mom's family? About your Cuban roots?"

With a shrug, she said, "I did, but I could see my mother's pain whenever I asked, so I stopped asking. Plus I was lucky to have my dad's big Italian family to fill that empty space."

"Empty space. Interesting, but I get it," he said rather matter-of-factly, even though she sensed there was more to it. There was pain behind his words, much like the pain her mother hid. Because of that, she wanted to hear more of his story.

"You said your parents came here during the boatlift?" she asked as the waitress came over and placed their burgers before them.

He nodded, took a bite of his burger, and after swallowing, he said, "Childhood sweethearts. Their families were neighbors in Havana. Somehow both families made it across the Florida Straits to Miami in a raft barely bigger than a rowboat."

"Where my grandmother hired them?" she said and swirled a french fry in catsup as he continued.

"She did, and as many other *Marielitos*—"

"*Marielitos?*" she asked, confused by the term.

Luis nodded. "The Cubans who left from Mariel Harbor during the boatlift. It was a tough time in Miami, with so many people flooding in. It almost destroyed the city," he admitted and stuffed a few fries into his mouth. "These are really good."

"My cousin will appreciate the praise," she said and finally took a bite of her burger before it got cold.

———— ❖ ————

Luis glanced around the place once again with a different eye now that he knew it belonged to her family. He couldn't find fault with the restaurant. While small, it was clean, well-thought-out, and, judging from the number of midweek customers, popular. So far, the beer and the food had both been delicious, which probably explained the crowd.

"You have a lot of family in Brooklyn?" he asked, although from his homework he knew that her dad's family was large and prosperous in various endeavors, mostly working-class businesses like Jessica's.

"A lot. Do I have a lot of family in Miami?" she asked, and it was obvious to him that the question was heartfelt.

He nodded. "Your grandmother. Two aunts. Assorted cousins."

"And you. I get that you're like family too," she said, and he couldn't deny the observation.

"I've known Carmen all of my life, and she's important to me. I don't want to see her hurt, but I don't want to hurt you or your mother either. You've got to believe that," he urged, laying all his cards on the table. It was the only way he could accomplish the mission that Carmen had entrusted to him because honesty was the best policy.

Jessica leaned back in her chair and gripped her beer glass tightly, her worry apparent. "I told my parents that I intend to go, but I know it will hurt my mom and that's the last thing I want to do."

With a sad nod, he said, "I understand. All I ask is that you give it some more thought before making a final decision."

She acknowledged his request with a dip of her head and said, "I will. That's all I can promise."

He raised his glass. "It's a promise I'll accept."

Chapter Three

AS HER MIND FILLED in the chorus to the elevator tune playing over the airport loudspeakers, Jessica tried to block the memories of her mother's pained features and her father's disapproving glare as she'd stormed out the door of her family's home a few nights earlier.

She would never intentionally hurt her family or cut them out of her life. That's what made it so hard to understand the reasons her mother had given for doing that to her own mother as well as her sisters. She was also trying to wrap her mind around the fact that her mother had never shared that Jessica's grandmother had reached out to her many times before the old woman had apparently given up.

It didn't make sense to her, nor had most of the story that her mother had offered to justify her actions. But it had been clear that her mom still carried a great deal of hurt from her childhood. That deeply buried and long-held anger was so different from the way she'd grown up around her father's Italian family, where tempers flared and voices were raised but fights were usually settled in short order. Holding on to such soul-deep hurt and anger for over thirty years…

Trying to understand the why of her mother's anger and have closure, if only for herself, was the reason Jessica had relented and agreed to her grandmother's request. And it was why she was trudging through Miami International on the way to meet family she'd never known about in a city she'd never been to before.

Her smartphone vibrated in her pocket, letting her know that she had a text. Fumbling with her purse, knapsack, and rolling bag, she rummaged through her jacket pocket and yanked out the phone. It was Luis texting her to say he'd be waiting for her right outside the baggage claim area for her flight.

She wanted to ask Luis how he'd located her baggage claim info so quickly, but after having read numerous articles about him online, she'd had no doubt he was capable of it. It seemed like he usually got what he wanted. She had no intention of being another entry in the win column whether personally or professionally. She pressed past baggage claim and walked out to the pickup area, but as she did so, the blast of heat and the weight of Miami humidity were almost a physical assault. Sweat immediately broke out across her body, making her yearn for the comfort of either air-conditioning or the early New York spring she had left behind.

A few steps away from the terminal door, she noticed Luis at the curb, chatting and laughing with one of the security guards. He was leaning against the fender of a shiny red fully restored 1950s Chevrolet Bel Air convertible. He wore a pale-yellow raw linen shirt with two rows of sewn vertical pleats running down the front of the fabric. The shirt hung loose around his slim midsection but stretched tight across wide shoulders. The color made his hair look darker and gilded his tanned skin.

She was struck once again by how handsome he was. How confident even in the casual clothes.

As she hurried toward him, he caught sight of her from the corner of his eye and his smile brightened. He straightened and clapped the other man on the back and met her halfway. They stopped short feet away from each other and just stood there, staring in an awkward silence, sudden tension shimmering between them as heavy as the humid Miami air.

"Well?" she said a little too sharply and immediately apologized. "Sorry. I'm just way nervous about this."

He nodded and said, "The same. I'm still trying to process that you're actually here."

"I am," she said and shrugged. "I made a reservation at the Tides in South Beach. Is it a long ride to the hotel?" she asked as she started moving toward his car again.

"*Por favor*, let me," he said and took the handle of the rolling bag from her. "Is this all you have?" he asked and looked back toward the terminal as if expecting an entourage. Most of the women in his circles would likely have at least a few bags packed with the latest fashion items and accessories.

"It is. I travel light," she said and followed him toward the vintage automobile.

<hr />

"I see that," Luis said. As he wheeled the bag toward the trunk of his car, he wondered if her lack of luggage was more about her being able to leave quickly in case things didn't work out, but he held back from asking that. He hadn't gotten to be president of a large company like Guerreiro Enterprises without learning to read people. He totally got that she was uncomfortable about being in Miami and meeting her *abuela* and the rest of the Guerreiro clan. Maybe even uncomfortable around him.

Not to mention that Jessica was nothing like the pampered, perfectly done-up women who normally populated his life. Whether professionally or socially, the women around him were what most Miamians would call CAPs—Cuban American Princesses. Jessica had a casual, no-nonsense style which was appealing in its own way. While he was loading her bag and knapsack into the trunk of his car, he asked, "Do you mind riding with the top down?"

"No problema," she said, which just bolstered his impression that Jessica would have no issue with getting a little mussed or painted with a spot of color from the blazing Miami sun. Today her caramel-colored hair was pinned up in a messy ponytail where wisps escaped to tease smooth, pale skin. The ponytail exposed the fine line of her neck and her heart-shaped face. He couldn't deny that she was attractive, but his primary obligation was to protect Carmen and her interests.

He swung around, helped Jessica into the car, and then slipped behind the driver's seat. As he did so, she again asked, "How far is it to the hotel?"

He sucked in a breath and held it, bracing himself because he suspected she would be less than happy with what he was about to tell her. He gripped the wheel tightly, shot a quick look in his side-view mirror, pulled out sharply, and said, "You're not staying at the Tides. We can call and cancel your reservation later."

"What? Where am I staying?" she said, raising her voice, and not just to combat the road noise as the convertible picked up speed.

"Your grandmother and I thought it might be best if you stayed with her. She's got plenty of room—"

"What if that's not what I want?" she challenged and glared at him.

"It would be the easiest thing, Jessica. Your *abuela* is eighty-three—"

"Bisnonna Russo is ninety-three and that doesn't stop her," she said, but as he turned onto the Dolphin Expressway, the car picked up speed and the road noise intensified enough to make talk difficult.

"Why not give it a shot? You might just like it," he said loudly and risked a glance at her again.

She shook her head and blew out a harsh breath but said nothing. Instead of continuing the conversation, he likewise fell silent and relaxed into the cushioned comfort of the leather bench seat. The sun was strong and provided welcome warmth against the slight chill from having the top down. A bright, fierce blue sky today had not a cloud in sight, but that could change quickly in typical tropical fashion. He almost wished the ride were longer because he was enjoying the quiet time with her and the beautiful weather.

She seemed to be enjoying it as well since she busily took in all the sights they passed along the highway. Low-lying buildings blanketed the areas all around and in the distance rose the taller downtown Miami skyline. In less than ten minutes they were riding across Biscayne Bay on the McArthur Causeway, surrounded by cerulean waters, and to their left, the Venetian Islands before the exit came for Palm and Hibiscus Islands. Too soon, he was driving toward the exit for Star Island, and the closer they got, the more his anxiety grew about what would happen once they got there.

He braced himself for Jessica's reaction as they exited and drove down the short road to the gate at the entrance to the private island. This was nothing like the world she was used to or what she might have expected. Even he sometimes felt overwhelmed by it all since it was so far removed from his own working-class upbringing.

The security guard stepped out of the guardhouse as he neared, but seeing who it was, the guard smiled, waved, and immediately opened the gate.

"Holy shit, what is this?" Jessica said as they pulled past security and the first elaborate entrance to one of the homes on the island.

"Star Island," he said and drove beyond two more entrances before turning in and going down the long, tiled driveway toward Carmen's waterside Mediterranean-style villa. As he maneuvered around the circular drive with the large fountain at its center, she said, "Seriously, what is this?"

He stopped the car, turned in his seat, and said, "*This* is home, Jessica. *Bienvenida.*"

Chapter Four

JESSICA STARED AT THE immense—no, make that *huge*—building before her. She couldn't really think of the structure as a house or a home because it was at least the length of a New York City block and she suspected its width wasn't much smaller. Earthen-colored terra-cotta tiles sat atop the two-storied structure iced with stucco. By her count, nearly two dozen windows graced the front, some in the distinctive rounded arches common to Spanish architecture.

"Home?" she said with a gulp and shot him an anxious look.

"Your *abuela*'s home, Jessica. As you can see, she's got plenty of room."

"Another understatement, Luis." She examined the grounds around her grandmother's massive home. The tropical gardens were perfectly kept, with luscious green lawns and tall palms whose bases were surrounded by vibrant flowers and colorful crotons. A fuchsia-colored bougainvillea vine arched gracefully over the front door. In the center of the drive, pale white water lilies floated in the bowl of a quietly burbling fountain.

"Give it a chance, Jessica. It will give you more time with her," he said and brushed the back of his hand across her cheek, but she pulled away from him.

"Please, Luis. Keep your hands to yourself," she reminded him, worried that she wasn't going to be able to handle him in addition to the other emotions warring inside her.

He raised his hands in surrender. "*Perdoname*, Jessica. Cuban. I use my hands a lot, but I won't touch again," he said with a dimpled grin.

"It's really hot and humid out here. Can we continue this discussion inside?"

"Of course, *mi amor*," he teased, apparently unable to keep from baiting her. She told herself again that he was way too confident for her taste.

She popped out of the car and as she did so, she noticed the carport off to one side of the intricately tiled driveway. It was in the same style as the house and held a Rolls Royce, Range Rover, and an empty space for a third car. Another reminder that she was way out of her comfort zone. Her beat-up pickup truck would stick out like a sore thumb.

"Ready?" Luis asked as he slung her knapsack over his shoulder and wheeled her bag around to her side of the Bel Air.

"No, but would that make a difference?" she said and wiped wet palms on her pant legs.

"No," he replied, not that she'd expected a different answer. Following him, she braced herself for what the inside of the house would look like. She couldn't think of it as home just yet. Maybe never.

Nothing could have prepared her for the opulence of the interior. On one side of the foyer, beyond the ornately carved wooden doors was an antique rococo secretary desk in what her expert eyes said was rosewood. An ornate baroque console with a large matching mirror above it had a spot on the opposite side of the foyer. Gleaming white marble tile spread out from the foyer into a living room that could have easily held her workshop and storefront within it. Maybe even her cousin's burger and beer restaurant. The furniture inside the living room was an eclectic mix of stark contemporary sofas, elaborate European antiques, and more rustic Spanish colonial pieces.

As they stepped inside, an older gentleman in a shirt similar to Luis's but in a pale blue thin cotton and not expensive linen

approached them. She'd seen many men on the street wearing similarly styled shirts, as if it was a kind of uniform for Miami males.

"Jessica, meet Manny. He's the majordomo and can help you
with anything you might need. *Gracias*, Manny," he said as the man
took Jessica's bag and knapsack from Luis.

Manny dipped his head. "*Bienvenida*, Señorita Russo. I hope
you will enjoy your stay with us. I will take your bags to your room
and set your things out for you."

"Please call me Jessica, and that's not necessary. I can take care
of my own things," she said and reached for her bags, but the majordomo shook his head.

"*Por favor*, Jessica. Señora Carmen is waiting for you," Manny
said and rushed off.

Luis motioned in the direction of the cavernous living room.
There were two distinct seating areas in the large space. One of the
collections of sofas and chairs was by stairs to an open second floor
that looked down on the living room. The other set of sofas and
chairs faced a large fireplace. The stone mantel around the fireplace
had a delicately carved design with an arch that echoed the shape of
the windows on the first floor as well as the arched doorways leading
to other parts of the home.

As they walked through the living room and toward one of the
doorways, she snuck a peek at the ceiling, which boasted a fresco that
looked like a beautiful summer sky with a few clouds scattered here
and there. She also took a moment to appreciate the many fine pieces
of artwork, as well as the furniture which called to the maker in her.
If she did stay for longer than the week she'd planned, she looked
forward to a more detailed inspection of the pieces.

"Right through here," Luis said and motioned to what appeared
to be a small reception area. At their entrance, a young woman
stepped out from a smallish office and smiled at them.

"You're here! Carmen will be so happy to see you. I'm Sylvia,

Carmen's assistant," she nearly bubbled and held out her hand. Dressed in a tailored black suit and white shirt, her hair in a stylish bob, she looked ready for business.

At Jessica's questioning look as she shook the young woman's hand, Luis explained, "Carmen no longer runs the company but likes to keep her fingers in some things. She's also involved with several charities in the area."

"She's still quite active then," she said, beginning to think that maybe Carmen was eighty-three years young and not as infirm as Luis had led her to believe.

"Carmen has more energy than some people—" Sylvia began, but Luis shot her a warning look. Sylvia finished with a stuttering: "She's been waiting for you. Please go right in."

Jessica didn't wait for Luis's urging this time. She marched right into an office where a tastefully dressed woman held court from behind a large mahogany desk. Behind the desk was a built-in unit chock-full of books and shelves boasting assorted awards, photographs, and knickknacks.

The woman didn't look a day over sixty, and as their gazes locked, Jessica realized this was her grandmother. They shared the same green eyes, high cheekbones, and thumbprint-sized dimple in the middle of their chins. Her grandmother rose but didn't step around the desk for a more intimate greeting. With a hand that had a slight tremble, she gestured to the two chairs before her and said, "*Gracias* for coming to see me, Jessica."

Jessica nodded and sat, not sure what to say next. She was also angry that Luis had misled her since, as far as she could see, her grandmother appeared to be in good health. Wanting him to know it, she said, "I didn't have much choice since Luis hinted that you weren't well."

Carmen looked in his direction, her head cocked at a regal angle. "*De verdad*, Luis?"

With a shrug and a chagrined look, he said, "I believe I said that Jessica should visit and 'set things to rights.'"

"Because we were running out of time," Jessica challenged with an arch of her brows.

"Luis," Carmen said, her tone chastising, but barely.

"A case of semantics," he said and raised his hands in defense.

Jessica blew out a harsh laugh. "Said like a lawyer. Are you a lawyer?"

He nodded and replied without shame, "I am, thanks to your *abuela* and her support."

"I'd call you a lying lawyer but that would be redundant, wouldn't it?" Jessica retorted, feeling like he'd played her for a fool by using her emotions against her. Especially since that had precipitated a nasty exchange with her mother, whom she loved more than anything. Even if she was still struggling to understand why her mother would cut off this branch of the family. But then again, if they were all as deceptive as Luis, it might explain her mother's motivation.

"Would you leave us, Luis? Give us some time alone before dinner?" Carmen said. It was clearly not a request, but a command. Obviously, Carmen was a woman used to giving orders.

"Of course, *viejita*," Luis said, but with affection and not anger.

As he rose, he glanced down at Jessica, his hazel gaze warm and filled with apology. "I *am* sorry if you feel misled. All I wanted was for you and your *abuela* to spend some time together."

Once he'd left, Carmen rose and walked around the desk to sit in the chair next to Jessica. She didn't fail to miss that her grandmother moved with sure steps and energy. In some ways Carmen reminded her of her Italian great-grandmother, who barely missed a beat even in her nineties.

She was dressed in a trim suit in a shade of green so dark, it almost looked black. It emphasized Carmen's slim but curvy figure and made the green of her eyes pop against her creamy skin. Her makeup was minimal on a face that was surprisingly unlined for a woman of her age. Carmen could easily pass for her mother's sister and not her mother.

The older woman fidgeted, twined her fingers together, and nestled her hands in her lap, clearly trying to contain herself. She examined Jessica and said, "Don't be too angry with Luis. He was only doing what I asked."

"He shouldn't have lied," Jessica replied and realized that she also had her hands locked together in her lap. *Just like your grandmother*, a little voice in her head pointed out.

———◇◆◇———

Carmen understood her granddaughter's anger with Luis. Maybe even with her, but *mi linda nieta* was finally here thanks to him.

"Luis wasn't lying when he said it was time to make things right. I'm not getting any younger and I really wanted to get to know you," Carmen said.

"But not my mother. You didn't want to end whatever is going on between you and my mother," Jessica said, her voice tight with anger.

Tension radiated from every line of her granddaughter's body, and her hands were clenched so tightly in her lap her fingers were white with pressure, much like her own. She unlaced her fingers and covered Jessica's hands. Jessica's skin was cold even though the temperature in the room was comfortable.

"I love your *mami*. I've never stopped loving her, but things between us… I did so many things wrong without meaning to," Carmen admitted, her throat so thick with emotion she could barely get the words out. Her body trembled from the strain of maintaining control.

"You spent too much time with politics and at work, building all this," Jessica said without hesitation and gestured with her head to the house around them.

"Is that what Lara told you?" Carmen asked, wanting to be clear about what her daughter had relayed to Jessica.

Jessica nodded and plowed on. "My mother said you left her in Cuba for over a year. And that when she finally got here, you were always running from work to meetings or having people in the house for parties and events. Then after her sisters came, there was even less time for her."

Carmen had to walk a tightrope because she didn't want to turn Jessica against Lara, but there was always more than one side to the story. Now it was time for her side to be heard. "It's true that she had to stay behind in Cuba when her father and I left. I can imagine that she felt that we had abandoned her, but we had no choice."

"Because of the secret police?" Jessica asked, obviously having been told at least that part of the story.

Carmen nodded. "Your *abuelo* and I helped put Fidel into power, and to this day I don't understand how we could have been fooled so badly."

"Sometimes we don't want to see what's right in front of our faces," Jessica said, a sudden note of sympathy in her tone as she looked down at their joined hands.

Carmen cupped Jessica's chin and with gentle pressure urged her face upward. "We didn't see it and let Fidel steal our world and that of millions of others."

"So you left Cuba?" Jessica said, clearly wanting to understand what had happened in Cuba and also between her mother and grandmother.

"We escaped," she clarified. "It was either that or prison or death, like so many political dissidents. We came here, but Fidel stonewalled getting your mother out of Cuba. He wanted to punish us for what we'd been doing."

"Is that why she was alone for a year?" Jessica asked, slowly pulling away from Carmen's reassuring touch.

Carmen folded her hands in her lap once again and nodded. "Lara wasn't alone. She was with her grandparents. My parents. But it wasn't an easy time, and I can understand how confusing and overwhelming it must have been when we were finally able to get all of them here in Miami."

Jessica appeared taken aback that Carmen wasn't denying most of what her mother had said. "Then why didn't you do something about it? Why didn't you help her when she finally came here?" she asked, her eyes brimming with unshed tears for her mother's pain.

"Because I was lost myself and struggling just to keep things together for my family," she confessed, recalling those early days in Miami and how turbulent that time had been. The many attempts to reunite her family while juggling work and helping others who were also suffering. Losing her husband when she had three small daughters who needed her.

"I was lost," Carmen repeated, the emotions of those days running as high as if she were still in 1960s Miami.

Chapter Five

Miami, May 1960

CARMEN DIDN'T BELIEVE WHAT she was hearing. They'd only just been reunited with Lara and had another baby on the way, and he wanted to leave again? She laid her hand over the growing bump and shook her head, not wanting to listen anymore. Not wanting to accept what her husband was proposing.

"It's so much to think about, Carlos," she said, and her husband laid his hand over hers as it rested on their unborn child. His touch was sure, his hand callused from his life as a police officer and the construction work he'd been doing since they'd arrived in Miami. He'd been her touchstone during *la Revolucion*, always at her side as they'd undertaken dangerous assignments—passing messages for the Resistance, picking up weapons and other supplies at Varadero Beach. *But had it been the thrill of danger or me that had kept him at my side?* she now wondered with this latest pronouncement.

"*Mi amor*, this is our chance to go home. To have a free Cuba like we imagined. A democracy and not this farce Fidel is creating," Carlos urged, his dark gaze glittering with emotion and excitement. He was a man of action at heart and the possibility of gathering with other like men to overthrow Castro was obviously more tempting than a peaceful existence in Miami. *A peaceful existence with me.*

"We were just starting to have a life here," she said, fearing what might happen if the CIA-backed operation failed, but likewise fearing what might happen if it succeeded and she had to uproot her family once more. Lara was just beginning to come out of her shell, and she worried for her daughter and the damage any more changes might inflict on her.

"And what will we do if the mission fails?" she pressed.

"It won't. We have the U.S. government behind us. We have capable men ready to do this. Others will join us in Cuba when they learn about our mission," he said and squeezed her hand to reassure, but it failed to convince her. Nothing in life was certain. What had happened in Cuba with Castro had taught her that.

"But if it doesn't…I don't want to lose you. Lose what we have now," Carmen said and laced her fingers with his.

He leaned close and his warm breath caressed her skin. He tried to comfort her. "You won't lose me, *querida*. When we're back in Cuba, a free Cuba, we'll look back on this and know we did the right thing."

She nodded, still unconvinced, but if it let them end their exile and go home… "*Comprendo*, Carlos. A free Cuba is what we dreamed of. Risked our lives for. It's what we want for our children," she said, skimming her hand across her belly and glancing toward where Lara sat gazing at them with accusing eyes. Eyes that seemed way too old for a five-year-old. Eyes that looked lost.

Carmen shook her head and looked away, tears shimmering in her gaze. "Carlos survived the Bay of Pigs but I think that by then I had already lost your mother. I just didn't realize it."

Jessica took Carmen's hands in hers and squeezed gently. "I'm sorry, Carmen. I don't want to hurt you with such sad memories."

Sniffling, Carmen nodded, her lips pursed as she fought for control. "It's long past time we talked about it, Lara and me. But she's not here and I'm not sure she ever will be. But I never wanted her to leave. When your father came into the picture, it caused even more problems," she admitted.

"Because you were afraid he was only in it for the money?" Jessica said, repeating what her mother had told her.

Carmen shook her head and laughed harshly. "I know Lara believes that, but it was only because I was afraid Salvatore would take *her* away. Money meant nothing. Lara meant *everything* to me." Sucking in a rough breath and with another shake of her head, she pushed on. "I contacted her many times to try and set things right, but she never returned my calls or letters."

Jessica applied gentle pressure on Carmen's hands again and softly said, "I know. Mom did tell me that."

With a dip of her head, Carmen peered intently at her grand-daughter, grateful that Lara had been honest in that respect. "*Gracias.* So where do we go from here?"

"I can take it one day at a time if you can," Jessica said, a tentative smile on her face, giving Carmen hope. Maybe in time, Lara would likewise be open to ending the rift in the family.

Happy tears nearly blinding her, Carmen nodded and somehow worked the words past the knot in her throat. "I can."

Luis bounced his heels on the ground trying to dispel some of his nervous energy as he waited for Carmen and Jessica to emerge. Worry filled him at what might be happening between the two women because he cared deeply for Carmen, and Jessica had likewise worked her way under his skin in the very short time he'd known her. He'd hate for her to be hurt as well.

When the door to Carmen's home office slowly opened, he popped to his feet and worriedly skipped his gaze over their features to gauge how they were doing. He was relieved to see both understanding and concern on their faces. Carmen met his gaze, hers slightly wet with tears, and said, "Would you mind showing Jessica to her room? I'm sure she'd like to freshen up before dinner."

"My pleasure, *viejita*," he said, and as Jessica approached, he laid a hand at the small of her back and hated it when tension immediately registered beneath his palm. He drew his hand away and gestured with his head in the direction they had to go. "This way," he said.

He walked a half step ahead of Jessica, and as he did so, she said, "What does that mean? *Viejita*?"

She had struggled slightly with the pronunciation and so he repeated it for her, emphasizing the syllables. "Vi-e-ji-ta. It means 'old lady,' but in an affectionate way."

Jessica laughed and shook her head. "It strikes me that while Carmen may be eighty-three, she's not an old lady."

He joined her laughter and nodded. "*Sin duda*," he said and directed her up wide marble stairs with elaborately worked wrought iron railings and banisters that evoked images of waves. They walked along the second-floor landing where more wrought iron railings protected the entire edge of the floor. Luis passed door after door until they got to a room at the farthest end of the hall, and he directed her to enter.

She barely contained a gasp, and Luis totally understood. He had always thought this was one of the best rooms in the house, with its amazing views from a side window and the balcony that faced Biscayne Bay. In the center of the room sat a king-size four-poster bed in carved rosewood with gently filigreed wrought iron rails interlaced with wood to serve as the posts. A brilliant white bedspread was trimmed in a pale blue that matched the color of the walls. Half a dozen pillows in assorted sizes and hues of blue completed the linens. Matching nightstands flanked the bed, and near the balcony was a seating area with similar furniture upholstered in a darker blue, accented with white and pale blue pillows. The colors gave it a very coastal feel to go with the priceless views of Biscayne Bay.

"This is…beautiful," she said and half turned to look at him, her astonishment clear. "And immense."

He chuckled and nodded. "Manny's laid out your things in the closet. It's right next to your bathroom," he said and held his hand out in the direction of two doors at the far side of the room.

Jessica walked toward the closet but stopped short as she peered into the bathroom. "Holy shit, this is bigger than my whole apartment."

"It's a sizable house," he said and followed her into the equally spacious walk-in closet, where he gestured to one wall where Manny had hung up Jessica's clothes. "I'm assuming your other things are in the drawers below."

Adjacent to Jessica's clothes were a number of new outfits, and at her questioning gaze, he explained, "Your *abuela* got you a few things. She wasn't sure—"

"If my things would be suitable?" Jessica said, fresh anger laced through her words. She whirled on him, her green eyes blazing fire and color riding high on her cheeks. "You may be used to all this excess, Mr. Rolex—"

"I wouldn't be caught dead wearing a Rolex," he shot back because of her tone, but immediately knew that wouldn't help defuse the situation or how Jessica was feeling. Trying to explain he said, "Your *abuela* wasn't sure that you'd know what to pack for Miami weather. *No*, I was freezing my ass off in New York last week," he said, and to emphasize his point, he rubbed his arms as if to chase away the cold.

Since that didn't seem to move her, he said, "Feel free to use them or not. It's up to you."

"Is it, Luis?" she said and walked over to a center island where there were rows of neatly arranged lingerie, probably courtesy of her grandmother as well. "Is any of this really up to me?" she asked, but her voice was filled with dejection now and not anger.

"I know you may be feeling a little overwhelmed." Hell, he wasn't feeling much different, trying to juggle the emotions of the two women.

"I'm not sure you can even begin to understand. My mother said that Carmen put money ahead of her, and now I'm surrounded by all this luxury, and it just feels so wrong. Like a betrayal of my father and my mother." She hurried to where her clothes hung, searched through drawers and an adjacent cabinet until she found her rolling bag and knapsack. She opened them and started tossing her clothes into the luggage.

He grabbed hold of Jessica's hand to stop her. "*Por favor*, Jessica. I understand, believe me."

She jerked her hand away from him and rubbed it as if it pained her. "Really? Mr. Wouldn't Be Caught Dead in a Rolex understands?"

He ignored her jibe and tried to persuade her again. "Do you think your *abuela* felt right at home when she came here? Or that I did, growing up in a Miami that didn't want people like me? No, we didn't, but we did it anyway, and look at where we are now because we took the risk," he said and held his hands wide to embrace all that was around them.

He had effectively boxed her into a corner. There was no way Jessica could compare her current situation to being forced to leave one's home or being unwanted, maybe even discriminated against. Thanks to her father's loving family, she had never experienced that kind of isolation.

"It couldn't have been easy for both of you, but this isn't easy for me either," she said, laying a hand on her chest.

Sensing that she was offering an olive branch, he graciously accepted her truce. "I know it's hard for you to deal with your mom, *abuela*, and all this. But do you know what Guerreiro means?"

She struggled for a second before shaking her head, and he explained, "It means 'warrior.' Your *abuela* is one, and that blood runs in you as well. I *know* you can handle this."

With a deep sigh, she said, "I'll try. And I'm sorry for being a brat."

He playfully ran a finger across the dimple in her chin, and this time she didn't pull away because his touch was soothing. "You're not a brat. Just wait until you meet your cousin Angelica. Her picture's in the dictionary right next to the word 'brat.'"

Jessica raised her gaze in pleading. "Please tell me I don't have to meet her tonight. I'm not up for that."

He chuckled and shook his head. "Not for a while. Your *abuela* thought you'd need time to acclimate and maybe see a little bit of Miami first, since you haven't been here before. That is if you'd like to play tourist."

"Are you going to be the tour guide?" she asked and started hanging her clothes again.

"I am, if you don't mind," he answered, his dark gaze skipping over her face, rousing unexpected emotions.

"I don't mind at all," she said and wondered if she was crazy to say so. He was an interesting man, but she had to keep that interest in check because no matter what, she was going home at the end of all this. Home to New York and to her Russo family. Back to a business that needed her.

These people here in Miami…she couldn't think of them as family at the moment. Not yet and maybe not ever. Only time would tell.

Chapter Six

LARA WALKED TO THE door of Jessica's old bedroom and paused, peering at the remnants of her daughter's young life that had been left behind years earlier when Jessica had moved into the loft apartment above her business. *The kids might leave home, but their stuff somehow never does,* she thought with a chuckle.

She strolled in and picked up a small plush elephant in happy colors of pastel pink and palest yellow that had somehow fallen off the twin bed in the middle of the room. Lara sat on the edge of the bed and ran her hand over the soft plush, remembering how Jessica would curl up with the toy. How she would sometimes snuggle with her young daughter for a quick afternoon nap.

Such happier times. Her gaze shimmered with tears. One slipped down her face, and she dashed it away with a shaky hand and looked around the room. Across from the bed a bulletin board held photos, ticket stubs, and other memories. A photo of Jessica, Lara, and Sal during a family vacation in Williamsburg, Virginia, was pinned in the center of the board. Smiles beamed from the image, so unlike the last time the three of them had been together.

The photo prompted Lara to recall one of her abuelo's favorite sayings: Never go to bed angry.

It had been a few nights of angry bedtimes since Jessica had stormed out of the house days earlier. In the days since then, Sal had reached out to both her and their daughter numerous times, trying to ease the upset between them, but neither of them was willing to budge.

In some ways—maybe more than some—both she and Jessica were way too much like Carmen. Stubborn. Headstrong. Determined. The Guerreiro genes were strong in both of them, no matter how much Lara tried to deny that she was anything like her mother. But in the ways that mattered, Lara was the complete opposite.

She had always been there for her daughter. Even when her career had been challenged by Jessica's birth, she had fought to balance her work and her family life. She had always put family first, which was why Jessica's desertion and flight to Miami hurt so much.

"Knock, knock," Sal said and tapped the jamb of the door with his knuckle.

She looked his way and realized that he had been standing there for some time. "I'm sorry. I didn't realize you were there."

He nodded, walked in, and sat beside her. Wrapping an arm around her shoulders, he drew her near. "You were somewhere else, my love."

She shrugged and stroked the plush toy again. "Did she get there okay?"

Sal nodded and laid his hand over hers to still the nervous motion. With a reassuring squeeze, he said, "She did. She's staying with your mother."

It occurred to Lara that she didn't even have any idea where her mother lived. When she had left for college—and then married Sal—her family had been living in an upscale suburb where many successful Cubans had moved to from Little Havana.

"Where?" she said, her voice cracking with guilt that she didn't know. Guilt that she somehow thought she was long past when it came to her relationship with her family.

"Where?" Sal repeated, obviously confused.

Lara shook her head in self-disgust. "Yes, where is Carmen living?"

He squeezed her hand again. "According to Jess's text, a big-ass mansion on Star Island."

"Wow, Star Island. The old lady must have really made it. Good for her. That's what she wanted more than anything," she said, bitterness driving away the guilt. Her mother—no, Carmen, not her mother. Carmen had only decided to become a mother to Lara when Carmen had wanted to control her life. Control where she would live and who she would love.

"You don't mean that. You know she loved you. She just didn't know how to show it," Sal said, ever the peacemaker.

Lara bolted from the bed, wrapped her arms around herself, and faced Sal. "You of all people should know better than to defend her. Have you forgotten how she treated you? What she tried to do to us?"

His brown-eyed gaze filled with pain and he nodded. "I remember, but some things are best left in the past."

"Really? What if I can't do that, Sal? What then?" she challenged, pacing back and forth like a caged animal as she waited for his response.

"Then you may lose your daughter. Are old hurts worth that?"

Miami, July 1977

"I don't understand, *mija*. You can go to law school here. The University of Miami has a wonderful program," Carmen said and reached out to her across the width of the desk, but Lara didn't take her hands. Her own were clenched in her lap, her fists tight.

"I've been accepted at Columbia," she said to end the discussion. Her mind was made up and nothing was going to change it.

Carmen sat back, obviously floored, but smiled and nodded. The motion was as stilted and as forced as her smile. "*Felicidades.* That's quite an accomplishment. I'm so proud."

"Thank you, but there's more. Sal has asked me to marry him, and I said yes," she blurted out in a rush of words and braced herself for her mother's reaction.

The smile disappeared as quickly as a camera flash. "He didn't ask me for your hand."

Lara laughed harshly, filled with disbelief. "Maybe because you would have said no."

Carmen sighed and shook her head. "I can't deny that, *mi'ja*. I don't know anything about him or his family."

Another rough laugh escaped her. Shaking her head, she said, "Maybe because you haven't tried. Every time we invited you to come up to New York—"

"I have obligations, Lara. The business. Your sisters."

Anger rose sharply in Lara, twisting her gut into a knot. Tightening her throat until she could barely speak, but she eked out the words. "*Siempre tienes algo mas importante que mi.*"

Carmen reached for her once more, palms up and open as if in pleading. "*No es verdad, mi'ja.* You are very important to me. That's why I've spent so much time building the business, so that you and your sisters will never have to worry about money or your futures."

Lara ignored her appeal, too caught up in her past to think about her future. Years of hurt had her lashing out, anger laced through every word. "You did it for yourself. Admit it."

Carmen shook her head again and looked away, her gaze crystalline with tears. "*No es verdad.*"

Lara leaned forward to drive home her point. "You wanted to prove you were better than they said, all those 'no dogs, no Cubans' people. You wanted to make up for the mistake you made in Cuba, supporting Fidel. Letting Papi go off to war." She paused to suck in a breath and in a voice that sounded almost childish to her own ears, she said, "You should have made him stay."

Carmen snapped her head around to nail Lara with her gaze. "I tried, Lara. *Dios mio*, I tried. And I struggled every day to make up for the mistake of leaving you in Cuba. Of not being there when you needed me."

The words drove the last of Lara's breath from her. She had longed for that admission for what seemed like forever, for an apology if that was possible, and maybe what her mother had done to build her business had been that apology. *Maybe*, Lara thought. Not that it would change the decision she had made.

Drawing in another breath to control herself, she said, "I am marrying Sal. He's kind and caring, and he makes me laugh. I'm staying in New York. I'm not coming back to Miami."

———⋄◆⋄———

"Lara?" Sal asked, peering at her, his gaze pleading.

"You don't understand. You don't know what she's like," Lara said, worried about how Carmen would ingratiate herself with Jessica. Maybe even convince her to leave Brooklyn. To leave them.

"I don't, maybe because I never got to know her or the rest of your family," her husband said, and it was too much to hear.

She rushed toward the door, but Sal met her there and blocked her way. "You cannot run away from this, Lara."

Body shaking with both anger and hurt, she said, "Is that what you think I did all those years ago? Do you think I ran away from home? From my mother?"

Sal cradled her cheeks with his rough, work-hardened hands and swiped away the tears she didn't realize were streaming down her face. "I'd like to think you ran to me. To our love and laughter, but a part of me...I feel like we can never be whole if *you* are not whole. And I think there's only one way that will ever happen."

Lara took hold of his wrists and drew his hands away. "You think I need to make peace with my mother? With my sisters?" she asked, the tone of her voice rising. Disbelief dripping from her words.

Sal stepped back, giving her the freedom to walk away as he said,

"You're a smart woman. So is Jessica. Between the two of you, I'm sure you will figure out what's the right thing to do."

The right thing? Lara rushed out of Jessica's room and hurried to her home office. Work always seemed to be her escape when things got to be too much to handle.

Like it was for your mother? the little voice in her head challenged.

I'm not like my mother, she shot back as she opened up the brief she had to read and approve for an important overseas litigation.

Aren't you? the little voice parried, but Lara only buried her head in the document. She had work to do, and this time, family matters could wait.

Chapter Seven

CARMEN STRAIGHTENED THE SUNFLOWERS in the vase beside the statue of La Virgencita de la Caridad and lit a candle while offering a short prayer for guidance as she had so many times in the past. Like the three workers in the boat being tossed about in the bay who had prayed to be rescued, Carmen had often found peace and salvation by talking to the Virgencita. And truth be told, by working. Work had been what had kept her focused when everything around her was unstable.

But not this week. This week was all about spending time with her granddaughter Jessica, who was finally here.

She murmured a prayer that all would go right with her granddaughter and then prayed for something she hadn't prayed for in a very long time: that Lara would come home soon as well. That she'd have her daughter to embrace once again before...

Fatigue settled into her core thanks to the emotion of the last few days which had been physically draining. *It's to be expected*, she thought, reminding herself that she was eighty-three as well and an afternoon nap was nothing to be ashamed of. It roused memories of afternoon naps beside Lara in the twin bed they'd shared when her daughter had finally arrived from Cuba. It had been a tiny one-bedroom apartment with a sleeper couch where Carmen's mother and father slept when the room wasn't being used as their living room or dining room. In the evening, Lara shared the twin and slept with Carlos while Carmen worked the night shift at a nearby grocery store.

As small as the apartment was, it had been home until Carlos had come back nearly two years later after the failed Bay of Pigs invasion. To this day, she could still recall that long vigil at the Dinner Key Auditorium, waiting for him to come home. Some of the prisoners had arrived the day before and been reunited with family, but Carmen hadn't been as lucky.

She had sat in the hard metal chair all night, praying to the Virgencita, counting the oversized tiles in the checkerboard pattern on the floor as news snaked through the hall about the arrival of the prisoners and how the Pan Am DC6s had landed at the nearby air force base. How the prisoners had met with immigration officials and medical staff before being processed and loaded on buses for the trip to Coconut Grove and the auditorium where the families waited inside. Outside the building, crowds of Cuban exiles and reporters had massed to cheer the returning heroes.

The Virgencita had brought Carlos home on the eve of Jesus's birthday, and later that day the family had shared a Noche Buena meal for the first time in years. The bridge table that was hauled out for family dinners had groaned with the weight of the roast pork, rice and beans, avocado salad, and assorted plantains for their Christmas Eve feast.

Tears came to her eyes as she recalled the joy on her husband's gaunt face as he beheld the meal and cradled his new daughter, Gloria, close for the first time. Lara had sat beside him, gazing with adoration at her father.

Happy times, Carmen thought as she stroked a hand across the sunflower petals almost as if it were Carlos's cheek beneath her palm. Or little Lara's, still baby-soft at seven.

What would Lara feel like now? she wondered, walking toward the divan at the far side of the room by the windows that faced Biscayne Bay. She toed off her heels, sat on the divan, and pulled a light blanket over her legs. The air-conditioning could be too chilly sometimes.

She settled her gaze on the gentle sway of the palms, royal palms like those in Havana. The azure waters blurred as her eyes drifted closed, and in her mind's eye she was back in Cuba during happier times. Before *la Revolucíon* and Fidel's subsequent betrayal. Before her world had shattered like Humpty Dumpty, never to be put together again.

Luis entered the reception area for Carmen's home office where the ever-efficient Sylvia sat at her desk, taking a call.

"*Sí, claro*. Mrs. Gonzalez Guerreiro understands how important the Brigade 2506 remembrance is," Sylvia said and looked up at Luis, as if asking for confirmation.

Luis shook his head. It was always tough to get La Viejita to go. It roused too many sad memories, and as strong as she was, it took a little piece from her every time she went. Plus with Jessica here, Carmen would likely want to spend all her time with her granddaughter in hopefully happier moments. He made a motion as if he were signing a check, and Sylvia nodded, understanding his instruction.

"I'm not sure Mrs. Gonzalez-Guerreiro is up for it this year, especially since she has family visiting at the moment. I'm very sorry, but Guerreiro Enterprises would be more than happy to provide financial support for the event," she told whomever was on the other end of the line.

That seemed to placate the caller, since Sylvia jotted down some information and then hung up. He had no doubt Sylvia would prepare all the paperwork for the donation, and the related publicity for the business, and have the information on his desk by the next morning.

"Is Carmen available?" he asked, not that he usually needed permission to enter. But if she was with Jessica, he didn't want to interrupt.

Sylvia hesitated, almost as if she'd be betraying a trust, but then said, "She's in her room. Resting. She seemed a little more tired than usual this afternoon."

Luis could well understand. The emotional roller coaster of the last week, wondering if Jessica would heed her plea, as well as her arrival just a few hours earlier would tax anyone. *No*, he was decades younger and he'd had many a sleepless night thinking about Jessica and her visit. Worrying about how it would go between the two women, but also wondering about Jessica.

In the short week that he'd known her, it was clear Jessica would not be easily controlled. Not by her mother. Not by Carmen. Not by him—and that intrigued him more than he liked. He went in search of the woman who had tangled into his dreams like the bougainvillea on the walls of Carmen's home. Beautiful but protected with sharp thorns. Invasive if you couldn't control it.

A quick peek out the living room windows and past the outdoor dining room revealed that Jessica was out by the pool, bent over her phone until she shook her head and dropped the phone on the table beside her chaise longue. She covered her face with her hands.

Is she crying? He hurried over, wanting to offer support, but as she heard the door open and his footfalls, she swiped away the tears and forced a smile. It didn't reach up into her green eyes, so much like Carmen's but not identical. Jessica's were a deeper green with traces of brown and a slight tilt that made them more exotic. More compelling because of the pain he saw in those shattered eyes.

Despite his worry and his interest, which would only tangle those thorny vines around his heart even tighter, he walked over and sat on the adjacent chaise longue.

"Are you okay?"

She nodded, but her voice was hoarse with repressed tears. "It was my dad. Trying to make peace, like he always does."

The words were telling. "I guess you and your mom butt heads often?"

She laughed harshly and looked away toward the waters of the bay. They were calm today and nothing like he imagined the emotions of the three women linked by blood.

After a long pause, she finally said, "You can say that. Maybe because we're a lot alike."

Much like he suspected Carmen and Lara were also alike. "Stubbornness runs in the genes."

Jessica laughed again, but softer and with more humor this time. "You think I'm stubborn," she said, but with little sting.

He shrugged. "Who says that's a bad thing? Maybe I should have said that you're all determined."

She smiled and this one did reach up into her eyes, making them glitter. "I like that word way better."

"Good. You'd think a lawyer would be better with words—"

"You'd think," she interrupted, chuckling and shooting him a side glance.

"For some reason, words sometimes fail me around you," he admitted, wanting to make up for her impression of his earlier actions to get her to Miami.

Her compelling gaze settled on him, inquisitive. "Not a lying lawyer, huh?" she said.

He spread his hands wide, inviting her in. "I'm an open book. Ask away."

"Have you always worked for Carmen?" she asked and turned so she was facing him.

"Pretty much. When I was a teenager, I worked part-time at whatever job there was, so I could earn money to pay for college."

"I thought Carmen helped you with that?" she said, puzzlement on her features.

He nodded. "That and law school, but I didn't know she would, and I intended to pay my way and not be a burden on my family."

"Stub—determined," she teased with a devilish grin.

He grinned back, grateful for the more lighthearted tone. "Definitely determined, and once I finished, I knew exactly what I would do with those savings."

"Which was?" she asked.

"I bought Guerreiro Enterprises stock, and I haven't been disappointed."

"Very determined. Loyal." She thought about that for a second and blurted out, "Persuasive. It explains a lot."

With a shrug, he said, "Not really, but I'm looking forward to the two of us getting to know each other better."

"Wow, direct as well. What if I don't want to share?" she said, but totally tongue-in-cheek. Or at least his ego told him it was.

"Persuasive, remember?" he said with a lift of a brow. Before she could deny it, he said, "What about you? What made you decide to start…what do you call it? Flipping furniture?"

She nodded. "It's called that. I just always loved working with my hands. I'd go with my dad on jobs sometimes—"

"He's a plumber?" Luis said, and the change in Jessica was immediate.

"Not anymore. He runs a successful contracting business now," she said.

Luis raised his hands as if in surrender. "Nothing meant by that. *Mi primo* is a plumber and he loves what he does. That's the important thing—that you love what you do. That way you never work a day in your life."

"I do love it," she said with a strong nod. "I love finding something that someone has tossed aside, but I see the history and the potential there. When I put my hands on it…"

He shifted in his seat as her words had him imagining her hands working the wood, her actions filled with fervor. "You're a lucky woman to be able to earn a living from your passion."

"I am. I love what I do, and I can't imagine doing anything else.

Being anywhere except where I am," she said, almost as if to warn him that her time in Miami was going to be short-lived.

"*Comprendo.* Miami has been home for all my life. Living somewhere else... It would be a challenge, but people like us love challenges, don't we?"

She narrowed her gaze, examining him before chuckling and shaking her head. "Persistent, aren't you?"

He grinned and nodded. "Are you going to deny that you like a challenge?"

Jessica smiled, slapped her thighs, and rose from the chair, her gaze peering past him toward the house. "I think I'll plead the fifth to that one, counselor," she said in almost a whisper so only he could hear.

He turned to look back over his shoulder toward the house. Carmen was walking toward them, smiling. He rose to stand beside Jessica, leaned down, and whispered, "Coward. I didn't expect that from you."

"Consider it a challenge," she whispered back, dragging a smile to his lips.

It's a challenge I will totally accept, he thought.

Chapter Eight

"Since it's such a beautiful night, I thought we'd eat on the patio if that's okay with you," Carmen said and motioned to the waterside table that Manny was setting for a meal.

"That would be lovely. It's not something we can do in New York City at this time of year," Jessica said and followed Carmen to the teak benches covered with inviting beige cushions and pillows in tropical hues of teal and coral. The benches surrounded a teak table that had been set with matching linens, fine china, and crystal. An immense offset umbrella offered protection from the last rays of the Miami sun. Brightly colored lanterns in matching hues were strung about the area to provide light at night.

"I imagine you must have your share of outdoor meals in the summer though," Carmen said, her tone inviting, and Jessica took up that invitation.

"The backyard is my father's pride and joy. It's big for Brooklyn, and we often have family barbecues there," she said.

Carmen took a seat at the head of the table, Luis to her left, and Jessica sat to her right, opposite Luis and facing the waters of the bay.

"You have a lot of family?" Carmen asked.

Jessica nodded as Manny and another servant poured water and sangria for them. "I do. My dad has four brothers and sisters, and they have a lot of kids and grandkids. Quite a few of them are named Salvatore after my dad's dad. Makes things interesting," she said with a laugh, picturing a sea of Sals answering whenever that name was called out at a family gathering.

Carmen laughed, as Jessica had intended. "It's why I didn't name any of the girls after relatives. Lara, Gloria, and Anna wouldn't create any confusion."

"Beautiful names," Jessica said and wondered about the aunts and other Miami relatives she knew nothing about. "What do they do? Do they work in the family business?"

Carmen shook her head and shot a side glance at Luis, as if for support. "Only some of your cousins work for me. Your aunts each have their own professions."

At Jessica's puzzled look, she explained, "After things with your mother went so badly, I did some soul searching. I realized it wasn't up to me to decide what my children wanted to do with their lives."

The admission shocked Jessica, considering how adamant her mother had been about Carmen's attempts to control her life. "You didn't push for my mom—"

"I did," Carmen admitted and reached for Jessica's hand. Like her Italian family, the Cuban half were also touchy-feely, and Jessica let it happen to keep the lines of communication open. She laid her hand palm up and Carmen slid her hand into Jessica's. Her palm was smooth, the skin almost papery with age.

"I did push, and it took me some time to realize how wrong that was," Carmen said. With a sad shake of her head, she added, "By the time I realized that it was too late. No matter what I tried to do, your mother refused to talk to me."

Jessica recalled her mother's upset and pain and rose to her defense. "She was very hurt. Angry about what you said about my father. He's a good man. A good father."

Carmen nodded. "*Sí, lo sé.* I was wrong about him."

Jessica accepted that peace offering. "Thank you. Maybe one day you'll be able to tell him that face-to-face."

"I pray to la Virgencita every day that I will be able to do that," Carmen said.

"La Virgencita?" Jessica asked, unsure but assuming it was something religious. She looked toward Luis for confirmation, who explained.

"La Virgencita is the Virgin Mary. La Virgen de la Caridad del Cobra is the patron saint of Cuba and there's a cathedral dedicated to her not far from here. Right near Vizcaya as well. I can take you there one day if you'd like."

With a shrug, she said, "I'm what you'd call a recovering Catholic, but I'd like that. What's Vizcaya?"

"It's John Deering's estate and quite amazing. I think you would love seeing the architecture and all the period pieces of furniture," he said.

"I *would* like that, as well as exploring some of the pieces here. That is if you don't mind, Carmen," Jessica said, shooting a quick glance at the older woman.

"*Mi casa es tu casa*, and I truly mean that. Whatever is mine is yours, *mi'jita*."

For a second Jessica wondered just how far that invitation went. She'd googled the business after her first meeting with Luis and discovered they were importers and exporters of all kinds of Latino food products and even had their own line of Latino fare. Even though she had no interest in a business like that, she wondered whether her Miami family would worry about someone like her suddenly coming onto the scene.

The discussion was interrupted by Manny and the servant arriving with the first course of their meal, a chilled gazpacho topped with a pile of crab meat.

"This looks delicious. *Gracias*," she told Manny, and Carmen and Luis echoed her thanks. She wondered if they normally did that or just took their service for granted.

But Manny smiled and said, "*Mi placer, viejita.*" His tone was filled with teasing, friendship, and that affectionate nickname.

After the majordomo had stepped away, she said, "Has Manny worked for you long?"

Carmen smiled and spooned up some of the soup. "Since 1980. He and his wife, Consuelo. They're like family."

The year rang a bell with her, and she once again looked toward Luis, who nodded. "Marielitos, just like my family," he confirmed.

It occurred to her then that 1980 would have also been shortly after the fight with her mother. *Had the Marielitos Carmen took in helped fill the void left by my mother's absence?*

Silence reigned for a few moments as hunger took over, but then she said, "What do my aunts do?"

Carmen paused with the soup spoon halfway to her mouth. "Gloria is a family physician and Anna is a psychologist who assists families with special needs children."

"And my cousins? You said some of them work in the family business?" Jessica asked.

"Some do. As for the others, they work at many different things, including contracting and owning restaurants, much like your Russo family. We're both immigrant families that have accomplished a great deal," Carmen said, her pride evident.

Jessica peered at her surroundings, thinking they were over-the-top and far removed from her Russo family properties, not that Carmen seemed to think less of them for that. It made her wonder about her mother's vehemence that Carmen had looked down on her husband-to-be and whether that had been an overreaction. Guilt suddenly swamped her that she was questioning her mother's beliefs.

"I'll have to take you to your cousin's Cuban restaurant in South Beach. Since you like your burgers, you'll have to check out his *fritas,*" Luis said as if to distract her from what she was thinking and feeling.

"What's a *frita*?" she asked as the first course was whisked away and a plate with an avocado salad took its place.

Luis grinned. "It's a small fried burger piled with lettuce and crispy shredded potatoes on soft, sweet burger buns." As he spoke, he mimicked piling up the items to make the *fritas* and then eating one, a big smile on his face. "*Delicioso*."

"Sounds tasty. I look forward to it," she said and meant it. There were so many things she didn't know about this side of her family, its history, and Cuban culture.

Over the years of growing up surrounded by her father's large Italian family, she'd wondered about her mother's family, why there was such a disconnect from them and from their traditions. But she hadn't asked, not wanting to see the hurt slip over her mother's features as it always did at any mention of her family or Cuba. Now, surrounded by it, she suddenly needed to know more. Needed to understand more. Maybe by doing so, it would explain the rift between mother and daughter. Between her mother and her sisters.

Maybe even between Jessica and her mother. Although they'd always been close, Jessica had sensed that a part of her mother had been closed off to her even before Luis had come to her with Carmen's plea.

———

Late January, 1998

The nuns in her catechism class had all been talking about the pope's visit to Cuba with excitement. *Historic*, they said, their joy apparent. *The first pope to ever visit Cuba*, the nuns would murmur, look skyward as if for celestial guidance, and offer up a prayer.

But as Jessica sat beside her mother that night, watching the television news, she was completely confused. There was no excitement there, only pain. Tears washed down her mother's face as she viewed the images streaming from Cuba. The pope was being greeted by thousands of Cubans along the streets of Havana, blessing the crowds with holy water while being held back by barricades and the military. The images were interspersed with footage of the bearded man she knew was Fidel, as well as ordinary Cubans going about their lives. Shopping at street-side markets where people paid with American dollars. Waiting on a tarmac while armed soldiers in white uniforms ceremonially lined up as the pope's plane landed.

Her mother shuddered and the tears grew heavier, becoming almost sobs.

Jessica laid a hand on her mother's arm and stroked it tenderly. "Mommy, are you okay?"

Her mother dashed away the tears and sucked in a deep breath, holding it for a long second to resume control before she said, "Mommy is okay. She's just sad."

"Is that Cuba?" Jessica asked, wondering as she had so often about the place where her mother had been born. Her mother never talked about it or her mommy and daddy. Jessica knew her mother had parents because, well, everyone had parents. She might be only six, but she knew that one thing for sure. Everyone had parents.

"It is Cuba," her mother choked out and then pointed to the screen and the image of a reporter on a street lined by old homes. "My mom told me our address once. The house where we used to live...I don't think it was all that far from that street," she said, voice hoarse. "I had a photo of my father with a car just like that one," she added as an old Chevrolet drove by on the road, followed by a number of bicyclists.

"Your dad? What was he like?" she asked, eager to finally hear more about her mother's family.

But only silence followed as her mother lifted the remote, shut off the television, and just like that, shut herself off once more.

"Are you okay with that, Jessica?" Luis asked, but it was clear to him she had been somewhere else during the entrée.

"I'm sorry. I was thinking about something," she said and turned her attention his way.

"I asked if you were okay with Luis showing you around tomorrow. Maybe even going to our corporate headquarters so you can meet some of the cousins?" Carmen repeated.

Jessica's gaze skipped between them. "That would be nice, but I'd like to spend time with you as well, Carmen. Find out more about you and my mother. Cuba."

The fear that had been in Luis since the day he'd flown to New York eased, replaced by hope. He hadn't known what to expect from Jessica. About how she would react, but so far, it was going better than he had thought it would. Jessica's words were a good sign that positive things would continue. But just in case, he decided to give them more time alone tonight.

He glanced at his watch. "I hope you'll excuse me, but I have to go."

A wry grin erupted on Jessica's lips. "Hot date?"

"Just some papers I need to review before an early morning meeting," he said and hoped his lie wasn't too obvious.

Carmen tsked and shook her head. "You need to leave time for personal things, *mijo*," she said and directed a less-than-subtle glance toward Jessica.

And there it is, he thought and chuckled. "*Viejita*, you should show Jessica some of those old family photos after dinner. I'm sure she'd love to know more about her Gallego great-grandparents and how they got to Cuba." He rose and brushed a quick kiss on Carmen's cheek before walking over to Jessica.

She stood and he did the same to her, keeping the kiss to a fraternal peck. "How about I pick you up around noon for that tour?"

Jessica nodded. "I'll be ready."

"*Hasta mañana*," he said and hurried off, glad that she'd be prepared for their tour because he wasn't sure he would be. Jessica was turning out to be a tempting puzzle. He had always loved doing puzzles and putting together all the pieces to reveal the final picture.

But this puzzle was different because he had no idea if he had all the pieces or a box top to help him see what the final picture should look like. His one hope was that he'd be able to make sense of the jumble in a way that completed that picture. *And not like a Picasso,* he thought with a harsh laugh as he left the two women alone to find their way together.

Chapter Nine

Instead of continuing with dessert on the bayside patio, Carmen asked Manny to serve it in her home office. As the older man set up the espresso and what Jessica recognized as flan on a coffee table in front of a leather couch, Carmen went to the built-ins behind her desk and pulled a thick scrapbook from one of the shelves. Her grandmother hugged it to her chest and returned to the sofa.

Whoa! How is it possible that in only a few hours I'm thinking of Carmen as my grandmother? She forced back that thought because it was too soon for the decades of her mother's pain to be wiped away so quickly.

The leather creaked as Jessica sat and was chilly from the air-conditioning. Carmen took a spot beside her and laid the scrapbook in the space Manny had left in the center of the coffee table. She gestured to the espresso and flan. "*Por favor.* Have your *cafecito* before it gets cold."

She picked up the demitasse cup and took a sip of espresso heavily laced with something thick, sugary, and milky. "Sweet," she said. *Teeth-achingly sweet.*

"It's my favorite. A cortadito with condensed milk," Carmen explained and tossed back the last of her coffee with a dainty tilt of her cup. After she set the cup down, she said, "Try the flan. Manny's wife, Consuelo, is an expert at making it."

She did sample it and couldn't argue with Carmen's assessment. The flan was smooth and creamy. There was a slight bitterness to the caramel it was swimming in, which balanced the sweetness of the dessert. "My *bisnonna* Russo makes something similar, but this is delicious."

"Your *bisabuela*, your great-grandmother, had a wonderful recipe for it. I'd be delighted to share it with you," Carmen said as she picked up her plate and spooned up a piece of the flan.

Jessica finished hers, laid her plate on the table, and stroked her hand across the leather surface of the scrapbook. "Do you have a picture of her in here? My great-grandmother?"

Carmen nodded, set aside her dessert, and opened the book. "*Sí*. And of other relatives as well, but not many. A great deal of it was lost during the Spanish Civil War and after, when we left Cuba."

A civil war? Like in the United States? There was so much she knew so little about, but she intended to learn. But first, it was learning more about Carmen's family. *Not my own family just yet*, she reminded herself.

Carmen rattled off names of the faces and places in the first several pages, people and locations a couple of generations removed from her great-grandparents. With the flip of another page, a face stared back at her that she couldn't deny. It looked too much like Carmen. Too much like her and her mother.

"Is that…?"

"Your great-grandmother Nieves. My mother. She and your great-grandfather left Galicia in the early 1920s, well before the Spanish Civil War broke out."

"What's Galicia?" she asked, unfamiliar with the name.

"It's one of the northernmost provinces in Spain. A Celtic nation," Carmen explained.

"Celtic? Like Irish?" she asked, more confused than ever about her ancestry.

"Some Irish and Scots are Celtic like your descendants, although there are Romans on your paternal grandfather's side. That part of

Spain was colonized by them as well, although the Romans found out that the Celts weren't easily defeated. We're fierce fighters."

So much to take in and learn, she thought and forged on to hear more.

"Why Cuba?" Jessica wondered in light of her own Italian grandparents' immigrant journey to the United States to improve their lives.

"My maternal grandfather always said he didn't want to spend his life as a 'dirt-poor farmer.' For him and many other Spaniards, Cuba was the land of opportunity." Carmen gestured to another photo of her grandparents posing stoically with a young child in some kind of costume. As she flipped the page, there was another photo of the same child similarly dressed, and as Jessica looked more closely, she realized it was Carmen.

"That's you as a baby," she said and peered at Carmen, trying to connect the sleekly coiffed woman sitting beside her with the young, too-serious child in the black-and-white photo.

A wistful smile came to Carmen's lips, as if she were remembering the moment. "It's me. And that's traditional Galician garb. Your Gallego grandparents made their dreams come true in Cuba. It was paradise for them."

Faster than a New York minute, her attitude changed. Hardened to stone. "And then it all became a nightmare because of me."

Havana, March 1956

Carmen pushed away the demitasse cup her mother placed in front of her. Lately the smell of coffee as well as a number of other foods made her stomach queasy. Beneath the hand resting on her swollen belly, the baby did a somersault that mimicked the tumble of her stomach. She almost lost it as her mother placed a plate of guava pastelitos in the center of the table. They were normally one of her favorites, but now the thought of all that buttery pastry and sweetness had her stomach revolting.

"*Gracias*, Mami, but I'll pass," she said in Spanish and held her hand up in a stop gesture.

"*Niña*, you have to eat. For the baby's sake," Nieves said, but didn't force the issue. There were bigger things to battle about as her mother shifted the plate away in deference to Carmen's request.

"It's for the baby's sake that I'm doing this, Mami. Castro says—"

"Whatever the people want to hear, like any good politician," Nieves argued and picked up her own coffee. The cup rattled against the saucer as her hands shook.

With anger or concern? Carmen wondered, but pushed on, trying to convince her mother.

"It's time for change in Cuba. Positive change, Mami. A democracy where we can be free and not under Batista's thumb," Carmen urged, wanting it more than ever for the child growing in her womb. A restive child who once again rolled and, for good measure, kicked her in the ribs almost as if punishing her for even thinking about what she intended to do.

Her mother forcefully set her cup down and coffee sloshed over the rim and onto the tabletop, her anger apparent now. "And what if you trade a thumb for a boot, *mi'jita*?"

Carmen couldn't ignore her mother's fear. The history of Cuba was rife with going from one oppressive regime to another. "It's worth the risk. For my baby and her future. For Cuba's future," she said and lovingly stroked her hand across her belly. A daughter, she was sure, and she would do whatever she had to so that she might have a better life.

With those thoughts, Lara—she had decided to name her unborn daughter Lara—seemed to quiet, as if accepting Carmen's decision. A blessing of sorts for the actions she intended to take. Actions that would finally give her daughter a better future.

There was so much pain in Carmen's gaze. So much grief that Jessica couldn't ignore it.

She laid an arm across Carmen's shoulders and squeezed. "You couldn't have known."

A sheen of tears filmed Carmen's eyes as she examined Jessica's features. "I wish it were that easy to forgive myself for so many mistakes. Fidel. Your mother, time and time again. Your grandfather Carlos and his restlessness. I just made it worse each time, no matter how hard I tried to make things better. I lost everything that ever mattered to me."

There was true apology there, but it wasn't Jessica who was owed that apology. "Maybe you need to tell my mother that, Carmen."

With several vehement nods and a loud sniffle, Carmen said, "I think it's time to call it a night. I'm tired."

Jessica wanted to press, but it was too soon, and Carmen was too fragile at that moment. "I understand. Maybe we can pick this up tomorrow."

Carmen nodded, rose, and smoothed her skirts. "*Hasta mañana.* I'll see you in the morning. Feel free to keep on looking through the albums," she said and rushed out of the room, leaving Jessica behind with her family's past spread out on the table before her like a body at an autopsy.

It was too much to resist, but would it be a Pandora's box that she could never close again once opened?

You should have thought about that before you decided to come to Miami, the little voice in her head chastised.

Well, the box was open, and Jessica was too intrigued to close it right now.

She flipped page after page, perusing carefully labeled photos and mementos detailing her family's history. At one point there was a photo of her mother looking so much like Carmen that she did a double take and had to flip back to the original photo of Carmen just to make sure it wasn't a duplicate.

They were like clones of each other, much like she and her mother. The Guerreiro genes did run powerfully. Warrior genes, Luis had said just earlier that day, and if this was a battle, Jessica intended to win. For her mother. For Carmen. For herself.

She came from a group of fierce fighters after all, she thought, recalling Carmen's words.

Returning to the scrapbook, she reviewed the pages carefully, almost as if to memorize the photos. From the shades of gray in the black-and-white images, she could tell there were a number of blonds and maybe gingers in the photographs. Celts, she remembered from Carmen's explanation. It probably explained the green eyes she, her mother, and Carmen all shared.

A man identified as Carlos Gonzalez, her grandfather. The Guerreiro name was her grandmother's—Carmen's—maiden name. Her grandfather was dressed in some sort of uniform; she guessed police. Much later on he wore the more familiar military garb of the U.S. Army and she wondered how he'd made that journey.

In between those uniform photos were ones of her mother with her sister Gloria and later, Anna. Sisters who no longer spoke. Aunts she didn't know with children who were also strangers.

Until tomorrow that is. Tomorrow she'd start meeting them, but for tonight…

She picked up the phone and dialed her father. She had texted him earlier that day to confirm she had arrived in Miami but needed to hear his voice and share some of what she was feeling.

He answered on the first ring, almost as if he'd been waiting for her call. But then again, that's how it had always been between them. Most times she'd run to him first with news, since her mother had oftentimes been busy at work.

Like mother, like daughter, she thought, hating the disloyalty in that realization.

"Hey, Dad," she said and leaned into the comfortable cushions of the sofa.

"Hey, yourself. How are you?" She closed her eyes and pictured him, brown eyes betraying his emotions so easily. If she had to guess, he was worried tonight despite his laid-back greeting.

"I'm tired. It's been a roller-coaster day, if you know what I mean," she said.

"I can't begin to imagine." He hesitated and then asked the question she had been expecting. "What's she like?"

She looked at the picture of a young Lara in the scrapbook before her. Pictured Carmen now. "Imagine Mom in twenty years."

"Ah. Stubborn," he said with a chuckle.

She joined in his laughter. "I think determined is a better adjective, but yes. They look alike, just like Mom and me."

"She's beautiful, then," he said, love for his wife in his voice.

"Some might say that. Definitely regal. Well-preserved," she offered since Carmen looked nothing like her age.

A long pause followed before he said, "What's it like? The 'big-ass mansion' as you called it."

She thought of the modest home in which she'd grown up. In which her parents still lived despite their financial success. They'd never felt the need to "keep up with the Joneses" and would never have moved all that far from family. Except for her mother's flight from Miami.

"It's hard to describe," she said with an amused chuckle.

"Try," her father said, a playful tone in his voice.

"Huge. Like *really* huge and on a private, gated island to keep out riffraff like me," she kidded.

"Send pics when you can. I promise I won't sell them to the *Enquirer*." He hesitated for a second. "You're really okay, right?" he asked, obviously worried.

"I am, Dad. I'd tell you if I weren't," she said and meant it. She had always been able to tell her father almost anything.

Another long pause followed, but then he said, "Love you." He didn't wait for her reply to end the call.

"Love you," she said to a suddenly dead line and stared at her screen where a picture of her and her mother smiling on one of their girls' nights seemed almost condemning.

She tapped the phone icon and her finger hovered over the picture of her mother in her Favorites list. She missed her already, but as she'd told her father, it had been a day of ups and downs.

She didn't know which it would be if she had a conversation with her mother tonight. She just knew she wasn't ready for it and swiped her phone closed.

Tomorrow. *Mañana*, she thought. She'd deal with her mother tomorrow.

Chapter Ten

WEAK SUNLIGHT LEAKED THROUGH the windows as the sun rose over South Beach, and Biscayne Bay came alive with color.

Jessica stretched in bed, the fine cotton sheets luxurious against any exposed skin. The light bedspread was a comforting weight she wrapped around herself as she lazed beneath it. Lazing was something she rarely did since she was usually up and about before the crack of dawn, either on her way to a flea market or dealer, or in her shop working on a piece.

She gave herself the gift of just lying there, appreciating the transformation of the bay as the sun touched it with light. Last night the water had been a midnight blue, accepting the kiss of moonlight on its waves. Now as the sun rose, bits of crystal danced on those same waves as midnight became indigo. Slowly the hues of dawn brightened. Summer roses, pineapple, and orange sherbet until the bay became a bright azure.

Transformation. She did it every day in her shop as years of grime and decay revealed the life and beauty of the wood. It usually took days for her to reveal that beauty. For the transformation to take place.

Yet in just a day, she felt that such a massive change was already underway inside her. Like she was no longer the woman she had been yesterday morning. But as she rose and sat on the edge of the bed, the spread wrapped around her body, she considered that the change had started much earlier.

It had started the day Luis had walked into her shop.

Luis. They were supposed to spend the better part of the day together, and while she looked forward to it, it also worried her.

He was far too charming and handsome. Too caring and considerate as well. Intriguing, but she ripped that thought out the way an avid British gardener tore out weeds while tending to her flowers.

She didn't know when Carmen normally woke, but assumed she had some time before she did. She'd use that time to check out some of those furniture pieces that had called to her when she had first walked into Carmen's home the day before.

After a long soak luxuriating beneath a rain-style showerhead and an endless supply of hot water, which was sometimes lacking in her apartment, she dressed for the day with Luis. While the collection of clothes Carmen had provided had been tempting—she had an eye for beautiful things, after all—she stuck to the serviceable khaki pants and teal camp shirt she had thought would be perfect for a Miami outing.

Down in the living room, the house was silent, but the clatter of pans drew her toward another wing where she found an older woman—Manny's wife, Consuelo, she presumed—preparing a pot of espresso. On one of the counters a pot of American coffee had already been brewed, spicing the air with its earthy scent.

"Good morning," she called out and the woman turned, smiling as she set the espresso pot on the stove.

"*Buenos días*, Señorita Jessica," Consuelo said with a broad welcoming smile. "What can I get you for breakfast?"

Jessica held her hands up in a "no need" gesture. "Just coffee, *gracias*."

"Americano?" she asked, and at Jessica's nod, Consuelo rose on tiptoes and took a mug from a cabinet. She poured the coffee and asked, "Milk? Sugar?"

"I can do that," she said, walked over, and took the mug. She realized there was hot steamed milk in a small pitcher and added it to the mug along with four heaping tablespoons of sugar.

"You are a Cubanita after all," Consuelo teased, and as the espresso maker burbled to warn the coffee was ready, she turned off the gas.

Jessica chuckled and sipped her sugary coffee. "I guess I am. Is Carmen up?"

"She's sleeping in today. The excitement of the last week has tired her." The barest hint of worry was in her tone.

"I'm sure. I promise I won't be too much trouble," she said to reassure, aware of the admitted friendship between the two women.

"She's very happy to have you here. Are you sure there isn't anything I can get you for breakfast? Some toast maybe?"

Jessica cradled the mug and held it up. "This will do. I'm just going to stroll around the house, look at some of the furniture, if that's okay."

"*Esta es tu casa*, Jessica. Feel free to explore," Consuelo replied.

"*Gracias*, Consuelo."

She left the kitchen and headed to the foyer and the first piece of furniture that had caught her eye. The console was in an elaborate baroque style with delicately carved flowers and scrolls covered with golden gilt. That motif was carried across the front of the piece, which was painted in a slate gray with a strong blue hue. The painted section was bordered in black. Marble with caramel, gray, and black veins topped the console. An intricately carved blue-and-black frame surrounded a mirror hung above it and matched the piece below.

Pulling open a drawer, she appreciated the finely done tongue and groove joints and the gilded drawer pull.

She was about to examine the rococo secretary desk across the way when the front door popped open and Luis walked in, clearly lost in thought as he rubbed his jaw while he entered.

He stopped short when he noticed her standing there. That

slightly distracted look immediately fled and was replaced by a broad welcoming smile.

"*Buenos dias*," he said, strode over, and dropped a quick peck on her cheek.

"*Buenos dias*," she repeated, thinking the Spanish might help her fit in better in this very different environment.

Luis waved his hand in the direction of the console. "I see you were inspecting the furniture."

She nodded and walked over to the secretary. "Lovely work. Rosewood. Such beautifully carved cabriolet legs and bronzework."

Luis nodded. "Carmen has a fine eye for quality, but she has one piece that's very special to her," he said, and taking Jessica's hand, he led her to a round Chippendale-style parlor table with a top inlaid with gold leaf embossed leather. The leather had the nicks and scars of use, and the wood was of a lower quality, but the piece was lovingly polished to a warm sheen.

The table sat by the door leading to the wing with Carmen's home office, as if guarding the entrance. She ran her hand over the piece, a reproduction from the 1940s or '50s if she knew her stuff, but still beautiful.

"I don't get it," she said and glanced at him.

He likewise trailed his fingers over the leather inlay. "It was one of the first pieces of furniture she was able to buy after coming from Cuba. She got it at a thrift store. St. Vincent de Paul, I believe. It was a big deal for her back then."

In some ways she understood, not that she'd ever wanted for anything in her life. "I often have people come into my shop for the first pieces they can afford. I see how special they are to them."

"And to you," he said. "I can see the love you put into restoring them."

The statement struck her as wrong somehow. "You saw that in, like, what…the five minutes you were in my shop?"

He jerked his hand away from the piece, clearly uneasy about her question, as if he'd revealed too much. "Your *abuela* asked me to come by early to get you for our tour. If you're ready, that is."

Worry worked into her gut again about Carmen's health. "She is okay, right?"

Luis nodded and laid a reassuring hand on her forearm, and she shifted away from the too-familiar touch. He understood and let his hand fall to his side. "*Perdóname.* Yes, she is fine. No need to worry. She's just a little tired. It was a very emotional day for her yesterday. For you too, I imagine."

"It was," she admitted. *Confusing as well,* she thought, recalling her early morning ruminations about the changes that had happened since her arrival in Miami.

"If you haven't had breakfast—"

"I haven't, but I don't normally do breakfast. Just caffeine," she said and held up her coffee mug for him to see.

In response his stomach growled, and he laid a hand over it and offered an apologetic smile. "Well, I do *do* breakfast and was hoping you'd join me."

His smile was so boyish and inviting that she couldn't refuse. "I'd love to. Just let me drop this off in the kitchen."

He flipped a hand in the direction of the door. "Meet me out front."

She nodded and hurried to the kitchen to drop off the mug. Inside, Consuelo and Manny were having breakfast and went to rise when she entered. She said, "No worries. *Gracias,*" and deposited the mug in the sink.

Rushing back through the living room and out to the driveway, she found Luis waiting there, arms crossed as he negligently leaned against the bumper of a Jaguar XJ in a metallic blue that gleamed beneath the Miami sun.

She raised her eyebrows and teased, "Boys and their toys."

He threw his hands up in a "why not?" gesture and gave her that boyish grin once more.

When she walked over, he held the door open for her, and she paused for a moment to run her hand across the soft grain leather. "My pops would absolutely love this," she said and sank into the seat.

"Maybe I can take him for a drive someday," he said, leaning close before he shut the door.

The citrusy fragrance of his cologne lingered for a moment, teasing her senses. He sat beside her, and she was enveloped in the combined scents of citrus, leather, and man.

"Do you mind?" he asked and pointed to a moonroof.

"Not at all. I'd love to get in as much sun as I can before going back to New York."

He grimaced but remained silent as he popped open the moonroof and pulled out of the driveway, the throaty growl of the engine vibrating through her when he accelerated.

In no time they'd pulled off Star Island and onto the causeway toward South Beach. Minutes later they were turning off Fifth Street onto Ocean Drive and cruised to a café across from a beachside park. Luis expertly parked in a spot that had fortunately cleared just as they arrived. There were no empty spots as far as she could see.

"That was lucky. Parking here can be tough, and if we're *really* lucky, we'll snag an outdoor table so we can people watch," he said.

They were *really* lucky, or maybe it was the fact that Luis was obviously well-known to the staff, since they were quickly seated at one of the coveted people-watching tables and handed menus.

With a quick look, they both ordered eggs, prompting Luis to say, "I guess we both love a lot of the same things."

Jessica smiled. "I guess we do. Makes me wonder what else we have in common."

He looked upward, as if giving it great thought and said, "Determination. Smarts."

"Humility," she teased to stop him.

With a shrug, he said, "Don't hide your light under a bushel. You've accomplished a great deal." The waiter came by at that moment with their coffees.

"And you know this because?" She sipped her Cuban coffee, which was sweet and creamy. She might just have to make this her morning staple. The sugar and caffeine would totally jump-start her workday.

He sipped his own coffee, paused, and said, "I never tackle any assignment without doing my homework."

For some reason, she didn't like that he thought of her as an assignment. She set her cup down sharply and it rattled in the small saucer. "Is that what I am to you? Legwork for Carmen's pet project?"

"Not anymore," he admitted and glanced at her with such force, unexpected heat flashed across her body like lightning before a storm.

Definitely time to change the subject. "Carmen and I chatted last night. I learned a little bit about my grandparents and great-grandparents."

"Spaniards one and all," he said with a touch of humor she didn't quite understand.

"You don't consider them Cuban?" she asked just as the waiter brought over the fried egg platters they had ordered.

With another Gallic lift of his shoulders, he said, "I have a friend whose father was first generation Cuban. In Cuba they were considered Gallegos because his grandparents were from Spain. When his family came here, Americans called them Cubans, naturally. He left the States to live with family in Spain where they called him 'the American.' He felt like no country ever wanted to claim him as one of their own."

"Poor man. It must feel terrible not to be wanted," she said and dug into her meal.

He did as well, but then paused, his fork in midair. "It hurts, but you get over it."

She realized he was referring to his own family's experience of not being accepted by the Cubans who had already been well-established in Miami when the *Marielitos* had arrived. It likely matched the experience of her own Italian immigrant ancestors in the early 1900s when they had landed in New York City.

"Do you get over it?" she wondered aloud.

"The best revenge is success," he replied matter-of-factly.

She considered him and the very obvious success he projected with his clothing, jewelry, and cars. He probably had an over-the-top home, not quite like Carmen's but still luxurious. It gave her a new insight into what drove Luis. Besides loyalty to Carmen. Which prompted her to ask, "Are we going to Carmen's business later?"

He quirked a brow. "You mean your family's business?"

She could argue with him but suspected it would be futile. No matter her mother's exile from her family, they were related by blood to this Miami branch. And she was quickly realizing there might be other connections that she wanted to know more about. A history in Spain. In Cuba. Here in Miami. Even though she knew nothing about them, they were as much a part of her as her Italian family's history.

"I'm looking forward to the visit," she said to head off an argument.

That arched brow challenged her again. "I mean it," she said. "But I thought you also said you'd take me on a tour? Show me some Miami sights?"

"If you'd like," he said, almost being too agreeable.

"*Gracias.* I'd love to see that church you mentioned. And the estate. If you have the time, that is."

He eyed her, that brown-eyed gaze intense. Compelling. "For you, I have all the time in the world."

Chapter Eleven

SINCE LUIS HAD COME earlier than expected, they went for a stroll along the winding path in Lummus Park, the seaside area opposite the Ocean Drive art deco hotels. A low stone seawall separated the park from the beach where tourists and locals alike took advantage of a beautiful early spring day. As they walked beneath sea grape trees and palms, in-line skaters whizzed past them, and in one area volleyball players engaged in a spirited game on the sand.

"This is nice. Not like Jones Beach or the Jersey Shore," Jessica said, taking in all the activity going on in the area.

Luis peered at her as she looked all around, clearly enjoying the vibe of the area. "When my family first came from Cuba, a lot of these hotels were home to welfare recipients and low-income families because they had gotten so rundown. My family lived in one for a couple of months before they saved enough to move out."

He gestured to one of the hotels across the way, right in the middle of the Ocean Drive scene. "That one," he said and waved in the direction of the building.

The hotel is anything but rundown, Jessica thought. The building rose higher than the nearby hotels and the cement walls were painted in an electric white with a central tower highlighted with extra wide stripes in shades of teal. A restaurant on the main level was busy serving breakfast on a veranda and a number of al fresco tables.

"It's in excellent shape now," she said, appreciating the work that had been done to renovate the location.

"*Gracias.* It took a lot of work for us to restore it to its original state in 1937. Do you know Clark Gable and Carole Lombard once stayed there?" he said, obvious pride in his voice.

Jessica paused for a moment, considering his words. "You said 'for us.'"

He nodded and smiled. "When I saw the area was starting to come back, I decided to jump into the real estate market and it seemed apropos."

More than apropos, Jessica thought. "The ultimate revenge is success, right?" she said, recalling his words over breakfast that morning.

That shrug came again. "Revenge and a wise investment. It's paid off so far, although we're starting to have problems again. Spring breakers and others just don't appreciate the history of the area. Tonight will be crazy busy as well."

"That's a shame," she said, but could imagine how the location would be a draw for party animals, what with the nearby beach and all the restaurants and bars along the strip. Especially on a Friday night, like tonight.

"It is, but we'll deal with it. Maybe we can do dinner there before you leave next Saturday?"

"Maybe," she said, worried that too much time with Luis would make him too hard to resist. Like the layers on the proverbial onion, each one that was removed gave her more insight into what made him tick, rousing unwanted emotions. They couldn't be more different, from lifestyle choices to geography.

Obviously disappointed that he hadn't exacted an outright yes, he deflected by shooting a quick glance at his watch. "Maybe it's time we head to the office so you can meet some of your cousins."

"Maybe," she teased.

He narrowed his gaze, his dark eyes contemplating her, but then a grin split his lips and he chuckled. "I think you just like being difficult at times."

"And I think you're too used to most people rolling over for you. I'm not most people."

"You are very definitely not most people." He ran the back of his hand across her cheek in a fleeting gesture, but even that slightest of touches felt too intimate. Too personal.

Voice shaky from her confusion, she said, "It's time to go."

"It is," he said, and in no time, they had doubled back to the causeway for the drive to downtown Miami, Luis playing tour guide as they drove past Bayfront Marketplace and Park to downtown. "This whole area has been designated as a landmark. Most of the buildings were built in the 1920s."

Her artist's eye contemplated the mix of architecture among the mostly low-lying buildings. One stuck out with its Spanish-style flavor. "What's that one?" she asked.

With a quick look, he smiled and said, "The Freedom Tower. Many of the Cubans in Miami came through there. It's kind of like Miami's Ellis Island. There are plans to possibly use it as a Cuban American museum in the future."

With its tall tower rising into the skyline and the distinctive columns below, it had the dignified look that suited a museum, especially given its history and meaning for the Cuban community.

"Did my family go through there? Yours?" she asked, wondering what it must have been like.

He shook his head. "Your *abuelos* and *mami* came before the U.S. government used it for refugees, and it closed before my family came. They were held in the Orange Bowl while being processed," he explained and turned off to park in front of another building. Tall, but not anywhere near as high as the almost Manhattan-like skyscrapers lining Biscayne Bay. She liked the feel of this area more because the various buildings had character that the immense glass structures couldn't match.

She was about to ask if this was her family's building, but a large brass plaque that ran just above the first three stories confirmed it: *Guerreiro Enterprises*. It made her wonder again why Carmen had decided to use her maiden name for the business rather than her husband's. She'd have to ask her grandmother. *Carmen*, she reminded herself, still stuck in that uncertain transformation that she'd sensed coming over her in the morning.

The building was located midblock and rose high above the lower-lying structures on the street. The first three stories were a combination of large glass windows and elaborate bas-relief panels depicting palms and tropical flowers. Each bay of windows and panels were flanked by columns that gave the structure the look of ancient Greece. Colorful hibiscus and a riot of cascading blossoms and vines in tall bronze-and-black planters at the base of each column softened the look of the building.

Luis came around and opened her door. "Ready?"

She didn't know if she was, but it was time to meet more of the family so she could decide for herself whether they were meant to be a part of her life.

The first two floors of the building had high ceilings, creating a bright, open space being used as an exhibition area for assorted artwork. "Lovely," she said, appreciating how the space had been modernized without destroying the 1920s feel of the lobby.

"It's a landmarked building, so Carmen really had to jump through hoops to get the look she wanted," he explained as they strolled to one of the two staircases at the back of the building.

They walked up the stairs to a roomy reception area boasting a few seating areas with comfortable black leather couches and low glass-and-metal tables for a modern midcentury feel. The receptionist's area was the exact opposite in style, with a large antique colonial Spanish desk boasting ornately carved wooden panels. Age had darkened the patina of the wood to almost black, which melded it with the more modern look of the other furniture.

The receptionist smiled at Luis as he entered but eyeballed Jessica as if sizing up the competition. "*Buenos dias*, Blanca," he said.

Jessica echoed his greeting and followed him through the glass doors as Blanca buzzed them in.

Luis held up one finger. "First stop, the mailroom."

"The mailroom?"

Luis nodded, and as they walked past the cubicles on the first floor, he greeted the various employees working there. "Carmen believes that everyone who wants to be anyone in the company has to learn the business from the ground up."

"Even family?" she questioned.

He dipped his head to confirm it. "*Especially* family, and before you ask, me as well. I did my stints in the mailroom, warehouse, cafeteria, you name it."

She furrowed her brow. "Cafeteria? Seriously?"

He grinned devilishly and, with his expressive hands, mimicked the toss of a spatula. "I flip a mean burger. Maybe I can show you some day."

There was that *maybe* word again and she was beginning to hate the indecisiveness of it because if there was one thing she wasn't, it was indecisive. "I'd like that."

Her words made him stop in his tracks. "Seriously?"

"Seriously," she said and added, "So which cousin is in the mailroom?"

"Carlos. He's named after his father, Gloria's husband, and your *abuelo*."

Another Sal situation, she thought and laughed silently.

The young man in the mailroom had intense green eyes, a dimpled chin, and the sharp nose she was coming to know as the Guerreiro look. Although she had expected some suspicion among her cousins at her sudden appearance, Carlos was friendly and welcoming.

"So nice to finally meet you, *Prima*," he said while effusively shaking her hand.

"Nice to meet you too," she said.

"I hope you're enjoying your time with Abuela. Is it your first time in Miami?" he said.

"It is, but Luis promised to show me around," she said.

Carlos's gaze skipped to Luis and then back to her. "If he's too busy, I'd be happy to show you around."

"I won't be too busy," Luis said and added, "It's time to go."

Then they were off and running to another section in the office to meet Angelica.

"*The* Angelica?" she said, remembering Luis's comments about her.

"*The* Angelica," he said with a chuckle and wry grin.

As it turned out, Angelica was on one of the uppermost floors, in the cafeteria Luis had mentioned earlier. The space was large and airy. On one side the floor opened to a rooftop patio set with tables, umbrellas, and planters bursting with colorful flowers and shrubs.

Inside, the cafeteria had an assortment of comfortable tables and chairs where employees at all levels mingled, from executives in suits to workers in overalls emblazoned with the Guerreiro name and logo on the breast pockets. An electronic menu board sat high above a 1950s-style stainless steel counter, and she noticed the prices for the menu items were more than reasonable.

"There are lots of places to eat in downtown, but your *abuela* wants her people to have their own place, and the food prices are subsidized by the company so everyone can afford them," Luis explained.

As they neared the counter, she noted the young woman helping to serve the orders that were placed at an assortment of electronic kiosks, in addition to an employee at an adjacent counter. Like Carlos, she had the Guerreiro look. Her hair was darker, almost jet black, which just made her green eyes pop against flawless white skin that was expertly made up. Her hair was done in an intricate bun beneath a beanie that matched the apron she wore. A dress that had to be designer peeked out from beneath the apron, and although she couldn't see Angelica's feet, she suspected her cousin had on designer pumps. An assortment of gold bracelets danced on her right wrist, and she sported a number of rings on her fingers. On her left wrist she wore a trendy and expensive wristwatch.

As Angelica set her gaze on Luis, it heated, and Jessica swore she detected a very feline purr in her voice when she said, "Luis. Always so good to see you."

"Angelica. This is your cousin Jessica," Luis said, his tone totally professional.

Unlike Carlos and his warm greeting, Angelica held out a hand as cold and limp as a dead fish. Her smile had no warmth, and that green-eyed gaze held the suspicion that Jessica had expected. "So nice to meet you," Angelica said, but obviously didn't mean it.

Jessica plastered a smile on her face and in exaggerated welcome said, "So nice to meet you also, Cousin."

Angelica turned her lips into a moue and extracted her hand from Jessica's. "I'm sure."

Luis barely contained his chuckle. He laid his hand on Jessica's back in a gesture that was becoming familiar as he applied gentle pressure to direct her toward a set of stairs to one side of the cafeteria. "We'll let you get back to work," he tossed at Angelica, who almost huffed and stamped her foot at having to return to delivering orders to her fellow employees.

"Entitled much?" Jessica said under her breath.

"More than all of the cousins, but your *abuela* won't put up with that. If Angelica wants to lead, she'll have to earn her place."

"Like you did," Jessica said as she climbed the stairs to the penthouse floor of the building.

That humble shrug came again. "Like Carmen did." He gestured to the space on the upper floor and said, "Everything here is because of her hard work. Because she earned it."

Jessica did a slow swivel, taking in the half dozen offices which were clearly for the top executives in the company. Like the gods on Olympus, they ruled the Guerreiro world, deciding the fates of all who belonged to their realm.

"Is this where you work?" she asked and followed him to the largest space on the floor. A central reception area was home to his administrative assistant. One side of the central space held his office while the other boasted a large conference room. All the walls were glass, providing views of Biscayne Bay and the skyscrapers along the water.

It was easy to picture him there as the king of the universe. *A benevolent king*, she thought, revising her first impressions of him. He'd been too open with her in the short time they'd been together, and from what she'd seen of the business so far, it took care of its employees. It was a philosophy that had been ingrained in her by her father.

Happy workers make good workers.

He held his hands wide. "This was Carmen's office, and I couldn't find the heart to remodel it."

Like the home on Star Island and the reception area, it was a tasteful mix of modern and antique. "You should make it yours," she said, trailing her fingers across the rustic surface of a colonial Spanish console along one wall. At his hesitation, she said, "You've earned it, haven't you?"

He delayed again and his humility wasn't feigned. *Or maybe it wasn't humility*, she considered and walked toward him. She cupped his cheek as she said, "Revenge is bittersweet, isn't it? I get that you still feel as if—"

"I'm not worthy?" he challenged with an arch of his brow, but he covered her hand with his. Twined his fingers with hers and urged her closer. "Maybe you can help me find something to call my own. The Design District isn't all that far from here. Or we can do a flea market."

She peered upward, locking her gaze with his. They were too close, and she stepped back because they were in his office. *No, Carmen's old office. It wouldn't be his until he really made it his.*

She smiled. "I would love to help you find something so you can make this *your* office."

"*Gracias.*" A second later his smartphone chirped to advise of an incoming call.

She stepped to the door of his office to avoid hearing his conversation, but as he answered whoever was on the other end, he looked in her direction. "*Sí, como no, viejita.* We were just finishing up here. I'll have her back in no time."

He swiped to end the call. "I think that furniture shopping will have to wait. Your *abuela* was hoping we'd be home soon. Are you ready?"

She wanted to say it wasn't home. She wanted to say that she had been enjoying their time together and didn't want it to end so soon. Instead, she said, "I'm ready if you are."

—◆◇—

Luis walked her to the bayside patio where they'd all shared a dinner the night before. Carmen smiled and motioned for him to join them, but he raised a hand and demurred. "I'd love to, but I need to go back to the office and catch up on some work."

She tsked and shook her head. "You work too much, *mi'jo,*" Carmen chastised again as she had the night before and sat back at the table.

Eyes gleaming with humor, he shot a quick glance at Jessica and said, "Actually I plan on taking the day off tomorrow to show Jessica around Miami since we weren't able to do it today. Visit La Ermita de la Caridad and Vizcaya. Dinner over in South Beach."

Carmen turned her attention to Jessica, a calculating look in her eyes. "Are you okay with that, *mi'jita?*"

"I'd like that, but I'd also like to spend more time with you. Get to know more about the family. I met Carlos and Angelica today," she said and hoped that her grandmother would provide insights into them and the other family members she would soon meet. She wasn't disappointed.

Nodding, Carmen said, "Carlos is a good boy. I have high hopes for him. Angelica as well, although it's going to be harder with her. She's too used to just getting things without earning them."

"Too many participation trophies," Jessica said, remembering her own experiences in school and sports.

That nod came again along with a twist of a smile. "That and my Anna. I may have indulged her a little too much since she was the baby."

"I get that as well. My mom and dad never denied me anything."

With a chuckle, Luis said, "You were spoiled, but not a brat like Angelica."

"*Mi'jo*," Carmen chided, but there was laughter in her voice. "Working with us will help Angelica improve her attitude."

Luis tilted his head and laughed again. "The stint in the warehouse will definitely help."

Jessica had to contain a laugh as she pictured her cousin in her fancy dress and designer shoes loading and unloading boxes.

"It will, Luis." Carmen was interrupted by Manny's arrival, who glanced at Luis in question.

"Should I set another place?" the majordomo asked.

Luis raised his hands in a stop gesture. "No, *gracias*. That's my cue to go."

He walked over to Carmen to kiss her cheek and then to Jessica, where he repeated the gesture and said, "I'll see you tomorrow."

"I look forward to it," she said, but hoped it wouldn't give Carmen any ideas about matchmaking. She suspected Carmen would be only too eager to see something happen between her granddaughter and her protégé, in the hopes that Jessica might stay in Miami. Only that wasn't going to happen. Her life was back in Brooklyn.

With a wave and wink in her direction, Luis walked away and

around the side of the house to get to his car. She watched him go, admiring his confident walk. He had the swagger of a man comfortable in his own shoes and sure of himself.

"He's quite a man," Carmen said, a gleam in her eye.

Shut it down, Jessica thought. "It was nice meeting the cousins today. Will I be meeting the rest of the family soon?"

Carmen saw through her ploy but went with it. "Later in the week, if that's okay with you."

While she appreciated how thoughtful they were being about making sure she was on board with their plans, it was almost too thoughtful, if that was possible. Not to mention that later was several days away when she hadn't been sure whether she was going to stay for the whole week. But so far, the time had been more pleasant than she had imagined.

"Whatever is good for everyone is fine with me, Carmen."

"*Bueno,* then I'll reach out to everyone about a Thursday night dinner. This way if you still want to leave after that—"

"When I leave," she stressed. She had a business to run and couldn't be away for much more than a week. *Or two,* the little voice in her head said.

"When you leave," Carmen echoed, her earlier mood dimming, which made Jessica feel like shit. She had never wanted to hurt anyone, but so far, she'd managed to hurt her mother and now Carmen. *Luis,* that annoying voice tacked on.

Manny came by at that moment with the first course of the meal, large crab claws that were a peachy-pink color with intense black tips. A simple slice of lemon completed the dish.

"These are Florida stone crabs," Carmen explained.

They were very different from the Maryland blue crabs she was used to eating. "No bodies?" she asked and opened the first claw to remove the snowy-white meat inside.

Carmen shook her head. "The bodies are too small and aren't

kept. They just pull off the claws and release the crab so it can regrow the claws."

"Sustainable," she said while enjoying the sweet meat from the claws.

"It's an important policy," Carmen said as she forked some crab, her slender fingers delicate and dainty.

"Are all your products sustainable?" she asked, wondering about the business Carmen had built since arriving from Cuba.

Carmen dipped her head. "We try to be sustainable, responsible, with all the food products we distribute and everything we manufacture ourselves."

As someone who'd built her own business, she was intrigued by Carmen's journey. "How did you get started?"

Miami, September 1960

Carmen sat at the bridge table, sorting through the pile of family bills and juggling who would get paid first and who she could hold off for just a little longer. Even though she had paid off a number of bills a week earlier, it seemed like the pile had only grown larger and not smaller. She dragged her fingers through her hair in frustration and sighed, wishing there was more that she could do for her family. They were barely breaking even, and it was a struggle to put food on the table every day, but somehow her parents and she managed to do it.

But for how long? she thought.

Her father, Antonio, left his beat-up recliner across from a tiny black-and-white television and sat beside her, his face darkened by a heavy day's-growth of beard and the worry in his hazel eyes. "*Mi'ja,* it will be fine," he said in Spanish.

"*Lo se.* I just wish…" *Wishing accomplished nothing,* she told herself. Only action accomplished anything. Even the smallest actions were better than the biggest of intentions.

"Is there anything I can do?" he asked.

She cradled his cheek, his beard rough beneath her palm. "Papi, you do so much for us already," she said and stroked his cheek lovingly. With Carlos away with the brigade, her father had stepped in as the man of the house. He'd even lied about his age, making himself a decade younger so he could work as a maintenance man at one of the food service companies at the airport. *What more could he do?* she thought.

With a work-rough hand, Antonio gestured to the papers spread across the surface of the table. "This will keep until tomorrow. Go get some rest. You have an early shift, and you have to think about la niñita." He motioned to her growing belly and the baby who would be there in only a few months. *Maybe Carlos would be home by then as well. Or maybe they would all be back in Cuba in their old home*, she thought, hope replacing some of her earlier despair.

But her father was right about getting some rest. She had a late morning stint at the supermarket before a short break and a run to a night job at a warehouse for one of their food distributors. Her father also had an early day, and right now she was keeping him and her mother from pulling out the sleeper sofa so they could get their rest.

She gathered up her papers and helped her father close the bridge table. He eased an arm around her waist, hugged her close, and she let herself savor the embrace, drawing comfort from his support. He and her mother had been there for her at every step of their exodus from Cuba, and she didn't know what she would do without them. It was thanks to her mother that she could work the two jobs, since her *mami* watched Lara for her.

Lara, Carmen thought, guilt clawing deep into her gut. She spent so much time away from her, but she had little choice if she was going to feed her family and keep a roof over their heads.

She kissed her *papi* on the cheek and went to the small bedroom she shared with Lara. Her mother, Nieves, was reading to her from a Spanish-language children's book Carmen had found at a thrift store in Hialeah. As she entered, Nieves rose from the small stool beside the bed with a slight hitch and a wince. *Her arthritis must be bothering her today*, Carmen thought.

She took the book from her mother and hugged her. Kissed her cheek as her mother left the room, closing the door behind her to give them some privacy.

"*Mi'jita*, I've missed you," she said and bent to bury her head against Lara's. She smelled of Castile soap as well as the orange water Nieves used on Lara's hair after her bath.

"Mami. Sing to me," Lara said and wrapped her soft, doughy arms around Carmen's neck, the embrace so loving, trusting, it made Carmen's heart constrict with joy.

"*Como no, amorcito*." She quickly changed into her pajamas and slipped beneath the sheet. She drew Lara close and began to sing.

"*Arrurú mi niña, Arrurú mi amor. Arrurú pedazo de mi corazón…*"

In no time Lara was asleep beside her, her body cradled tight. The new baby trapped between them. Another girl, she was sure. *I'll name her Gloria*, she thought, but even as that thought came, so did worry. Another mouth to feed. More burden on her parents, who were already well into their sixties and dealing with their own struggles of being in a new country that was so different from Cuba.

She had to do more, and as she lay there with her two daughters close to her heart, she prayed to the *Virgencita* to give her the strength to do what she knew she had to do.

As she drifted off to sleep, she could swear she heard the Virgencita say that she and her three daughters would be fine.

Three daughters? she wondered but accepted it because the Virgencita had said it would be so and she was always right. In her darkest moments, she'd worried about her family ever being together, but the Virgencita had told her things would work out and they had.

Armed with that belief, she joined her daughter in sleep.

Chapter Twelve

"THREE DAUGHTERS? BUT YOU only had my mom and the baby on the way," Jessica said as she finished up the delicious paella Consuelo had made.

"I thought the same thing, but I've learned that the Virgencita has her own ideas about how things will turn out," Carmen said, and the tone of her voice brooked no disagreement.

Carmen truly believed in that divine intervention and Jessica wasn't about to dismiss it. Sometimes life moved in ways that were hard to understand, like the break between her mother and grandmother. Her mother's sisters. *How different would all our lives be if that schism hadn't happened?* she wondered.

"My mother used to sing that *arrurú* song to me," Jessica said, latching on to a happier moment. Her father had told her years later that her mother had only known Spanish lullabies, not English ones since Spanish had been her first language.

"It was her favorite and mine," Carmen said, a wistful tone in her voice.

Jessica reached out and laid her hand over Carmen's. It wasn't as cold today, maybe because she'd been able to rest earlier in the day. "It's my favorite as well. That and the *barco chiquitico* song."

Carmen smiled. "That's a cute one as well," she said and sang the first verse, rousing happy memories that had both of them laughing as they finished singing together.

Carmen clapped her hands, joy radiating from her green gaze.

"You remembered most of it. Maybe one day you'll sing it to your children."

Jessica hadn't thought about a permanent relationship, much less children, thanks to how busy she'd been building her business. *Just like your grandmother*, the little voice chided, but Jessica didn't feel guilty about it. But did Carmen? Did her mother?

"Do you regret it?" she asked.

The joy fled and Carmen looked upward, as if searching for either divine intervention or the answer in the stars. When she finally met Jessica's gaze, she said, "I regret how I hurt your mother, but I'll never regret what I did for my family. How I guaranteed their future."

Jessica couldn't deny she had done just that and in ways most could not imagine. Carmen hadn't just achieved the American Dream, she was the *AMERICAN DREAM*, and as a businessperson, Jessica wanted to know more.

"You used to work for an import/export company in Cuba?" she asked.

Carmen nodded. "I did, and when I saw how things were working at the supermarket and the warehouse, I was convinced I could take what I was learning and start my own business."

She finally asked the question that had been in her mind. "Why Guerreiro and not Gonzalez for the company name?"

Carmen chuckled. "Gonzalez is like Smith in English, plus I thought a warrior on the label would be eye-catching." She paused to remove a smartphone from her pocket, and with a few swipes, she showed Jessica the logo. She remembered seeing it at the company's office earlier that day.

"It is eye-catching," she replied, agreeing. Powerful and strong, much like the company's founder.

Carmen pulled the phone back, took a look at the image herself, and smiled. "We were inspired by a portrait of El Cid, El Campeador, on his white horse, Babieca, his sword, Tizóna, raised high." She mimicked that raised sword but winced a little, dropped her arm, and rubbed her shoulder.

"You okay?"

"Arthritis, but I'm very healthy so I can't complain," she said.

"Contrary to what Luis said—"

Carmen jumped in with "I hope you're still not angry with him."

Jessica thought about all the time they'd shared in the last couple of days and rolled her eyes. "No, I'm not, and before you go there, I'm not interested." She couldn't let herself be interested.

A long pause followed, and Carmen apparently knew better than to press, so she changed the subject. "If you'd like to know more about the Cuban diaspora or our family's history, I have a number of books I can lend to you."

She had come down here to learn more about this part of her family and their history. Nodding, she said, "I'd like that."

Chapter Thirteen

AFTER CARMEN AND SHE had spent another few hours lost in the family photos, Jessica had even more questions, but it had grown late and both of them were tired. She had gone to bed with Carmen's promise that she would share more photos and stories the next night as well as a book about Cubans in Miami.

She'd been lying in bed in the morning, enjoying the rise of the sun over the bay, when her phone chirped to warn she had a message from her mom. They were both early risers and often shared breakfast together before they'd go off to work or school. Even on a Saturday, like today, they were up early.

Are you okay? her mother asked.

Her usual "fine" was anything but usual or simple. It could mean so many things to her mother, most of them not good. Plus texts and emails were so often misinterpreted. She hovered her finger over the call icon on the message, fighting with herself about whether to phone because she wasn't in the mood for an argument. But she missed her mom and had as many questions for her, maybe even more than she had for Carmen.

She tapped the call icon, and the phone rang only once before her mother picked up.

"Hi, Jess," Lara said. Hesitant. Unsure.

Her response was as uneasy. "Hi, Mom. How are you?"

A long pause, heavy with emotion, was followed by a rough sigh. "I'm hanging in there. And you?"

Way better than she had expected to be, but she wasn't sure if her mother was prepared to hear that. Despite that, she said, "Fine, actually. Everyone has been very nice so far."

Silence greeted that response and another deep inhalation. "That's nice. How is she?"

She. Not Carmen. Not "my mother." Jessica didn't want to be angry with her mother, but it was getting harder the more that she got to know Carmen. But her mother had many more years of upset, and Carmen had likely been on her best behavior with Jessica.

"She seems to be doing well. I've learned a lot about her. About the family." *About you.*

"How are…Gloria and Anna?" Lara asked, the names spilling from her almost as if it pained her to say them.

"I haven't met them yet. Carmen is organizing a family dinner for this coming Thursday."

"So far away? What have you been doing in the meantime?" her mother said, almost accusatorily.

"Chatting with Carmen. Seeing the family business's building. I met two of my cousins yesterday. Carlos and Angelica. We all look alike."

"The Guerreiro genes are strong," her mother said with a strangled laugh.

"Luis said something like that to me too," she said with a chuckle, but after she did, she wanted to bite her tongue. Her mother was sharp and might pick up that there was more there that she wasn't saying. More that she didn't want to think about.

"Luis? Is he the lawyer who—"

"Yes, Mom. He's the lawyer who came to New York," she replied, more snarky than she wanted.

"Ay, chica. Are you sure this makes sense?" her mother said.

"Nothing is going on with us or will go on with us," she quickly defended, even though in the last couple of days… "Absolutely nothing," she repeated with total conviction to shut down that line of questioning.

"I don't want to argue with you, Jess."

"Then don't," she said abruptly, but then shook her head and sighed. "I love you, Mom. I miss you, but I have to go."

"I love you too, Jess. Don't forget that, okay?" she said, her tone pleading. Worried.

"Come on, Mom. How could I forget that?" she said, emotion clogging her voice.

"Please, don't be angry with me," her mother said, her voice strangled with emotion.

"Seriously, I'm not. I love you. I gotta go," she said and hung up.

Jessica's hand shook as she lowered her phone and stared at it. Stared at their smiling faces on her home screen.

"I'm so sorry, Mom," she murmured to the image, as if by doing so her mother would hear.

But despite her apology, she had no regrets about coming to Miami. If anything, she wished that learning more about her family and her mother would only strengthen their relationship, not tear it apart.

Her one hope was that her mother would see that as well.

She hopped out of bed, needing something to do to drive the argument from her brain. She suspected Carmen's neighbors wouldn't take too kindly to someone walking around in front of their properties. She hadn't noticed a gym but was sure there was one since the home seemed to have everything else. Of course, there was the pool, and water always called to her. Her mother used to tease her that the reason she loved the water was because she was a Pisces, and maybe it was.

Even the sight of the bay just beyond the windows was soothing. The last couple of nights she'd gone to bed and risen with that sight, and it had helped calm her. Helped her process all the thoughts going through her brain so she could make sense of what she was finding out about her mother and her family.

She quickly dashed through her morning routine, slipped into her bikini, and eased on the soft terry robe that had been left for her in the spacious walk-in closet. She dropped her smartphone into the pocket, grabbed a towel from the bathroom, and detoured to the kitchen where Consuelo was already at work, preparing coffee.

"*Buenos dias*, Consuelo," she said, and the older woman turned and beamed a smile.

"*Buenos dias,* Señorita Jessica. Can I get anything for you today?" she said while she spooned sugar into a small container.

Jessica went over to the coffeepot and poured herself a cup. "Just an Americano for now."

Consuelo nodded and eyeing the towel and robe said, "If you change your mind, there's a phone by the pool. Just call and let me know what you'd like."

"I will. *Gracias,*" she said and finished prepping her mug. She hurried to the pool, eager to get in a swim. Maybe even some water aerobics because the pool wasn't intended for laps, just leisure.

She dropped her towel on a chaise longue, slipped out of the robe, and placed her coffee mug on the edge of the pool. She hurried to the stairs, dipped in a toe, and sighed. The pool was heated. She walked in, let herself sink beneath the water and drift to the shallow bottom. Floating there, silence enveloped her. Opening her eyes, she watched the rays of sun pierce the water and seemingly almost reach for her.

With a powerful thrust of her legs, she pushed to the surface and sucked in a breath of salt-kissed air from the bay. The early morning sun was already bringing heat. Well, at least what a New Yorker would call heat. She suspected most Miamians would be still wearing heavier jackets when any Northeasterner would be in a T-shirt and shorts.

Laughing with the thought, she pushed through the water, jogging a dozen or more laps around the perimeter. She stopped to grab a few gulps of coffee before adding some squats and lunges for good measure. The heat of the pool loosened muscles and relaxed her. She went back to the edge of the pool for her coffee and as she did so, she noticed Carmen walking toward the pool, holding a tray.

Carmen smiled and greeted her, joy gleaming from that green-eyed gaze so like her own. "*Buenos dias, mi'jita.*"

"*Buenos dias*, Carmen," she said, still unable to call her grandma.

Carmen set the tray on a table by Jessica's chaise longue and sat on the edge of another chaise. "I brought you a little something you might want to try."

Jessica laid her hands on the edge, propelled herself out of the pool, and grabbed her mug. She snagged the towel to dry off a bit, slipped on her robe, and sat opposite Carmen, the tray on the table between them. Long, flattened pieces of toasted bread slathered with butter sat on a plate beside mugs of café con leche.

At her questioning look, Carmen picked up a piece, dunked it into her coffee, and ate it, dabbing at her mouth with a napkin as some of the coffee dribbled from the toast. Murmuring with satisfaction, she said, "*Por favor,* try it."

She did, copying what Carmen had done by dunking her bread into her mug. She brought the messy, coffee-sopped bread to her mouth and ate a bite. The mix of coffee, sugar, milk, bread, and butter was delicious, and she repeated it quickly, scarfing down the toast.

"Delicious," she said around a mouthful.

Carmen smiled and gestured to the coffee, where a slick of butter now swam on the surface of the coffee. She drank it and again the melding of the various ingredients improved the flavor. "I guess you guys invented keto coffee ages ago," she teased.

Carmen chuckled. "I guess you could say that." She paused for a second. "You're going sightseeing with Luis today?"

Jessica nodded. "He'll be here at nine. You don't mind, do you?"

Carmen shook her head and did another dunk and taste of the coffee-soaked Cuban bread. "Not at all. I think you young people can have more fun together than you would with an old lady like me."

For a moment her mother's words about Carmen being manipulative flashed through her brain. She tried not to let that influence her too much even though she had always trusted her mother's judgment and ignored it at her peril.

"Fun is all it is, Carmen. Don't forget that," she warned.

With a hunch of her shoulders, Carmen said, "An old woman can dream, can't she?"

Much like she hadn't wanted to argue with her mother an hour earlier, she didn't want any conflict with Carmen. But she also had to dissuade her from any matchmaking.

"Not if that dream involves me staying in Miami. Not going to happen, Carmen. My life is in Brooklyn."

With another shrug, she said, "Comprendo, Jessica. But you never know what life is going to throw at you."

She didn't want to continue the discussion. "Is that what happened to you? In Cuba? Here?"

The earlier happiness that had been in Carmen's gaze faded and she straightened her spine and pulled her shoulders back. "It is, but I think that discussion is for another day." She shot up from her chair, surprisingly nimble this morning despite her arthritis. But Jessica recalled her Bisnonna Russo complaining that it always got worse at night and before she started moving in the morning.

"I understand, and I want to hear about it, Carmen. I really do," she said, wanting to restore the earlier closeness they'd been sharing.

Carmen smoothed her hands over the fabric of the linen pants she wore. "*Bueno.* I'll leave a book in your room that might interest you, and I want to learn more about you as well. About your business and your Russo family."

"Thank you, Carmen. I think you would like them if you met them."

Carmen smiled, but it was sad and laced with emotion. "Since they raised a fine young woman like you, I'm sure I would. Hopefully, I'll see you later, but if you get in too late, we'll chat tomorrow."

She didn't wait for Jessica's response. With a brave smile and a quick wave, she hurried off.

Jessica wanted to chase after her, but at that moment her phone chirped to announce an incoming call. She eased her hand into the robe's pocket and pulled out the phone.

Luis. She swiped to answer the call.

"Luis," she said, her voice a little too husky to her own ears.

"Jessica," he said, strumming the strings of interest that had slowly been tangling around her brain despite her best intentions. "Are we still a go for today?"

"We are. I'm looking forward to it," she said and meant it.

"See you at nine," he said and didn't wait for her sign-off to end the call.

"See you," she said to the dead phone, and seeing that it said there was only an hour left before his arrival, she got herself in gear to shower and get ready.

She wasn't one of those girly-girl Barbie-doll types, but she also wasn't what her dad would call a schlub. She had her pride, after all.

Pride goeth before a fall, the little voice in her head said, but she soundly ignored it.

She had to get ready for Luis's arrival.

After a quick shower and blow-dry of her hair, she walked into the closet that was almost as big as the entire living area in her Brooklyn apartment. Flipping through her clothes, nothing screamed at her for their outing. She refused to think of it as a date. That would put too much emphasis on what was only a sightseeing tour of Miami.

But she wanted to look her best, and as her gaze skimmed over her clothes, a bright splash of color in the corner of her eye snagged her attention. A Lilly Pulitzer sundress in a riot of tropical colors. One of the outfits her grandmother had bought for her "just in case."

She guessed this was as much a "just in case" as any and grabbed the dress. Holding it up to her, she looked in the full-length mirror built into the gap between two closet units. The colors complemented the slight bit of color that she'd gotten in her few short days in Miami and her green eyes.

Slipping it on, she realized it was a perfect fit. The bodice hugged her breasts and made them look fuller. Sleeveless, the dress exposed arms toned by hard labor. The skirt hit just above her knees, displaying an ample length of lean leg.

She looked feminine but powerful, and she had to admit she liked the look.

She paired the dress with her own sandals, and her thin gold chain and bracelet. The slightest touch of blush and mascara completed her regular routine.

With minutes to spare, she grabbed the straw purse she had brought from New York and headed out to the living room to wait for Luis, but he was already there, chatting with Consuelo. Or maybe it was better to say charming her, and the older woman was loving it.

"Señor Luis. You are too kind," she said with a girlish giggle and playfully tapped his arm.

"But it's true, Consuelo, only don't tell my *mami*. She'd be very upset to know your flan is better than hers," he teased with a smile.

"*Gracias*," Consuelo said with another giggle.

Too charming maybe? she asked herself.

Luis must have seen her since he turned toward her, and that smile became even broader.

"Jessica. You look lovely," he said and walked toward her, hands outstretched and reaching for her.

She slipped her hands into his and, as girlishly as Consuelo, said, "This old thing?"

"*Que linda*," Consuelo said, but hurried away to give them privacy.

"*Sí, bien linda*," Luis said. His gaze was intense as it traveled up and down her body, but finally locked on her face. "You're beautiful."

"*Gracias*. You don't look too bad yourself," she said and eased her one hand away to slip it down the smooth linen of his Cuban-style shirt.

"This ol' thing?" he teased and mischievously swung their joined hands. "Are you ready for our…tour?"

The slight hesitation in his words had her questioning if he too wanted to avoid calling this a date. Despite her own reticence about that, a nugget of disappointment formed that he didn't want it to be a date.

"I'm ready," she said, even though she wasn't. She was confused. It was the best way to describe the feelings that had been growing about him, but maybe this day with him would help her resolve the conflicting emotions she had.

"Maybe" seemed to be the one word that kept on popping up in their relationship. If there was even a relationship there. Maybe today would tell.

Chapter Fourteen

THE FIRST STOP ON their tour was the cathedral the Miami diocese had erected right along the edge of the bay. Beside the water, a small park and path provided a place for churchgoers and others to enjoy the views. Luis and she paused by the seawall to look toward the church, a modern, conical structure rising high above the bay.

She leaned against the wall and listened as he explained.

"This church is very special to Cubans since La Virgen de la Caridad del Cobre is Cuba's patron saint. The church is actually situated to look toward Cuba," he said and waved his hand toward the water and the views southward.

In the distance, there was land, and she motioned to it and asked, "What's that?"

Luis peered in the same direction and chuckled. "Not Cuba, although rumor has it you can see Cuba from the Key West lighthouse. That land is probably Virginia Key and Key Biscayne."

"Can we go inside?" she asked.

"Sure," he said and held out his hand for her to take.

She slipped her hand into his, recalling his warning that he was touchy, but she had come not to mind it. If anything, she looked forward to that simple and oftentimes reassuring touch. Together they walked into the church which was as modern inside as out. Bright ceilings soared up into the conical structure as did a mural painted behind the altar. Sitting before the mural was a statue preserved beneath glass, and as Luis noticed her attention on it, he said in a hushed whisper, "That's a statue of the Virgencita that was brought from Cuba."

She narrowed her gaze to examine it more carefully as they approached the altar. "My mom has a medallion with her on it," she said, recalling the gold medal her mother never removed. She had worn it so often the edges of the image had been smoothed to be almost indistinct in spots.

"Cubans keep her close. She gives them hope that one day *volveremos.*"

"*Volver…?*" she asked, stumbling.

"*Volveremos.* We will return," he said.

She stood there, the silence in the church broken only by the quiet murmur of some parishioners praying in a nearby pew and their own low-volume discussion. The air was redolent with the scent of candles from a small adjacent chapel.

We will return, she thought, only it had been over sixty years and they hadn't gone home. Such a long wait required a great deal of hope and faith. Hope and faith like that which the parishioners of this church might have. Love for their homeland completing that well-known trinity. *Faith. Hope. Love.*

She didn't know if she could have such hope and faith and wondered if Carmen and Luis still believed they would one day return.

"Do you think you'll go back?" she asked.

He shrugged, but it struck her as one of confusion and not indifference. "This is my country and my home, but I think Carmen and my parents think about going back."

"To live? For good?" she asked, puzzled by why anyone would return to a place that had brought them so much unhappiness.

That shrug came again along with a rough, almost disgusted laugh. "I don't really know."

He urged her to turn then, and when they walked out, he said,

"I don't believe in living in the past. I believe in looking toward the future instead."

She wondered what that future entailed but held back because she wasn't sure she wanted to hear if he thought she might be part of it. "Where to next?"

"Vizcaya. I think you'll love it," he said and walked her to his car.

In no time they had made the short trip to the former Deering estate, and Luis explained that the Miami diocese had actually purchased some land from Vizcaya in order to build the shrine to the Virgencita.

Much as Luis had expected, she loved exploring the estate with its mix of Italian Renaissance and Mediterranean revival architecture and gardens.

The rooms inside paid homage to the luxury and glamour of an earlier time. The silk, bronze, and gilt of rococo and baroque pieces mingled with tapestries, rugs, urns, and furniture from even earlier eras. Rich woods—mahogany, walnut, and more—had been crafted into timelessly beautiful desks, screens, and tables. The roughness of limestone walls and arches in some areas complemented gorgeous frescoes and plastered ceilings inlaid with heraldic tiles. Throughout the home, images and figures of seahorses formed an almost playful motif for the otherwise elegant villa.

The gardens outside were immaculate, and in the areas that faced the bay, mangroves protected the waterfront along one section while a large stone barge served as a breakwater for the more exposed areas along the bay. Immense mermaids adorned the barge but had suffered the ravages of time thanks to the softer limestone from which they had been carved.

"This is truly amazing. *Gracias*," she said as they walked toward his car after they had finished their walk through all the rooms, gardens, and a grotto-like pool area.

At the passenger door, he opened it and leaned against the top of the door. "I'm glad that you enjoyed it. It's truly spectacular. Are you up for lunch?"

She risked a quick glance at her phone and realized they had been at Vizcaya for hours and it was well past noon. As if to suddenly remind her of the time, her stomach growled noisily. "I'd like that," she said, covering her midsection with her hand to quiet the rumblings.

"Great. I think you'll find Little Havana interesting as well." He eased behind the wheel and they were soon driving to the area so many Cubans had called home upon their arrival in the sixties. He drove competently, those hands whose touch had become so familiar cradling the leather-and-burl-wood steering wheel. The inside of the car was filled with the scents of citrus, leather, and him.

Short minutes later he pulled into the parking lot of a restaurant with a large green-and-white sign that proclaimed: Versailles Cuban Cuisine The World's Most Famous Cuban Restaurant.

She gestured to the sign as he parked in front. "Is that true?"

Luis peered at the sign and rolled his eyes. "*Sin duda*. If anything is happening in Cuba, you can be sure to see a news crew parked in front or at La Ventanita. That fast-food window over there. It's where you'll be sure to hear any news about Cuba, no matter where it comes from. Miami. Havana. Washington. If you want to know, you go there."

Chuckling, she said, "It's like my Italian grandmother. She's always got her police radio and the news going. If you want to know what's happening in the neighborhood, just ask her. Even the local news crew interviewed her about it when she was in the park one day."

Luis tilted his head and considered her. "You really like her, don't you?"

Jessica nodded with an enthusiastic dip of her head. "I do. She's always been there for me and, more important, my mom."

———◇◇◇———

Do I hear the condemnation there or is it only in my imagination? Luis wondered. He opted not to challenge her on that statement because so far they were having a really good time.

Too good, he thought. He hadn't enjoyed his time with a woman like this for way too long. Possibly because he had been too busy with work, and he warned himself that what he was feeling was like a rebound romance. Except he was rebounding from work and not another woman. And this wasn't a romance and could never be. They were way too different in so many ways. She worked with her hands. He worked at a desk. She knew little about her Cubanidad and he lived and breathed it.

"It's nice that your mom and your father's mom get along so well. Lots of women wouldn't say the same about their mothers-in-law."

"No, they wouldn't," she said, humor apparent in her voice. Her words were chased by another rumble of her stomach.

"Let's go eat a Cubano," he said, then popped out of the car and walked around to open her door.

"Nom nom, a Cubano. They're quite popular in New York," she said.

"We have managed to export it everywhere, but now you can say you had it in the heart of Little Havana. No visit to Miami would be complete without a stop here."

There was nothing glamorous about the inside, which carried over the white and green of the outside sign on the walls, floor, and even the plates. Etched mirrors on the walls helped brighten the space illuminated by crystal chandeliers. The tables were basic white covered by paper placemats emblazoned with the restaurant's name. Padded metal chairs were comfortable enough, although he remembered sticking to them as a child in shorts during hot summer months.

When the waitress came by, he said to Jessica, "Do you mind my ordering?"

She flipped her hand to tell him to go ahead.

"*Dos sándwiches Cubanos, maduros, y un batido de mango y otro de guayaba,*" he said. The waitress jotted down the order and stepped away to place it. At Jessica's raised eyebrows, he clarified. "The Cubanos, ripe plantains, and some shakes. Mango and guava. You can try both and see which one you like best."

"*Gracias,*" she said and perused the restaurant, taking it all in. "Has this place been here long?"

"Forever, but in reality more like fifty years, I'd say. We always came here as kids and when family visited from Jersey."

"Jersey? As in New Jersey?" she asked.

He nodded. "Lots of Cubans up in Union City right across from New York City. Now all my family has moved to other neighborhoods, but Little Havana is still a hub for la Cubanidad. A touchstone to their past."

"I guess like Little Italy in Manhattan, although there's little of it left with the expansion of Chinatown," Jessica said with a frown.

"Things change, sometimes not for the better." While he hadn't meant it to sound bitter, he realized it had.

"Don't like change?" she asked, inching up an eyebrow in emphasis.

"Actually, I normally don't mind, only…there's been a lot of change lately. Carmen leaving the business. More on my plate," he said and paused for a long moment before locking his gaze on her. "You. It's only been a few days, but it's been a change having you around."

She reared back, almost as if slapped, and he held his hands up in supplication. "Not in a bad way, Jessica. It's just that having you around is…different."

His words seemed to mollify her. "It's different for me too, Luis."

The waitress returned at that moment with a large serving tray loaded with their food. She quickly laid their orders out on the table and hurried away to assist other diners.

Hunger curtailed their earlier discussion as they both dug into their sandwiches. After a few bites, he forked some ripe plantains onto her plate and gestured for her to sip one of the shakes, the pinkish one the waitress had placed before her.

She swallowed, ate a maduro, and smiled. "Tasty. Sweet."

She grabbed the shake and took a big sip through the straw, immediately wincing as the cold hit her. "Brain freeze and whoa, way sweet. Is everything Cuban always sweet?"

He chortled and, as she put down the glass, swapped it out for the orange-colored shake. "That was the guava shake. Try this one. It's mango."

She did and grinned. "Love the mango and it's not as syrupy."

"Keep that one. I love guayaba, but it is an acquired taste for some," he said and took a long drag on the straw. "Dulce."

As it had before, hunger replaced talk and they quickly demolished the sandwiches, shakes, and plantains. Sugary, milky cups of espresso—cortaditos—finished off the meal.

Jessica leaned back and laid a hand on her stomach. "I am so full."

"Is it time for a walk, you think?" he asked.

"For sure."

He hesitated for a moment, thinking about where to go next and knew where she had to visit without fail.

Chapter Fifteen

JESSICA STOOD BEFORE THE tall memorial where an eternal flame burned to honor those who had lost their lives during the ill-fated Bay of Pigs Invasion. Gold lettering proclaimed something in Spanish, and Luis translated at her questioning look.

"Cuba. To the martyrs of Assault Brigade 2056. April 17, 1961."

She was silent, considering the words. Martyrs. *My father was betrayed by Kennedy*, she remembered her mother saying on one of those rare occasions when she had talked about Cuba.

"My grandfather—Carmen's husband—he took part in this," she said, piecing together what few tidbits she'd overheard as a child.

Luis perused her intently, seemingly surprised by the statement. "Your *abuela* hasn't told you about him yet?"

"No, she hasn't. Was he one of the men who died there?" she asked, recalling the photo she'd seen of him in the army uniform.

Luis shook his head. "No, not there. He survived and was imprisoned by Castro. Then he came back and eventually went to Vietnam where he died. That's all I know. Carmen doesn't really like to talk about it," he admitted, obviously uncomfortable.

Just like my mother didn't really like to talk about it, Jessica thought.

Two women so alike. United by history and emotion, but also torn apart by it, she suspected.

"Would you like to go inside the museum?" he asked, sensing her upset and reticence.

Would it be another Pandora's box? she wondered, but that was why she'd come to Miami, after all. "Yes, I would."

Inside the nondescript building with the white stucco walls and terra-cotta roof tiles were two large rooms. One contained a long table and bookcases filled with books. The main area in the small building was the space that commanded attention. In the center of the front wall, a bright yellow flag for the brigade was protected beneath glass. Above the flag were photos of two men and an emblem like you'd find on a soldier's arm. On either side of the altar-like presentation were an American flag and a Cuban flag.

The adjacent walls were covered with photographs of men, so many men, with small plaques beneath to identify them. They drew her, and she found herself searching the faces until one jumped out at her. She walked over and rose on tiptoes to stare up at the photo.

My grandfather, she realized, confirming it with a quick look at the plaque. He was a handsome man with a strong, chiseled jaw, full lips, and slash of a nose. Dark eyes which seemed fathomless even from the black-and-white photo.

Comforting hands gripped her shoulders and kneaded gently. "You okay?"

She wasn't, which surprised her since she really had no connection to the face up on the wall. But it was moving to think about a man who believed so strongly in something, in a free Cuba, that he'd risk his life for it.

"I'm okay," she choked out, her voice tight with emotion. "Can we go?"

Luis nodded and eased his arm around her waist. He once again drew her close in comfort. "Sure. Let's go."

They exited the building and walked to the car, but Luis didn't drive them home. Instead, he headed down Eighth Street—Calle Ocho—back toward the restaurant where they'd eaten, until he stopped at a park along the street. A fence made of white stucco columns and wrought iron was topped with a wrought iron sign that said DOMINO PARK.

"You can't leave Little Havana without seeing this," he said with a smile, trying to lighten the earlier pall that had settled over the day due to their visit to the museum.

She wasn't quite sure she was up for it, emotions still running high, but up until the last stop they'd been having a lovely time. If she was being truthful with herself, she didn't want the day with him to end just yet.

"I'm game," she said.

His grin broadened and his hazel gaze glittered with humor. "I'll take you up on that."

Puzzled, she nevertheless walked with him into the park, where men and women gathered around at various tables, playing dominos. Some were taking it seriously, but for the most part there was laughter and friendly chatter. The shuffle of the pieces and player's selection of their dominos were followed by the sharp snap of dominos hitting the tabletop.

They walked around, watching the games, and when a couple of spots opened at one table, Luis grabbed her hand and led her to the empty places. "Can we join you?" he said in Spanish to the men seated at the table.

"*Como no*," the men replied in unison, but as Luis tugged her hand toward the table, Jessica pulled back.

"I don't know how to play," she said, worried that the more experienced players wouldn't want her to slow their game. She recalled the anger of poker players at an Atlantic City table when an inexperienced player pulled cards that ruined their hands.

"*Niña*, we'll show you," one man said and held his hand out in invitation toward the empty space.

With a quick look at Luis, who urged her on with another smile, she sat at the chair and Luis took the spot beside her. He leaned close and explained as one of the men shuffled the dominos on the table-top, gnarled fingers shifting the pieces around. At their prompting, she selected a number of pieces and glanced at them, seeing nothing but lots of dots.

"The idea is to match your piece to one that the players before you place down," Luis said. "Same number of dots together."

"What if I can't?" she said and jumped, startled, as one of the older men slammed a domino down on the table to start the game.

Luis and the other two men gestured to a pile of dominos that had been left over after their selection of pieces. The one older man mimicked eating, bringing that gnarled hand to his mouth, and Luis said, "You eat pieces until you get a domino you can match."

The dots in front of her coalesced into a pattern and as the older men placed their pieces on the table, she calculated which of her dominos to play.

As she did so, the game progressed in earnest with everyone laying down their dominos until one of the older men had to take from the pile. His friend laughed and made the eating motion with his hand, making the other man wave him off with a disgusted huff. But he did pick up a number of pieces until he could match one to the dominos already on the table.

Over and over that action repeated until it became obvious that no one could lay down another piece. They'd reached a stalemate.

"What now?" she asked Luis.

He turned his pieces upward to reveal what he had in his hand. "We add up the dominos and whoever has the lowest number wins."

She flipped over her three pieces, which up until then had been zealously guarded with the other dominos she had used. As all the men looked at her dominos, one of the older men scoffed and pushed away his pieces.

"You won," Luis said and huffed out a laugh.

"I won?" she said, but then glanced at all the pieces and realized she had dominos with the lowest number of dots. Smiling, laughter in her voice, she said, "I won. I really won."

"¡Sí, niña, ganaste!" said the friendlier of the two men while the other one blew out an exasperated breath and waved, as if to brush her away.

The friendly man leaned forward and in a mock whisper said, "He hates losing, especially to an Americana."

She laughed and said, "My mother's Cuban."

At that, the grumpy man lifted his hands and shrugged as if to say, *That explains it.*

Luis leaned toward her and said, "Time for us to make a strategic retreat."

He popped out of his chair and grabbed her hand. "*Señores, muchissimas gracias,*" he said.

"*Muchissimas gracias,*" she repeated hesitantly, earning a smile from the friendly man and another disgusted wave from his exasperated friend.

At the car, she looked at Luis and said, "Why retreat? I won. I won!"

"You did at that, *chica,*" he said and dropped a quick kiss on her cheek, but as she turned her head, her lips brushed against his. They stood there for the longest time, staring at each other. They were so close. They moved closer, gazes locked.

The blare of a car horn shattered the moment.

They jumped apart and Jessica escaped into the car. Luis walked around and slid behind the wheel. He gripped it tightly, his hands flexing on the wheel. "I'm sorry. I didn't mean to make you uncomfortable."

She sat there awkwardly, hands fisted in her lap. "You didn't. If anything, you've made me feel…not uncomfortable," she finally said, fumbling her description.

He blew out a harsh laugh. "Not uncomfortable. That's a ringing recommendation."

She hated that she was making him feel awkward when he'd gone out of his way to be friendly. To be a source of support for her in a situation that was rife with emotion and possible conflict. Turning toward him, she laid her hand on his jaw and applied gentle pressure to urge him to face her.

As he did so, she stroked his cheek. His beard was rough beneath her thumb. The line of his jaw was hard, and under her palm, his muscles were tense.

He was a strong man but caring. Serious, but also capable of playfulness. Honorable despite the way he'd gotten her to Miami. Loyal. To Carmen, but also to her, she sensed.

And she was tired of denying that she was attracted to him. That she found him intriguing and exciting and too damn interesting.

She urged him near and kissed him, and he kissed her back before pulling away.

Luis gripped the wheel again, hands flexing off and on until he nailed her with his gaze. "I'm not sorry."

"I'm not either," she said with a decided bob of her head.

He gave a slower, almost hesitant nod. "Where do we go from here?"

She understood what he was asking, but it was a place she totally didn't want to go at the moment. "You mentioned my cousin makes a mean burger?"

He chuckled. "You're hungry?"

She wasn't hungry but needed something to change the mood of what was happening. It was too soon, and there were too many problems with taking whatever was going on between them to the next level.

"I am. I'm hungry."

He eyed her, his gaze determined as it traveled up and down her body. "Where do you put it all?"

She shrugged. "I work it off. I'm not used to just sitting around doing nothing."

"Not a lady of leisure?" he asked, one dark brow flying up like a crow's wing in flight.

Dipping her head to the side, she fixed her gaze on him and said, "No. Not at all. Is that a problem?"

He grinned. "Not at all."

They ended up walking around South Beach instead of heading straight for the burgers.

"*Fritas*," Luis corrected as they strolled along the wide sidewalk on Lincoln Road. On a Saturday, the pedestrian mall was alive with people visiting the various stores and restaurants that lined the several blocks that made up the mall. In the center of the mall a combination of lush gardens, fountains, and eating areas provided spaces for weary folks to stop for a rest or to people-watch.

"*Fritas*," she repeated and playfully swung their joined hands. She tugged him to the window of a nearby shop to look at the bathing suits displayed there. Although "bathing suit" was a generous description of the strips of cloth that would barely cover strategic parts of her body.

"Do women—"

"And less," he quickly said. "People go topless on the beach."

"You mean *women* go topless. You guys are always topless," she said with a chuckle and drew him away from the window before things went somewhere uncomfortable.

He raised a hand as if being called upon to testify and said, "Guilty. I go topless on the beach."

Trying to avoid any thoughts of him shirtless, she said, "My cousin's place is here on Lincoln Road?"

Luis lifted his chin and motioned toward the end of the mall.

"Way down toward Alton Road. He lucked out because there's new construction happening that should bring him lots of business. It's been tough for him and other mom-and-pop shops because the rents have gotten too high in this area." He gestured in the direction of one vacant storefront nearby that had at one time housed a toy store.

"It's tough to run a small business. I had to take a risk and buy in an iffy neighborhood. Now you can't touch the area it's so pricey," Jessica said. In fact, she'd received more than one offer from a developer to sell her building so they could put up another of the sanitized, glass condominiums that were now peppering the area.

"I hope it's better for him, but wouldn't Carmen—"

"David isn't the kind to ask for help. Like you—"

"And like you," she said, gazing at him intently.

He dipped his head to acknowledge it. "Like us. He wants to make it on his own, but we're family so we try to support him in any way we can."

It was telling to hear him say David was family because Luis wasn't a blood relative. She had no doubt, however, that he was as much a Guerreiro as any family by blood.

"The Guerreiros are tight-knit," she said matter-of-factly.

That familiar shrug came again. "Just like the Russos, I suspect. Let's agree on one thing right now," he said, but the humor in his voice was obvious.

"Sure. What is it?" she asked.

"I've eaten your cousin's burger, and now you're going to eat David's *frita*. We have to agree to be honest about which one is better."

She shook her head from side to side, pondering his offer. Lifting her index finger, she said, "On one condition."

He shot her a side glance. "Only one?"

Nodding, she said, "Just one. No matter which one we think is better, we never tell either David or my cousin Sal."

He offered his hand for a shake. "Deal."

Chapter Sixteen

LUIS WHEELED HIS JAGUAR in front of Carmen's home and killed the engine. He faced Jessica, seemingly hesitant about the end of the night, much like she was. She sat there, waiting. Tension built between them. She swallowed, her mouth suddenly dry, and said, "Would you like to come in for a drink?"

He expelled a relieved sigh. "I'd like that. A lot."

He hurried around to open her door and they walked inside hand in hand again, but when they got there, she stopped short in the foyer, unsure of where she could provide the promised drink. "I'm sorry. I'm not sure where they keep the liquor," she said, facing him.

With a slight tug on her hand, he urged her close, cradled her cheek, and said, "I'm not sorry and I *am* sure."

Before she could say anything, he kissed her again. He moved his mouth against hers, his touch mobile. Insistent. She took a step closer, and it was like a homecoming. Every inch fit his every inch, like two pieces of a puzzle joining.

Joining, she thought, anticipation growing until the reality of their situation sank in.

Jessica stepped back from him but continued to hold his hand, loath to break the connection. She struggled to find the words, the right words, but they escaped her.

Luckily Luis was not as tongue-tied. "I'm glad we got to spend this time together."

"I am too, only…" It was way too confusing.

He swung her hand and smiled, but it didn't reach up into his eyes, which were sad with the unsaid. "It'll work out, Jessica."

He said it as if he believed it, but in only a few days things had gotten way more complicated than she had ever expected. Instead of finding the controlling, demanding mother who had driven away a daughter, she had encountered an interesting woman who appeared to be fully aware of the mistakes she had made. Apologetic about them, even.

And Luis…

Everyone around him obviously liked him. Carmen thought the world of him, to the point that he was like a member of the family and her apparent heir in the business. But despite that…

"I wish I could believe that, but things are getting too complicated, and I don't want to get hurt. And I don't want to hurt my mother or Carmen either."

"I don't want to see you hurt, Jessica. You have to believe that," he said and cradled her cheek.

"I believe that, Luis. But maybe this," she said and motioned back and forth to the two of them, "maybe we need to stop before this becomes more than either of us wants."

He nodded. "I agree. I should go."

He should, but after he gave a final reassuring squeeze on her hand and walked out, his absence hit her roughly. A sudden blast of icy, air-conditioned air swept through the foyer and she wrapped her arms around herself to combat the change in temperature.

Chased away by the chill, and suddenly feeling almost insubstantial in the large open area in the living room, she hurried to her bedroom, needing a safer haven. Inside her room, she noticed a trio of books lying on the bed.

The books Carmen thought I might find interesting.

Unable to sleep anyway, since she was so wound up from her

encounter with Luis, she changed into her pajamas, selected one of the books, and settled herself in the bed to read. An hour or so passed as she read about the Cuban diaspora. About their exile in the United States.

Before coming to Miami, she had done a little homework and seen the word *exile* used more than once to describe the Cubans who had arrived in the 1960s. But as much as she wanted to keep on reading, she was soon fighting off sleep.

She set the book aside and turned off the light. Snuggling deeper into the pillows, her mind whirred with so many thoughts. Carmen and her exile. Her mother's self-imposed banishment. Luis and the separation she'd just requested.

So many hearts driven apart by both circumstance and choice. Exiled from each other.

A forever exile, or is it possible for them to come together again? she wondered as sleep finally claimed her.

———————————— ◇ ————————————

Lara stood beside Sal's mom, Rosa, as she stirred the Sunday sauce in the large pot. On a range beside it, water heated toward a boil after the addition of a mound of dry pasta.

"This is all going to work out, Lara," Rosa said as she moved the wooden spoon around and around in the thick sauce, searching for the meatballs and sausages that were an integral part of Sunday dinner. As she found one, she scooped it into a serving dish.

Lara wished she could be as certain. Her emotions were like the water heating on the range: calm on the outside but bubbling beneath the surface until the water would spill over angrily, spitting and hissing.

"I'm not so sure about that, Mom," she said. In the years since leaving Miami and marrying Sal, Rosa had become her surrogate mother. Always there with advice, complaints, and a good pot of Sunday sauce a couple of times a month.

"You don't understand," she added when Rosa didn't immediately reply.

A long side-glance challenged Lara. "I do understand, and check the pasta while you're just standing there doing nothing," she said with a laugh.

Lara grabbed the pasta fork and whipped the lid off the pot. The water was close to boiling over after the addition of the pasta, and she gave it a stir, then set the lid back on.

Rosa balanced the spoon across the lip of the sauce pot and faced Lara. Arms akimbo, she said, "My sister Stella and me, we had a fight years ago. We didn't talk for a few months about something that turned out to be stupid when we really thought about it."

The sputtering and hissing from the stove warned that the pasta needed attention. Lara snatched the lid off and gave it a stir. "This wasn't about something stupid, Rosa. It was major."

Rosa shook her head of dyed black hair, but it didn't budge with the movement, helmeted into place with a can of hair spray. "Nothing can be that 'major,'" she said with air quotes, "that you haven't talked to your mother or sisters in thirty years. Thirty years, Lara. That's a lifetime."

Like the pot that had boiled over, her emotions spilled from her. "My mother is nothing like you, Rosa. You were always there for Sal. For me. You as good as adopted me after…" She paused to suck in a breath, control those roiling emotions. "My mother was never there for me until she decided to control my life. Who I was going to marry."

"And I gather it wasn't my Salvatore. He's such a good boy," Rosa said affectionately with a peek at Sal in the dining room, where the rest of the family had been gathered for a few hours, eating and chitchatting. Arguing loudly but laughing even more exuberantly.

She tracked Rosa's gaze and smiled as Sal laughed and playfully rubbed his great-niece's hair. "He's a good man and a wonderful father. I'm lucky to have him."

Rosa wrapped an arm around her waist and drew her near. "He's lucky to have you and Jessica. Family is everything, isn't it? You can never have enough family."

She was convinced Rosa should have been a lawyer instead of an accountant because her mother-in-law was effectively leading her to a conclusion she wouldn't be able to avoid.

"Not all families are like yours, Rosa" was the only thing she could think to say.

"Get the *scolapasta* into the sink, please," Rosa said, and a second later, the timer dinged to warn it was time to drain the pasta. Rosa grabbed potholders, pulled the pot off the heat, and spilled the water and pasta into the colander Lara had dutifully placed into the sink.

A wall of steam rose up before Rosa gave the colander a shake, spilled the pasta back into the pot, and spooned some of the sauce over the pasta to keep it from sticking. She leaned back against the counter and met Lara's gaze full-on. "We have no idea what your family's like because we've never really met them."

No, you haven't, Lara thought. A dinner one night during their last parents' weekend at college didn't really count. But in some ways, the Russo and Gonzalez families were very similar. Hard-working, maybe too much so at times. Proud Americans who were also proud of their immigrant roots.

Rosa grasped her forearm and squeezed reassuringly. "We'd like to meet them. Get to know them and make them part of our family. You can never have too much family," she repeated.

"Rosa, is that pasta ready? I'm dying here," Sal's father called out from the dining room, and others joined his plea with their own.

Sal's older sister, Diana, hurried in but stopped short as she caught sight of the two of them. Hazel eyes a shade darker than Sal's narrowed. "You two okay?"

Rosa said nothing, waiting for Lara to answer. "We're just fine. It's time for pasta," Lara said.

"You sure?" Diana asked, even as she grabbed a pasta bowl from the stack on the counter behind Rosa.

"I'm sure. Things are going to be fine," Lara said and followed Diana's lead, grabbing a bowl so the pasta could be served to her family.

My family. It had to be fed and not just with food. You could starve a family with a lack of contact. With the deprivation of emotions. Not like the Russo family who, despite arguments and disagreements, fed their family's soul with these Sunday dinners and more.

As she placed a heaping bowl of spaghetti before Sal, he looked up at her and smiled. He ran his hand across her cheek, and she leaned into it, taking solace from that touch. A touch she had lacked so often as a child from a mother who was always too busy. Too distant. Too everything to her sisters and others, but not to her.

Even now the request had been for Jessica to visit. Not her. Never her, only...

What had she expected, given how she had cut off her mother and sisters? Cut them out of her life the way a surgeon cut out a cancer. Except they weren't as bad as that, she had to acknowledge. Especially her sisters. They had been friends. Confidantes at one time. She had missed them more than once over the years.

As she finished serving and sat beside Sal, she looked around the table at all his family and imagined her sisters sitting there. Their children, her nieces and nephews, joining them. *Because you can never have enough family*, she thought, echoing Rosa's earlier comment.

But I can't erase thirty years of pain in a second. It takes time. Healing. Maybe Jessica's visit is a start, Lara thought.

"What do you think?" Sal asked, peering at her.

She shook her head. "What? I'm sorry. I was elsewhere."

Sal brushed back a lock of her hair. "We're trying to decide who's going to do Easter this year. I thought we might do it."

Easter. A time of rebirth and resurrection. It somehow seemed appropriate in so many ways at that moment. "I think I'd like that."

Miami, April 18, 1965

Lara peered at her sisters in their Easter bonnets and dresses that matched hers. Her *mami* and *abuela* had worked for weeks to sew the dresses so they would have new outfits for the special day, their first real celebration since her *papi* had passed. She hadn't really known what that meant at first, but as friends and family had come to visit, she understood.

Her *papi* was gone and wouldn't be coming back from that faraway place. She'd even looked it up in the encyclopedia at the library: Vietnam. It's where her *papi* had gone and not returned, but she wouldn't be sad today. *It is too special a day*, she thought, peering at the new dresses she and her sisters were wearing.

The dresses had light-yellow tops with frilly skirts the color of bright-green grass. The skirts swirled like a ballerina's tutu when she spun around. Her sisters and she had spent the morning spinning and twirling and laughing. Excited about the new dresses and because they were going to an Easter egg hunt and a movie in a real movie theater. Not their little TV that her *abuelo* sometimes had to play with the antenna to get the grainy black-and-white pictures.

Her *mami* had also surprised them with white straw hats gaily decorated with spring flowers and a tiny, glittering Easter egg. Each egg was a different color, so she and her sisters wouldn't look entirely alike. As the eldest, she'd gotten her hat first with the egg in her favorite color: blue.

Abuelo had driven them to church and, after mass, to a park where her sisters and she had raced around collecting colored plastic eggs from the lawn into the paper bags her *mami* and *abuela* had brought from home. Bags were filled to almost bursting with the brightly hued eggs, and then it was time for the movie.

The Sound of Music. She had sat sandwiched between her *mami*, who was cuddling a sleepy Anna, and an antsy Gloria. Her sister had been shifting and fidgeting in her chair until the film started on the big screen and she had finally settled down.

Lara had sat there mesmerized by the colorful images and songs on the screen. By the sight of the von Trapp children in their curtain clothes, looking so much like her sisters and she in their matching outfits. At the end, a mirror of her own life except she had crossed an ocean and not snowy mountains.

She whispered to her mother, "It's just like us."

A loud sniffle greeted her, and she looked to find her mother wiping tears from her face. "It is, *mijita*. It is just like us," she said and wrapped her arms around Lara to draw her close. "We'll have a happy ending too, *mijita*. I'll make sure of that."

Lara wanted to believe that. She really did, only it had all been so sad since coming here. She had seen so many tears. So much anger and upset. Loss.

But as the happy music and scenes on the screen played out, Lara let herself believe that they could be like the von Trapps also. That they too would soon find happiness in this very different land.

Chapter Seventeen

CARMEN SAT BESIDE JESSICA at the dining room table on the covered patio. It had been too windy to sit at the bayside table, but the day was beautiful enough to stay outdoors.

They had just finished a light Sunday dinner. The dining room table was strewn with an assortment of family photos and scrapbooks. The scrapbooks were ones with family photos from the late sixties and seventies as well as others with news articles Carmen had clipped about what she had thought of as key moments in her life. The Bay of Pigs Invasion. The Mariel Boatlift. The pope's first visit to Cuba. Fidel's death. The key moments of Carmen's very existence, but with her granddaughter now sitting beside her, they all seemed inconsequential somehow.

"Great-Grandma Nieves took care of my mom in Cuba?" Jessica asked, the final part of that question left unsaid even though it was branded on her soul. *After I left. After Carlos and I left*, she thought, because for some reason Lara had always fixated on her being the absent parent, maybe because her daughter had always revered her father. He could do no wrong in Lara's eyes.

"She and my dad. They were my bedrock when they came with Lara, and after when I became pregnant with Gloria and Anna."

While she hadn't said it, Jessica clearly picked up on the vibe. "But not your husband?"

The last thing Carmen wanted to do was speak ill of the dead, especially when it would only alienate Lara even more if she got wind of it. But she wanted to be honest with her granddaughter because one couldn't build a solid relationship on lies. "I loved Carlos with all my heart, but he changed after we left Cuba. Or maybe I never saw his wandering spirit there because we were so involved with *la Revolucíon*."

Jessica paused, the picture of a smiling Carlos in his police uniform in hand as well as the more serious one she'd seen the day before. "We went to the museum yesterday. His picture was up on the wall."

Carmen nodded. "He was very proud that he'd taken part in the invasion, and the exiles here treat those men like heroes. Which they were, don't get me wrong," she said and raised her hand to stop Jessica from assuming otherwise.

"But it must have been very difficult for you. Then and after. Luis told me Carlos left again for Vietnam," Jessica said and settled her gaze on Carmen, searching for her reaction.

The years fell away, and Carmen remembered the day she had watched him leave, never to return. Lara had been standing beside her, tears streaming down her cheeks, but silent. She'd had Gloria on her hip beginning to whine as she picked up on Lara's upset. Her mother and father had formed bookends around Carmen, almost physically supporting her. In truth, her knees had been weak, wavering as she stood there, trying to be strong because she had needed to be the bedrock for her family.

In a nearby cradle, Anna slept peacefully, unaware that the father she would never know was walking out the door.

"He did serve in Vietnam," she said unemotionally, because all her emotions about him and about everything that had happened back then were worn-out. All used up except possibly one, and for the first time in her life, she confessed to it.

"I know it sounds selfish, but I was so very angry with him. My little babies needed a father. I had a company that needed my attention so I could build a safe and steady life for my family. I needed him beside me, but instead…"

As Jessica switched out the photo for one of an older Carlos in his army uniform, tears blurred his image. Carmen swiped at them as they washed down her cheeks and Jessica laid a hand on her shoulder, soothed her with a gentle caress.

"I'm sorry, Carmen. I didn't mean to make you cry," she said, guilt heavy in her tone.

Carmen again raised her hand to stop her. "It's okay. Hopefully you came here to learn more about your family. I know Lara idolized her father, but a child's love is so different from a woman's."

"From what little she said, I know my mother thought the world of him. He's still a hero in her eyes," Jessica said, but continued her caress, reassuring Carmen to continue.

"He was a hero, but even heroes make mistakes. He went to Vietnam thinking that if he helped fight communism there, it would renew the battle for Cuba. That it would help topple Castro so we could go back one day. End our exile."

Exile. That word again, Jessica thought. It occurred to her that it was as good a time as any to change the subject and avoid upsetting Carmen even more.

"Why do Cubans think of themselves as exiles?" she asked.

"*Volveremos*," Carmen said, repeating the word Luis had said the day before. "When we came here, we never expected to stay. We thought that in time, the nightmare that was Fidel would end and we could go back to our homes and lives that were generally better than the ones we first found here. Many of us were teachers, lawyers, doctors. Educated. Middle class for the most part. Refugees."

"But it didn't happen," Jessica said matter-of-factly.

Carmen expelled a harsh breath and wiped away the last of the tears from her face. "It didn't happen. Not after the Bay of Pigs. Or the failure of the sugar harvest in 1970 or Fidel's disastrous plan to grow coffee trees around Havana. Every time something happened in Cuba, the community would hope for him to fall and for them to return."

It was there behind the words, but Jessica had to hear her confirm it. "But not you."

A shrug followed, so much like Luis's that it made her wonder if he'd picked up the habit from Carmen. "I hoped as well. I wouldn't be Cuban if I didn't hope to one day see Cuba again, but I also understood that this is my home now. It's a home that has given me so much. More than I would have had in Cuba, I think."

"But it took so much away also," Jessica challenged, thinking of her mother and her hurt.

"Not it. *Me*," she said and tapped a finger to her chest. "*I* lost your mother."

Miami, 1967

Lara huddled at the top of the stairs, peering through the balusters at the people gathered below.

Earlier in the day, they had been sitting around a table, arguing about people and money. Or at least that's what she understood. They needed money for people. People who wanted to come here. To leave Cuba.

She hadn't wanted to leave home and come here, only that's where her abuelos had brought her so she could be with her *mami* and *papi*. Except her *papi* had left and Mami was so busy she hardly saw her. And some of the people here were mean, with words she didn't understand, but their nasty looks made her want to shrink and hide, like she had when the soldiers came in Cuba. Only there was no place to hide here. No place to avoid the unkindness or the sadness.

She and her sisters were supposed to be sleeping, but she'd heard the music that had replaced the yelling, drifting in through the closed door of their bedroom. Music and laughter. It drew her because there had been so little laughter in their lives. Especially since Papi had gone away and not come back. She had asked her *mami* time and time again when Papi would return, but her *mami* would tell her he had passed and start crying. Lara had stopped asking.

Opening the door just enough to crawl past, she kneeled behind the balusters, wrapped her hands around them, and peered down.

Her *mami* sat off to one side by herself, still wearing black for her *papi*. The other couples were dancing, twirling like the little ballerina in the jewelry box she'd gotten for her birthday. The people spun and stepped across the small room, hips and feet shifting to the beat. Beautiful. Graceful.

She didn't know how long she huddled there, face pressed to the wood. Smiling at how happy they all seemed for a change. But then that sad song came on. That song that always made them cry.

Cuando salí de Cuba, dejé mi vida dejé mi amor.

The dance vanished as they held one another and sang. Swayed to the music like palms in the breeze. Cried and looked away.

Are they looking for Cuba? Lara wondered. *Can I see Cuba if I close my eyes?*

She screwed her eyes shut and tried to remember her room in their pretty little home with all the wonderful flowers in the yard. With the palm trees that danced with the breeze and rustled noisily when the wind grew angry. The *pop-pop-pop* of heavy rain on the rooftop and the cool that usually followed such a storm.

But then the image came to her of that bearded face peering beneath her pink bed skirt, reaching for her, and she jumped up, wanting to hide.

She suddenly found herself tumbling head over heels, *thump*, *thump*, *thump* down the stairs. She landed with a rough thud, scared by the fall. Crying.

Her *mami* was immediately at her side, picking her up and cradling her close. She smelled of talcum powder and oranges as Lara burrowed against her. Kissing her head, her *mami* wrapped her arms tight around her. "*Mi'jita*, are you okay?"

She buried her head deep into her mother's soft breasts and nodded, comforted by her hug and presence. By the soft kiss her mother dropped on her head again and her *mami*'s soft whisper.

"*Te quiero, mi'jita. Te quiero.*"

"*Te quiero*, Mami," she said, and with her mother rocking her, she felt loved for the first time in a long time.

She finally almost felt safe.

Chapter Eighteen

IT WASN'T UNUSUAL THAT on a Sunday, when either Carmen or Luis weren't with family, he'd go over to Carmen's for dinner. She was like family after all, as well as an amazing sounding board for any ideas or problems with the business.

But after last night with Jessica, he'd opted to cancel the invitation he'd accepted earlier in the week to have dinner with Carmen and her granddaughter.

Her granddaughter. Jessica.

She was way more than he'd counted on. Way more fascinating and complex. Sexy.

No, *so damn sexy and nothing like any other woman I've ever been involved with*.

But you're not involved with her, the little voice in his head goaded.

He couldn't argue with that, and since he'd basically promised to keep his distance, it was unlikely they'd get involved unless…

He sat down at his computer with a Cubano he'd picked up for a quick dinner. There was one idea that had been bouncing around in his head for the last couple of years, and it was as good a time as any to finish the research he'd started months earlier. As good a time as any to flesh out his idea and see if it merited his bringing it up with Carmen and, after, an in-depth analysis.

With the various reports spread out across the large surface of his home office worktable, he added the information to his research, building the proposal a piece at a time until it became something more—it became a real plan for the future. A way to continue to grow Guerreiro Enterprises so that Carmen would not have to worry about her family once...

He wouldn't think about that. He wouldn't think about the day that Carmen wouldn't be there, because it would hurt as much as if he lost his own mother or father. Truth be told, in some ways he was as close to Carmen, maybe closer, than his parents. Between his work and now Jessica, he possibly spent more time with her than with his family.

Guilt swamped him then, because his mother and father, his grandparents, had sacrificed so much for him to be in the position he was in today. Successful. Financially secure.

Alone, he thought as he tapped out the last few words into his report and saved the document.

He shoved away from his worktable and strolled into his living room. The modern and almost spartan aesthetics of the open-concept floor plan had seemed clean and uncluttered at first, but now struck him as cold and barren. Empty. Too, too empty.

Luis poured himself a scotch and walked to the wall of windows that faced his backyard. A covered outdoor entertainment space complete with a seating area, television, and pool table opened onto a pool and surrounding deck. Beyond that, a nice patch of grass and garden led to the dock for his boat and Indian Creek.

He strolled outside and kept on walking toward the dock and a riverside patio. In the distance the lights of the homes on Indian Creek glittered as bright as the night stars above. Peering south, the waters of Biscayne Bay sparkled like diamonds beneath the moonlight, and in his mind's eye, he pictured the ride to Carmen's along the water. He'd done it a few times, navigating past the causeways and Venetian Islands.

Maybe he'd do it again and take Jessica for a ride. Bring her to his home...

Danger, danger, danger, his little voice warned, and he didn't ignore it.

It was too much too soon, even though the plans he'd just finished working on said otherwise. Said that he was thinking that there was the possibility of more with Jessica.

And while he was thinking of more, he whipped out his smartphone and dialed his mom. He hadn't talked to her in days and his earlier thoughts had him feeling decidedly guilty. Guilt being something that Cuban parents seemed to be able to dish out at will.

But that guilt vanished as soon as he heard her voice over the line, replaced by comfort. It was something he had always been able to count on, and tonight was no different as he told her about all that he'd been doing that week. Everything except Jessica and his time with her.

It made no sense to share that because in a few days Jessica would be on her way back to Brooklyn. Back to her own life, so he could get back to his.

He finished the call and slugged back the watery remnants of his scotch. The expensive liquor tasted harsh as it burned down his throat.

And as he returned to his home, it felt even emptier. Less like a home and more like the kind of showcase intended to flaunt his success. A hard-won success. It was what he had at one time thought would be a satisfying revenge, only now it tasted as harsh as the whiskey.

He threw the glass against the stone wall by the fireplace and headed up to his empty bed.

He'd clean up the broken bits in the morning, much like he'd pick up the pieces of his life once Jessica left.

———— ❖ ————

It has been an enlightening day with Carmen, Jessica thought. She'd learned so much about her grandfather and how the family had survived during those many difficult years in the United States. How her grandmother had taken the information she'd known from her work in Cuba, combined it with what she had learned at the supermarket and warehouse to build a business that specialized in the distribution and manufacture of Latino food products.

It had all been fascinating, but also emotional. Especially her grandmother's hurt about losing her daughter and her husband. Although Jessica had sensed there was more there about her grandfather Carlos. More that Carmen wasn't yet prepared to share.

But maybe her mother might.

She tapped the phone to call her mother, who answered immediately. "Jess, how are you?"

"I'm fine, Mom." She paused, unsure of how to continue. *Banal or direct?* she wondered, but then the words exploded from her. "We talked about your dad today."

Silence. Except for the sound of a television program in the background until her mother apparently muted it.

"What did she say?" her mother asked, her tone as chilly as icicles on a gutter in winter.

She needed to melt that ice. "That he was a hero. That you adored him."

Another stilted silence followed, but this time her mother's tone was warmer. Friendlier. "I did. He was…larger than life. So handsome."

"Yes, he was," Jessica said, recalling the photos of the almost beautiful man in his police and army uniforms. His power and confidence had been obvious and must have been so much more powerful in person. Especially to a young child.

"Carmen said he was a man of action," she said, wondering what her mother remembered about him. After all, she'd been so young when he'd passed. She'd only just turned nine.

A loving chuckle drifted across the line, surprising Jessica. "He was an all-action guy. When he was home, we'd go to the playground and he'd chase us around until we were so tired we could barely walk. Then he'd scoop us up in his arms and carry us home. Effortlessly. He was so strong. So very, very strong."

Jessica joined her mother in laughter. "All three of you?" she said, picturing her grandfather hauling the toddlers and a little baby around Little Havana.

"Well, just Gloria and me at first. Then Gloria and Anna because they were little. I'd hold on to his belt and walk beside them, but Papi…" Her mother choked up then but pushed on. "Papi would always make sure to look at me and smile. He let me know that he saw me. That I was loved."

Unlike how you felt with your mother, Jessica thought.

"It must have been hard after… I can't imagine," she said, struggling because she couldn't conceive of not having her parents in her life. They were so much to her. Parents. Mentors. Best friends. It hurt her heart to think about them not being there.

Hesitation, almost painful, ended quickly. "You know your dad and I aren't going anywhere, Jess. We're going to be here for a long time."

"I know that," Jessica said but charged on, even knowing that it might be difficult. "Your mother…Carmen. She was there, just not how you needed, Mom."

"I don't want to talk about this, Jess," she said, her tone icing over again.

"But we have to, Mom. We have to talk about it—"

"I knew it was a mistake for you to go there. I knew Carmen could be persuasive. I guess you're thinking about staying there," Lara said, loud enough that Jessica had to shift the phone away from her ear.

Jessica had her mother's temper, but she battled it to calmly reply, "No, Mom. I'm coming home to Brooklyn. As for persuasive, she couldn't persuade you to stay in Miami, could she? She couldn't persuade you to talk to her and your sisters after you left."

The chill from earlier became a full freeze. Colder than an arctic winter. "I think it's time to end this call before we both say things we'll regret."

"I love you, Mom. You know that. But I've always sensed that there's a part of you closed off to me. A part of the past—"

"And how can we build a future without knowing our past?" her mother jumped in.

Jessica wavered, wanting to avoid kindling the anger again. "There really isn't a right and wrong here, Mom. You're a lawyer. You know the story's sometimes right in the middle."

With a resigned sigh, her mother said, "It is, Jess. And I promise I'll try to think about the past. Try to see things her way."

Her way, Jessica thought, pessimistic about that outcome, but she tried to put a happy face on it. "Please, Mom. I want for you to find peace. To heal."

"Fine, Jessica," her mother said in a way that was more reminiscent of a hormonal teenager than her normally brilliant lawyer mom.

"Love you, *Mamacita*," she said, wanting to restore peace between them.

"Love you more, *Chiquitica*," Lara said and hung up, giving Jessica hope that she'd succeeded on some level.

Jessica lowered the phone and stared at the happy image of the two of them on the screen. A happy face that hid the hurt very well, she now understood.

Her trip to Miami was exposing that wound, but her one hope was, as she had told her mother, that it would help her heal. Help her deal with the past so the future would be free of the pain. Maybe even filled with her Miami family so her mother's exile could end.

And what about Luis? Will he be a part of that future? she thought, but quickly forced away that idea. First and foremost, she had to think about her grandmother and her mother. Only after that could she consider anything to do with her own future.

And whether it would include a very smart, honorable, funny, and intriguing man.

Chapter Nineteen

JESSICA HAD BEEN CHECKING in with her employees off and on and everything had been going fine. But the store was her baby and she had been itching to get back to work since she wasn't used to being a woman of leisure. Work kept her balanced, especially when she was trying to restore a piece that time had damaged or attempting to reimagine one into something different.

Carmen was sleeping in since they'd stayed up late the night before, so it was the perfect time to call the shop and see what was happening. Her part-time manager Sandy answered immediately.

"Hi, Jessica. How's the vacation going?" Sandy asked.

Jessica wasn't quite sure she'd call it a vacation, but it wasn't work either. "I'm having a nice time, thanks."

"How about Mr. Trouble?" her manager teased.

Still trouble but in a different way, she thought. "He's actually been quite nice. He's taken me sightseeing. Miami is very beautiful."

"Hmmm," Sandy said. Her part-time manager had tried to match her up more than once with one of her single male friends, so Jessica decided to head off that discussion.

"How's the shop? Sell any more pieces?"

"We did. That folding table you finished right before you left, two bar carts, and a coffee table. Oh, and that ladder bookcase you made. We also got a call about a commission for a new dining room table."

Commission work is always good because it makes me more money,

Jessica thought. "Did they send photos of what they might want? When they'd need it? Budget?" she asked.

"Got it all, boss. If you want, I'll send it to you."

"Thanks, Sandy. I'd appreciate that," she said and ended the call. Within minutes the information was in her mailbox, and she smiled as she glanced at the photos and the budget. The young couple wanted a farmhouse-style table, preferably oak. The problem was that any standard table would be too wide for their space, so they'd come to Jessica to customize a piece for their Manhattan loft.

Jessica remembered the couple, a duo of financial hotshots, had bought a few other pieces from her, also in a farmhouse style. The young woman had said that the furniture gave her a homey feel in their otherwise stark and modern Soho loft.

Smiling, Jessica emailed the couple to say she'd love to do the work for them and to also ask for other information, like what their timeline was and color preferences for the painted table legs.

With that finished and itching to do something besides lounge by the pool, she decided to examine some of the other furniture in her grandmother's home and maybe also take her up on her invitation to look through any of the scrapbooks in her home office. Strolling to the living room, she examined the intricate baroque pieces as well as the much older colonial Spanish furniture with its hand-wrought hinges, drawer pulls, and square nails.

But it was the piece that guarded the entrance to Carmen's home office that drew her again. A reproduction with lower quality mahogany, despite that the table had elegant character and would grace any home. She could picture it being a special piece, especially if you'd worked hard to earn the money to buy it. She could also imagine passing it down in the family since it had such meaning.

Which made her think about the scrapbooks in her grandmother's home office.

With a final stroke of her hand across the surface of the family table, she went to Carmen's office. Sylvia had just arrived and was getting ready for a day at work. The young woman smiled as Jessica approached.

"*Buenos dias*, Señorita Jessica. Is there anything I can do for you? Some coffee possibly?" Carmen's assistant asked.

Jessica smiled and nodded. "A cup of Americano would be nice. *Gracias.*"

Sylvia nodded and walked away to fulfill her request, and Jessica entered Carmen's office and went straight to the bookcase that held an assortment of framed photos, mementos, and books about Cuba, as well as scrapbooks and photo albums. But it was one leather portfolio whose surface had the kind of patina that said it had been handled often that called to her.

She grabbed the well-worn portfolio and walked to the sofa and coffee table. Much like she had done several times with Carmen over the last few days, she set the portfolio on the table and opened it, only it didn't contain photos, just paperwork.

Puzzled, Jessica laid out the papers, trying to make sense of them. Pages with names and addresses. What looked like a ledger and meeting minutes as well as a passbook for a bank account that had been closed out long ago.

Unfortunately, many of the documents were in Spanish, confounding her. She regretted not having kept up the language after learning it in high school. But combined with the Italian she'd learned from her Russo family, she could make sense of some of the words since the two languages were so similar. Some words, but not enough.

Luckily, Sylvia returned with her coffee just then.

"If you have time, could you help me with this?" she said and gestured to the papers.

Sylvia glanced at the papers and her eyes narrowed in puzzlement. "Certainly, but these are new to me," the young assistant said, but took a spot beside Jessica, knees primly pressed together in deference to her pencil skirt.

"*Dios mio*," Sylvia said as she skimmed her hands over the papers, shifting them into some kind of order. "I'd heard about this from my grandparents, but thought it was all talk. You know the old ones always make everything about *la Cuba de ayer* seem perfect. If everything they said was true, most of them were millionaires in Cuba."

"What's *la Cuba*…" She paused, fumbling with the language.

"Yesterday's Cuba. The old Cuba they left behind," Sylvia explained.

Jessica motioned to the papers, still a little surprised by Sylvia's almost condemning response. "What is this?"

"*Mis abuelos* said that the Cubans who came here would often help other people escape Cuba. It looks like your *abuela* Carmen and some people from her old company in Havana helped other employees come to Miami. See, these are the names and addresses of people who were able to leave," Sylvia said and motioned to one page before gesturing to another. "This is a list of those employees who were still stuck in Cuba."

Intrigued, Jessica passed her hand across what she thought were the minutes since the ledger and passbook were self-explanatory. "And these?"

"Minutes of their meetings," Sylvia confirmed, and her eyes widened in surprise as she flipped through the papers. At Jessica's prompting, she ran her finger across a few handwritten lines. "It says here that Carmen wanted them to get together to start the business, but they voted it down. Wow, imagine that."

She could imagine it and also understand. Much as she had learned from Carmen in the past few days, they'd all been busy trying to keep their heads above water. Adding a start-up business to all that was already going on must have seemed impossible, and yet…

Her grandmother had done it. Alone. She'd risked it all to improve her family's life, but at what cost?

The answer came to her immediately: her mother.

The price for Carmen's success had been the relationship with her oldest daughter.

Would I have done it? she wondered, and the answer came without hesitation. *Yes.*

In fact, if she thought about her life, she already had sacrificed what a lot of her married friends with children had. Family, although she'd always had her parents and the large Russo clan that filled her few free moments to temper the void of not having her own family.

My own family.

It was something she hadn't thought of in a while. Not since her last unsatisfying relationship. Not since the last friend's wedding she'd attended solo only to face the well-meaning matchmaking of her married friends. She hadn't let it ruin her night, but days after, as she'd worked on a commission for a secretary desk for a young child, she'd lost it, lamenting whether she'd ever have a child of her own.

In the months since then, she'd driven that sadness from her brain. Driven away the fact that she'd been so focused on building her business she'd let her personal life flounder. It occurred to her yet again that she was a great deal like Carmen in that respect.

Like your grandmother, the little voice in her head chastised and she had to acknowledge that relationship because, in the last few days, she'd come to like the old woman. Come to admire what she had accomplished in her life. Even to understand some of the choices she had experienced in her own life, namely putting work before her personal life.

Like my grandmother, she admitted to herself. And like her mother if she was honest. Her mother's legal career had often pulled her away, although her mother had made it a point to spend as much time as she could with Jessica.

"Thank you for explaining," she said to Sylvia and gathered the papers to return them to the portfolio and its spot on the bookshelf. "*De nada*. If you need anything else, just let me know," the young woman said and exited to answer the phone that had started ringing.

It made her wonder what else Carmen was involved in now, as Luis had mentioned she worked with several charities. She made a mental note to ask, returned the portfolio to the bookshelf, and took down another scrapbook to appreciate.

Like the others, the photos had been carefully labeled with information about who was in the photo. This scrapbook also had original documents from Cuba, carefully preserved. Her mother's birth and baptismal certificates. An identification card for her great-grandfather at some kind of medical clinic. Driver's licenses. Her grandparents' marriage license and a photo of them signing it at what looked like a government building. It was followed by a photo of them walking down the aisle, looking as glamorous as movie stars.

Her grandfather had been a very handsome man and Jessica could see how her mother might have idolized him. He looked so strong and powerful. She could picture him carrying his daughters around with ease, just like her mother had said.

Her grandmother was lovely, her hair done up in some kind of bouffant that held her veil. A brilliant smile on her full lips instead of the sad smiles she'd seen in the last few days. Jessica was again struck by how much her mother looked like Carmen, and it made her wonder whether her aunts, Gloria and Anna, had the same strong Guerreiro genes.

More photos later on confirmed the family resemblance, although Anna leaned more toward her father than Carmen. She had his sharp blade of a nose and angular jaw, but the light Guerreiro eyes, high cheekbones, and dimpled chin. Some of the early photos had the girls all dressed in similar clothes made with the same fabric.

Obviously homemade, which made sense. There must not have been a lot of money for store-bought clothes in those early days.

Not much farther into the album there was a picture of the entire family, grandparents, Carmen and Carlos, and the sisters in front of a small building with a sign that said *Guerreiro Enterprises*. Even without all that she'd learned, some things were obvious. Her mother, Lara, was tucked tight to her father, unsmiling, almost angry. A stoic Carlos rested his hand on Lara's shoulder while he cradled a very young Anna in one arm. Gloria, her smile beaming, chin upturned with pride, beside her mother and grandparents who were also smiling.

This had to be at the early beginnings of the business and the beginning of the end for so many other things. Her mother's relationship with Carmen. Her grandfather, who would soon leave for Vietnam and never return.

She dragged herself away from the photo, moving on to happier times as the family and the business grew. But as before, the distance between her mother and grandmother leaped from the photos, the physical space between them a testament to the emotional break that hadn't healed to this day.

In another scrapbook, her mother was gone from the photos as life in Miami went on without her. Other celebrations, babies, weddings, and more, all without Lara, and it was unfathomable to Jessica considering how she had been raised surrounded by Russo family. Surrounded by her helicopter parents who had always been there because, according to them, family was everything.

"I see that you're going through the scrapbooks," Carmen said from the doorway, her slim hand shaky on the doorjamb.

Jessica nodded, but couldn't keep in the one question that had been stuck in her brain ever since Luis had come to New York. "I just don't get it. Why would she cut you all out of her life? Out of my life?" she said, tapping a spot above her heart.

Carmen almost physically recoiled, but then straightened her spine and tilted her chin up, much like little Gloria in some of the photos. "Don't be so harsh on her, *mijita*. She had a very difficult time when we got here, and as I've said before, I didn't know how to deal with it. With her hurt. Her fear. She was just so afraid."

Jessica shook her head, trying to imagine but failing. "Family has always been everything to us. I couldn't imagine not having them in my life."

Carmen nodded. "The Russos. I'd love to know more about them. Maybe you can tell me about your family while we have lunch."

Lunch? she thought, but a quick look at the brass clock on one of the shelves, a gift from the City of Miami for some donation Carmen had made, confirmed that it was midday. Time for lunch and also for a visit from Luis.

Her heart sped up with that realization, but she reminded herself that all beginnings had endings, just as the many photos in the scrapbooks had documented.

"I'd love to tell you about the Russos," she said and rose from the sofa. She walked over to Carmen, who slipped her arm through Jessica's. Together they walked out to the bayside patio tables and sat just as Luis strolled out of the home and toward them.

The sight of him in his charcoal and white-striped suit and brilliant white shirt, open at the collar, stole her breath. She realized she was in over her head considering how little time had passed since she'd met him. But then again, her parents had always said it had been love at first sight for them.

She told herself that it wasn't love. That this was nothing like her parents, and her feelings were in overdrive because of the very emotional week.

He gestured for them not to rise and walked over to drop a kiss on Carmen's cheek. "*Viejita*, how are you today?"

"I'm fine, *mijito*. Jessica was just going to tell me about her

Russo family," she said and gestured with a delicate wave in her direction.

He quirked a dark brow and swept around the table to place a kiss on her cheek. A kiss that lingered a little longer, together with a husky whisper of her name. "Jessica."

That whisper strummed alive unwanted emotions, and she corralled them and said, "Luis. It's so nice to see you again."

He removed his jacket and took the spot opposite her at the table. As he unfurled his cloth napkin and placed it in his lap, he said, "I'd love to hear about the Russos as well. And your parents, of course."

"My parents," Jessica said with a smile. "Great parents. Always there for me."

"You love them," Carmen said, and she answered without hesitation.

"I do and I can't imagine not having them in my life."

———◇◆◇———

Those words again, much like Jessica had said just moments earlier, Carmen thought.

"You're very lucky to have that kind of relationship. They're very lucky to have each other," Carmen said, but couldn't keep the hint of question from slipping into her words.

Jessica nodded. "They are lucky to have each other. My father is so supportive of her. Of me." She paused and smiled. "He makes her laugh. Mom can be too serious at times."

Carmen chuckled. "Lara was always serious. Too serious for a *pequeñita*." At Jessica's puzzled look, she explained. "Little one. *Pequeñita.* She had such old eyes even as a baby. Like she had seen too much of the world already."

Luis reached over and covered her hand, offering comfort. Carmen smiled sadly and her eyes sheened with tears. "I'm glad he makes her laugh. It's the laughter that keeps you going once the passion is gone. Remember that," she said and glanced between the two of them, aware of the sparks flying between her granddaughter and a man who was as good as her grandson.

Jessica, clearly sensing the mood had grown too somber, said, "He makes her laugh all the time and she's happy. Very happy with him and the rest of the Russo family."

"Tell me more about them," Carmen said, eager to hear about the people who had become such an important part of her daughter's life. A life she knew so very little about.

With a dip of her head in acceptance, Jessica said, "The matriarch is Bisnonna Russo and whatever she says goes. And there's no stopping her even though she's ninety-three. She's a lot like you that way."

Carmen smiled and chuckled. "I hope I'm just like her at ninety-three."

Luis patted her hand and joined in the laughter. "*Viejita*, you are well on your way."

Jessica nodded and continued. "My grandparents are just like my dad. Funny. Loud when they speak Italian so that I don't know what they're saying."

Carmen totally understood. "Our first real home was an apartment we rented from an Italian family. Betty, the landlady, once told me, 'You don't speak in Italian, you scream in Italian.'" She emphasized her words with broad gesticulations and added, "And you speak with your hands too."

Luis shook his head and said, "Italians and Cubans. Not very different in some ways."

Carmen nodded. "Not very different at all. Except they can go home again if they want."

Luis nodded. "Very true. Between the embargo and how the Cuban government treats us, it's too hard."

"How do they treat you?" Jessica asked.

"We have to go on our Cuban passports which means we have to pay for the assorted renewals and other fees. They also don't recognize our U.S. citizenship once we get there," Carmen explained.

"It was too hard to leave. No reason to risk being trapped there again," Luis said, and she was totally on board with his fears.

"No reason. Anyway, Betty and her family understood the problems we were having getting an apartment and were willing to rent it to us. They were also very generous in other ways."

"My *bisnonna* sometimes mentions how her family was ostracized when they came here from Italy. People are afraid of things that are different," Jessica said.

Luis's entire body tensed with her words and Carmen understood. He had experienced the pain of that rejection, of that hate, firsthand. Much like she had, although the wound was far newer in him. Maybe still unhealed, she had thought more than once as she saw Luis fill his life with all the trappings of success but without the most important thing: family.

"That's no excuse for what they do," he said, tones harsh and alive with pain.

Jessica reached out to him, and he slipped his hand into hers, confirming what Carmen had suspected. Something more was happening between these two, and she hoped it wouldn't end up hurting them while at the same time hoped it would become more. That whatever it was would keep Jessica in Miami.

"What happened?" Jessica asked, obviously wanting to know, but possibly also sensing that talking about it might help him heal.

With his familiar shrug, he cocked his head, looked away, and said, "I guess I was about nine. My little brother was six. There were some older boys in the neighborhood who picked on us. Almost daily. There was one who beat on us because we were Marielitos."

His gaze shifted back and settled on Carmen. "I came with my dad to work one day, bruises on my face, and Carmen saw me. Took me to the side. Do you remember that day, *viejita*?"

How could I forget? Carmen thought. He'd looked at her that day like Lara had, with lost eyes. With soul-deep pain and fear.

"I remember, *mijito*."

"What happened? What did you do?" Jessica asked, leaning toward him.

"La Viejita raised her dainty little hand like this," Luis said and clenched his other hand into a fist. "She told me that bullies only understand strength. That I had to stand up to them for myself and my little brother."

"Did you?" Jessica said, and Luis faced her full-on. Nodded.

"It took just one punch and they never bothered us again. I wasn't proud of that moment, but it taught me that other people couldn't put me down unless I let them put me down."

"It made you a stronger man," Jessica said with another comforting squeeze of his hand.

Luis nodded. "I'll never let that happen again. Never."

The moment was shattered as Manny and his assistant wheeled over their lunch.

And maybe that was a good thing and time to prod Jessica to continue her stories about the Russo clan as well as her decision to go into the furniture flipping business.

Chapter Twenty

Luis sat back as Manny placed the plates with lunch before them and poured glasses of fresh lemonade.

"*Gracias*, Manny. It looks delicious," he said, admiring the artfully prepared plate of poached red snapper beside roasted asparagus and fingerling potatoes.

"It does. *Gracias*, Manny," Jessica said and smiled at the older man. After she ate some of the fish and potatoes, Jessica murmured her approval and said, "If I keep on eating like this, I'm going to gain a hundred pounds."

Luis laughed and shook his head. "I imagine you can work it off on a typical day in your shop."

Jessica nodded and chuckled. "I probably could. It can be hard work."

"What made you decide to go into that business?" Carmen asked while she ate her own meal.

Jessica shrugged. "Like your dad, Luis, my dad would sometimes take me with him to one of his contracting jobs. It was fascinating to see them building a home. How it all came together."

"Why not an architect, *mi'jita*?" Carmen probed, obviously intrigued by her granddaughter's choices.

Jessica's hands flew into motion while she explained. "What I liked best was working with my hands. Feeling the wood. Feeling its history and giving it a new life. New purpose."

Sheepshead Bay, Brooklyn, 2003

The sander sat on the top of the oak table her father and she had found at a local consignment store. Her mother had been complaining about their kitchen table being too rickety, but despite visits to several furniture stores, nothing had seemed to please her.

"Your mom says nothing she's seen so far has character," her father said and ran his hand across the surface of the old farmhouse table. "*This* has character. And those," he said and pointed to the chairs they'd found at a different secondhand store.

He walked over to them and ran his hands over the curved top of the chair and then down the spindles to the worn seat. "These are Windsor chairs."

"Windsor like the castle?" Jessica asked.

Her father smiled and nodded. "Exactly like the castle and the nearby town, but it's Americans who took them over the top. I think your mom will appreciate that," he said with pride.

Jessica had no doubt she would. In some ways her mother was more American than most Americans, maybe because she understood the blessing that was America. "She'll like them, Dad," she said and gestured to the sander.

"What do we do next?" she asked.

Sal dipped his head in the direction of the table. "We've stripped off the old varnish. Now we sand and stain. But first, protection," he said and handed Jessica a mask to guard against the sanding dust and ear plugs to deaden the sound.

She slipped them on and walked to stand beside her dad to watch him sand, but instead he laid her hands on the sander. "You do it. With the grain. Always with the grain," he said, patient. Gentle as he guided her, helping her sand the tabletop to a smooth finish. The noise of the sander was a low murmur, almost musical as she moved it over the wood. The vibrations sang up her arm, another melody.

"That's it," her father said and shut it off.

Jessica stared down at the tabletop that had once had assorted scratches and nicks on it. Now it had new life and a fresh beginning with her family. Maybe in time, another family would also be able to sit around the table, sharing a Sunday dinner. Gathering together just as her family did.

"I knew right then and there, that's what I wanted to do. I wanted to save those things that had meant something to someone so they wouldn't just be tossed away," Jessica said, and Luis completely understood.

"It's a family's history. Something that was lost for a lot of us," he said, recalling the few photos that his family had of their home in Cuba. The humble pieces of furniture and other items that had been left behind during their escape to the United States.

Jessica nodded and shot a worried look at Carmen. "I think my mom always felt that way. Like she'd lost a lot of her history."

Carmen's knife and fork clattered against the china as she laid them down, hands shaky. She sighed heavily and said, "She did. I blame myself for that. Every day, if you want to know. I helped put that man in power. I made the mistake that stole our family's future."

Jessica reached over and laid her hand over Carmen's. "I didn't mean to blame you. That's not what I meant."

Carmen nodded, but her eyes held the sheen of tears and her full lips had tightened to a knife-sharp slash. "*Lo se.* If you'll excuse me, I'm not really all that hungry."

Before either Jessica or he could say anything else, Carmen awkwardly pushed away from the table and hurried back into the house.

"Shit," Jessica muttered and shook her head. "I didn't mean to upset her. To blame her," she said and peered at him, as if searching for absolution. "I didn't," she urged.

"I know you didn't, but it's a sensitive topic for her. Even after sixty years, she still blames herself for Castro. For the pain your mother suffered."

Jessica blew out a harsh breath and met his gaze. "That's a lot of guilt to carry around."

"A lot of guilt and pain," Luis challenged and held his breath as he waited for her reaction. *Would Jessica be like her mother? Filled with accusation and disdain for the woman who had sacrificed so much for her family?*

She looked away, back toward the house, and he heard a sniffle. "Too much pain," she said, her voice pinched tight with emotion. Her gaze shimmered with tears as she looked back at him. "For my mother too, Luis. How I wish…" She sucked in a breath and blurted out, "I wish I could make it stop. Make it better. For both of them."

There was no doubting Jessica's sincerity. No doubting the guilt and pain that had now settled on her shoulders, torn as she was between the grandmother she'd only recently come to know and the mother she loved and had been with her all her life.

"You've started the healing, *mi amor*. Coming here, as tough as it was… It was the right thing to do for both of them," he said.

She offered up a smile, but it didn't quite reach up into her eyes, still wet with unshed tears. "Thank you, but it doesn't feel so right at the moment. But maybe in time."

"Maybe," he said and hated repeating the word that had almost become a mantra lately. He wasn't a man used to maybes. He was a man used to making things happen, much like he had in convincing Jessica to come to Miami, making him as responsible for the current situation as Jessica.

"Give Carmen a little bit of time, but don't be afraid to ask the hard questions. To understand what really happened back then."

"Because knowing the past is what you need to understand the present and build the future," Jessica said, and he couldn't disagree.

"It is. The past shaped us. Made us who we are, for good or bad," Luis said, hating that his past and present seemed to be shaping a bleak future for himself. One filled with mostly work and not much else.

Jessica seemed to sense his upset. She laid her hand over his and urged him to twine his fingers with hers. "I don't see any bad there, Luis."

He chuckled, a harsh sound that seemed to surprise her. "I'm not a lying lawyer anymore?"

She tightened her lips. "I'm sorry I said that. I was angry because there was so much going on with my parents. With my grandmother." She recoiled a little, seemingly surprised with the last bit of her statement.

"She is your grandmother," Luis challenged and squeezed her hand. "I'm glad you're willing to admit that."

Jessica firmed her lips even more but nodded. "She is, and she's a fascinating woman. A strong woman who had to overcome so much. I know that now and yet…"

There was no doubting her sincerity or her upset. He finished for her. "And yet your mother left her and never looked back."

Jessica pulled her hand away and laced her fingers together tightly. With her hands in her lap, she looked down at them and in a barely audible voice said, "She had her reasons and I get some of them. She felt abandoned and not just for the year she spent alone in Cuba."

"But she was here with her family. How could she have felt abandoned?" Luis wondered, wanting to understand what had driven Jessica's mother away from Miami and her family.

Jessica shrugged and, almost in slow motion, raised her face to meet his gaze once more. "My mother said that Carmen was always busy. Away from the family with work. Going to parties and events, and even when she was home, a lot of the attention went to her sisters because they were younger."

Luis nodded. "From what I know, that's true. But understand that Carmen was founding the business and trying to help others escape Cuba. Dealing with losing her husband. It couldn't have been easy for her, especially with three little girls."

———————◇———————

It couldn't have been easy, Jessica thought. "I can't imagine what she was going through."

"Don't just try to imagine. Ask her about those years. The ones that caused the pain that never went away."

"But I don't want to hurt her."

Luis cupped her jaw again and strummed his thumb across her cheek. "I know you don't, but it might help both your grandmother and mother to finally heal."

"It might," she agreed reluctantly, unsure of how it would but determined to understand what had really happened and how it had shaped her mother's world. "I will," she added and once again twined her fingers with Luis's, taking comfort from that touch. Too much comfort. He was becoming too special to her and that was bound to cause both of them pain.

"Thank you," she said and broke her connection with him, even if it was too late to avoid the hurt.

He nodded but was obviously upset by her action. As he resumed lunch, he jabbed at the food on the plate almost angrily, before he finally set aside his knife and fork and said, "I really should go. I have a pile of work on my desk and lots to do before Thursday's big family gathering."

Bolting to his feet, he stared at her, hesitating for a moment. "I guess I'll see you soon."

She dipped her head. "I guess you will."

He rushed off, leaving her sitting there alone on the patio, accompanied by only her half-eaten lunch and the thoughts bouncing around in her brain. Thoughts of pain and hurt. Guilt. Her guilt at having come here and reopening old wounds.

For so many years she'd avoided asking her mother about her family because she'd seen the hurt there, time and time again. No matter how much she'd wanted to know, she'd held that want inside her to spare her mother the pain. Now she'd exposed those wounds, that pain, but despite that, she knew Luis was right. That *she* had been right to come here to learn more about her family's past.

Armed with that, she rose and went in search of her grandmother.

Chapter Twenty-One

BACK IN BROOKLYN, JESSICA would know just where to look for her mother if she was upset.

Since she suspected the apple hadn't fallen far from that tree, her first stop was Carmen's home office.

Sylvia was at her desk, working at her computer as Jessica entered. When the younger woman glanced at her, it was clear she was distressed about something.

"Is my grandmother here?" Jessica asked and gestured toward the closed door.

"No, your *abuela* came by a short time ago but left," Sylvia said, her words curt. "She was quite upset," she blurted out with an accusing glare in Jessica's direction.

"I'm sorry she was upset. I need to talk to her," Jessica said.

Sylvia hesitated, obviously torn, as if by revealing where Carmen might have gone was a betrayal. Finally, reluctantly, she said, "She's in her bedroom."

"Thank you."

She turned to walk out, but as she did so, Sylvia said, "Please don't hurt her any more. She doesn't deserve it."

She paused and pivoted to face the younger woman again. "That was never my goal. Please believe that."

Sylvia peered at her, as if to gauge her sincerity. Then she nodded slowly, acknowledging Jessica's statement. "I believe you. But please be kind to her. She means a lot to many of us."

With a nod, Jessica hurried out and she was struck yet again by the loyalty and love that Carmen had inspired in strangers while her own daughter wanted nothing to do with her.

In the living room, Jessica pondered where Carmen's bedroom was located, since in the four days she'd been here she'd had no cause to go there. Luckily, Consuelo walked into the living room with a tray holding a carafe, a cup, and some pastries.

"Are you taking that to Carmen?" she asked.

Consuelo nodded. "*Sí*. I know your *abuela* didn't finish lunch and thought she might be hungry," she said with an almost condemning tone.

"I'll take it to her. Which way should I go to her room?"

Much as Sylvia had done earlier, Consuelo delayed, clearly upset with Jessica, but then the older woman relented. She handed the tray to her and said, "Down that hall to the right. All the way down to the end."

Tray in hand, Jessica marched to the room but paused by the door. Sucking in a deep breath, she balanced the tray against her side and knocked but received no reply. She knocked again, a little harder. Louder, but was again met with only silence.

Worried, especially considering how upset Carmen had been, she tried the knob, and it gave easily beneath her hand.

Slowly, tentatively, she entered, not knowing what to expect inside.

The room was of a size similar to the guest room she'd been given. A queen-size bed sat between two french doors that opened onto patios beside Biscayne Bay. Similar to the European and colonial Spanish furniture in the rest of the home, the bed was dark walnut with elaborate scrollwork carved into the headboard and footboard. But it was the sitting area beyond the bed that drew her attention.

Her heart pounded in her chest as she walked to the sitting area and laid the tray on the coffee table there. She pushed on the writing table just feet away against the wall. Her hands shook as she ran them across the floral scrollwork that graced the front of the piece. It had taken her hours to clean out the layers of paint that had been slapped on by various owners, muddying the fine lines of the carving. She traced her fingers down the curved lines of the legs to the claw feet, now also free of paint. In her mind's eye she recalled the dowels she'd had to reconstruct to strengthen and stabilize the trestle that supported the heavy walnut tabletop.

This had been one of the first commission jobs she'd ever done after opening her shop and the buyer had paid a hefty price for the time Jessica had spent locating the piece and renovating it. The money had come at a much-needed time, since she'd only just opened her business and had had a wealth of expenses to cover.

The sound of the french doors opening had her turning to find her grandmother walking back into the room, a weary expression on her face that became one of surprise. Eyes wide, her grandmother wrung her hands together, clearly unsure of what she might be thinking at the discovery of the writing table.

"How? Why?" she asked, trying to make sense of it. She'd been a little surprised by the commission at the time, wondering how someone had found her shop for the job, but grateful for the money it would bring in. Not to mention that the interior decorator who had hired Jessica had been thrilled with the quality of the work and now regularly gave Jessica commissions for other jobs.

With that all-too-familiar shrug, her grandmother said, "You're my granddaughter," as if that would explain everything. Carmen motioned to the love seat by the coffee table and Jessica joined her there, heart still pounding heavily. Her hands still a little shaky as she poured Carmen a café con leche from the carafe and handed her the cup.

Carmen was likewise a bit unstable as she took the cup and a sip.

Jessica pressed on. "How did you know about my business? About what I do?"

"I've tried to follow how you're doing. How Lara and Sal are doing. There's a lot of information on the internet, you know," she said with a sidelong glance. "You did a press release when you opened the shop, and it came up in an alert I set up."

Jessica blew out a laugh. "Pretty savvy for an eighty-three-year-old, or did you have help?"

With a wry crinkle of her lips, Carmen said, "I have to confess that Luis helped, despite his objections."

"Because it was spying," Jessica said, her tone reproachful rather than harsh.

Carmen looked upward, considering the condemnation, but then said, "Is it spying if you make it available for all the world to see?"

"Like my Facebook page? Instagram?" Jessica wondered aloud.

Another shrug answered her. "I might have followed you to see how you were, who you were. And I was very proud of what I saw. You've accomplished so much."

Despite her grandmother's praise, Jessica was trying to balance the revelation that her grandmother had been spying on her, only… was it really spying if, as her grandmother had said, she put it out there for all the world to see?

"So you knew about the shop. Anything else?" she asked and grimaced, trying to recall what she might have posted about her life on her personal profile.

Carmen set aside her cup and did air quotes as she said, "Your 'relationship status' has been single for some time. And you really should be more careful about who you friend on those sites."

Jessica chuckled even as heat flooded her face. "I should, otherwise someone as disreputable as you might be spying on me. Are you even sorry you did it?"

Bright color painted Carmen's cheeks. "I'm sorry, but not sorry. I was happy to be able to be a part of your life even if I really couldn't be a part of it. And I'm not sorry for having you restore that writing table for me. I've sat there many a night, writing in my journal."

"You keep a journal?" Jessica wondered what her grandmother would write about. *Her life? Business? The break with her daughter?*

"It's something I started recently. I wanted to write down my thoughts about things before memories faded. I'm not getting any younger, *sabes*." She hesitated and dragged in a breath through her nostrils, which flared with the action. "I just wanted you to understand how I felt in case you wouldn't come."

Her grandmother paused again, took a sip, and picked up the plate of confections. She held it up to Jessica, obviously trying to distract her from the discussion.

Jessica played along for a moment and took a flaky pastry from the plate. She nibbled on it, enjoying the buttery flakiness that was chased by the fruity sweetness of the filling. "Delicious."

"It's a guava pastelito. It's one of my favorites," Carmen replied and took another pastry for herself.

Jessica waited to press about the journals, polishing off her own pastry and delaying until Carmen had finished hers and a cup of coffee. After Carmen had poured herself a second cup, she glanced at Jessica. "Would you like some? I can have Consuelo bring in another cup."

Jessica shook her head. "No, thanks." She laid her hands on her thighs and rubbed them back and forth anxiously before she blurted out, "Did you write about my mom in the journals?"

Carmen peered at Jessica's hands and then laid her hand over them. "I think it's what I wrote about the most. I keep on going back to those early years and all that happened. I keep on asking myself what I did or didn't do. How I could have done things differently so that I wouldn't lose her."

Jessica thought back to what little her mother had said about feeling abandoned. About how Carmen had always put others ahead of her, including her sisters. How her grandmother had almost admitted as much to her over the last few days.

"You told me that you were lost as well in those days," she said, hoping to restart the discussion in a way that wouldn't make her grandmother defensive.

"I was," Carmen said and sipped her coffee, almost as if using it as Dutch courage. But then she said, "I need something stronger."

She popped off the couch and walked over to a bar where she poured not one but two glasses of liquor. Returning to the coffee table, she set one of the glasses before Jessica and said, "Matusalem twenty-three-year-old rum. I like to support fellow Cubans."

"*Gracias*," she said, picked up the glass, and held it tightly, waiting for her grandmother to continue.

Carmen sat back down, took a substantial sip of the rum, and finally began. "We had very little money when we got here and most of what we had was spent on trying to get Lara and my parents out of Cuba."

"Is that why it took a year?"

Carmen huffed out a harsh laugh and shook her head vigorously. "No, it was Castro. All Castro. He wanted to punish us, so he made life as difficult as he could. Even here," she said, confusing Jessica.

"How?" she asked.

"When your *abuelo* came to meet me at the airport, we were pulled aside by Immigration. While we stood there, we noticed one of Castro's people walking by. He tipped his hat and smiled at us. The kind of cold, lifeless smile a shark gives you before it attacks," she said and downed the rest of the rum in one quick toss.

"Someone had notified Immigration that your *abuelo* and I had supported Castro. That we were communist sympathizers and because of that, Immigration was threatening to send us back to Cuba."

"But they didn't, right?" Jessica said and pressed her glass of rum into her grandmother's hands.

"No, they didn't because I told them we wouldn't leave. That they could put us in jail here because that would be far better than going back to Cuba, where they would either imprison us or kill us," she said, her voice trembling with anger.

"But you were able to stay, so what took so long to bring my mom and my great-grandparents here?" Jessica wondered.

"Castro again. When we didn't come back, he took away the family's passports, basically trapping them in Cuba. That started another battle. I spoke to every agency I could, but that accomplished nothing. I couldn't get any help legally."

"If you couldn't get help legally…"

"I reached out to people who had other connections. It took time, but I was able to get fake passports and rush the family out of Cuba, but there was no legal way to enter the U.S. at that time, even though my husband and I had requested political asylum."

Jessica's mind was reeling with the information and what her grandmother must have been feeling as she tried to reunite her family. "Where did they go? Where did they stay?"

After a sigh and a smaller sip of the rum, her grandmother said, "With distant family in Nicaragua, but they were poor, and the living conditions weren't good. Then they went to Mexico, and by then the U.S. laws had changed and Cubans could enter the country legally. A friend helped us get them over the border, and Immigration assisted in getting them to Miami." With a shaky breath, she said, "I remember sitting in the Immigration office, waiting for them. One of the officers came out and told me that I had a beautiful daughter."

Her voice grew even huskier as emotion threatened her narrative. With a sharp laugh and a swipe of the tears from her face, she said, "I was so out of it with worry and anticipation that I didn't make the connection. I asked him how he knew, and he told me that it was because she was in the room next door."

Jessica wrapped her arms around Carmen and drew her near. "I can't imagine how that must have felt."

"It was amazing. I was so happy. I thought that the pain and separation were all over. That we were going to have our happily-ever-after, but I was so wrong," she said and burrowed her head against Jessica's shoulder.

She wondered if her mother knew this story but assumed that she did. How could she not? And if she did, how could she think that her mother had abandoned her in Cuba?

"I'm so confused, Abuela. How could my mother—"

"Don't, Jessica. Don't judge her harshly. She was too young to remember so much from those years, and after...I *was* busy with others. I had to be because I had to pay it forward. There were people who helped us escape and be reunited. I had to help others in the same situation."

Pay it forward. It was something her mother had stressed to her more than once. That they had been blessed with so much that it was only right they help others. But Jessica had always understood that it was thanks to her parents' hard work, Carmen's hard work, that they had those blessings.

"Those parties and events...that's how you did it?" Jessica wondered.

Carmen nodded. "It is. In the first year it was just a few times, but after the Bay of Pigs, a lot of it had to do with trying to get Carlos home."

"And building the business," Jessica added, recalling some of the stories her mother had told her as well as Carmen's recollections.

With another nod and a sniffle, Carmen shifted back on the love seat to face her. "And building the business. With Carlos gone, money was scarce, and I knew I had to do more to help my family."

The images of the spreadsheets, address list, and other minutes from the exiles' meetings flashed through Jessica's brain. "You were helping others, but you also asked them to help you start the business. They didn't want to take part in it."

"They didn't, but I understood, no matter how hard it made it for me not to have partners. But they all had their own problems they had to focus on."

It was all Jessica could do to keep her voice calm. Steady and not condemning, despite what she was feeling inside. Despite what her mother must have felt as a lost and lonely child. "You had problems too."

Carmen clearly knew what Jessica had meant. "I failed Lara, but not intentionally. I thought that as long as she had a roof over her head and food on the table, I was being a good mother. By the time I realized that she needed more, I think that it was too late."

Jessica had heard her grandmother admit it more than once already, which made her wonder about what she might have said to her mother. "Did you tell her that?"

Hesitating, Carmen looked away, as if considering how to respond. After a long pause, she said, "Not at first, because it took me a long time to realize it. Once the business took off, I had to devote even more time to it. To compensate, I would take the girls to the office with me on weekends, and we would make a day of it."

She rose, more slowly this time, and went over to the desk Jessica had restored, grabbed a small album off the surface, and brought it over. She opened the photo album and flipped through a number of pictures until she got to one of the family in what was clearly an office. "This is us at our first location," she said and tenderly ran her hands across the black-and-white images in the photograph.

Jessica's mother's face was grim in contrast to that of her two younger sisters, who were both happily smiling as they posed in front of a desk piled with papers.

"I would let the girls do small chores to earn their allowance.

Making copies. Stapling papers. Since your mother was older, I'd let her file papers away so she could improve her alphabet."

Like mother, like daughter, she thought. "My mom took me to her law office if she had to work on a Saturday. I'd do little odd jobs and she'd pay me for them. After, we'd explore the city together. Maybe go to a museum or park."

Carmen smiled and it was a happy smile that reached up into her green gaze. "I did that with the girls often. I'm so glad Lara did it with you."

"I'm glad as well," she said and pondered why the actions that had brought her closer to her mother hadn't done the same with her mother and grandmother. But then again, there had been bone-deep hurt there already. What would it take to overcome that kind of hurt?

"My mom...she was upset about the time you spent on the business and everything else. And she was...devastated by losing her father."

"Losing Carlos," Carmen began and shook her head. "I felt like I kept on losing him, but then again, how do you lose something you never really had?"

Puzzled, Jessica said, "I don't get it. He was your husband. You had him."

She shook her head more vigorously. "I thought I did, but it was an illusion. In Cuba he was so involved with both his job and the Civic Resistance to overthrow Castro. I didn't realize it because I was just as involved. But when we came here, I was ready for a different kind of life. A peaceful one for my family, but he wasn't. First it was the Bay of Pigs and then Vietnam. After I grieved, I was angry with him for putting everything ahead of us. Ahead of his family."

Like mother, like daughter, Jessica thought again.

"Do you think my mother sensed that anger? She adored him," she said.

"She did adore him. She would look at him with such love. She never looked at me like that," Carmen said, sadness dripping from every word.

"I'm sorry," Jessica said and laid her hand on Carmen's forearm. "Abuela," she said, trying out the word for the first time. Finding it not as foreign as she might have thought. "I'm truly sorry."

Carmen smiled and covered Jessica's hand with her own. "*Gracias, mi'jita.* Tell me about Lara. How is she doing? Is she happy?"

Chapter Twenty-Two

IS MY MOTHER HAPPY? Jessica asked herself and couldn't be quite certain. "I think she is. She loves her job. She's done well at it, although she grumbles about how it's still an old boys' club."

"It can be in many law firms from what I've seen, much like with what you do," Carmen said and patted Jessica's hand in sympathy. "I'm so proud of you for not being afraid to follow your own path that way."

"Thank you. Did you know my mom wanted to be a writer?" Jessica asked, wondering what it was that had set her mother on such a different path in life.

A slightly guilty look slipped onto her grandmother's face. "I did. She wanted a typewriter as her high school graduation gift, but like many immigrant parents, I wanted her to have a profession. A career that would let her take care of her family. That's what made me so happy when she said she was going to law school."

"She never wrote that book, just briefs," Jessica said, sad that her mother had left one of her dreams unattained.

"Mmm," Carmen said, obviously thinking about something but seemingly unwilling to share that thought. That became clear as she said, "The family is coming over on Thursday so you can meet them. That still gives you a few days to relax or see some other sights with Luis. Maybe even spend time with your cousins before you go home."

Even though she'd already met three of her four cousins, the thought of all the family together was a little daunting. Especially when combined with meeting her aunts for the first time. But her grandmother would be there for support as well as Luis.

Luis, she thought with a sigh. She told herself she was counting on him too much, maybe because her emotions had been running so high since he'd first landed on her doorstep. Or maybe it was something else. Something she didn't dare admit to because it was too complicated.

"Well? Does that sound good for you?" Carmen pressed, tilting her head to consider Jessica after her prolonged silence.

"It's a little nerve-wracking, but that's why I came here. To meet all of you," she said, but didn't add *to understand why my mother cut you out of her life.*

"Wonderful," Carmen said and clapped her hands. "I think you will really enjoy your aunts and cousins. They're an interesting group."

"The cousins I've met so far have been quite nice," she thought. *Except for Angelica.*

The sharp rise of a brow greeted her. Her grandmother obviously could read her quite well, but she remained silent. "*Bueno.* We'll finalize those plans, and I'll let you and Luis decide what to do over the next couple of days. Maybe he can take you for a boat ride."

A boat ride with Luis. "That sounds nice," she said, while also worrying about how risky it would be to her emotions.

"I'll ask him to take you," Carmen said and looked at Jessica in a way that almost dared her to refuse.

She didn't, despite the fact that Carmen's obvious matchmaking could only cause problems for both her and Luis. But they were two consenting adults. Two intelligent and sensible adults who could handle it.

Or at least she hoped they could.

Even though the family gathering was a couple of days away, Carmen, Consuelo, and Manny jumped into preparations with unparalleled enthusiasm the next day.

Manny brought in additional staff to tidy what was already an impeccable home and to place more tables and chairs throughout the gardens, patio, and pool. A small dance floor had been set up as well, because how could it be a party without dancing, Carmen had advised.

Carmen and Consuelo spent hours chatting about the menu for the special gathering, and afterward coordinated with Manny to arrange for the help that would serve the assorted appetizers and multicourse meal the two women had dreamed up for Jessica to be able to sample the best of Cuban cuisine.

She found herself drawn into all the planning, walking the house and gardens on behalf of her grandmother to make sure the layout made sense. Taste-testing some of the dishes that Consuelo intended to prepare until she felt like she might burst from all that she'd eaten.

It bordered on madness, but Jessica understood the why of it. Her grandmother wanted it to be a perfect evening before she left. And she would leave despite what her grandmother hoped. She had her business to run. She had her parents and the Russo family that would be missing her.

But she would be back. She had no doubt about that. She wanted to build a connection to this part of her family.

To Luis, the little voice in her head said, and as much as she wanted to deny it, she couldn't.

It was what had her calling him after the whirlwind of preparations had driven her to hide in her room after dinner. A dinner where he had been conspicuously absent, considering how often he had been coming by in the days since she'd arrived.

Is he avoiding me? she wondered as she flopped onto the bed and waited for him to answer.

It took a few rings and the hesitation worried her. "*Hola, mi amor,*" he said when he answered, his voice low and slightly husky, as if she'd woken him.

"I'm sorry. Were you asleep?" She shot a quick look at her watch and winced as she realized it was after ten. She hadn't realized how late it was with all the activity that had been going on all day and, clearly, well into the night.

"No, just reading in bed," he said.

"Oh. Sorry. I can call back."

"No, not a problem. I'm sorry I didn't call today. It was a crazy busy day at work," he said.

"It's been insane here as well with getting ready to have family over on Thursday since I'm leaving on Saturday," she said, even though as Carmen's right-hand man, Luis would know everything.

"I can only imagine that they've been crazily getting ready," he said with a laugh.

"That's an understatement. You have to save me, Luis. I don't think I can take another day of this insanity," she said, but with humor.

He laughed again and teased, "I thought modern women saved themselves."

"I am. You're going to take me for a boat ride. Tomorrow."

His hearty chuckle drifted across the line. "I like a woman who can take charge. I'll pick you up at nine. *Buenas noches, mi amor.*"

She echoed his good night. "*Buona notte, amore mio.*"

---◆---

Luis stared at the phone, slightly puzzled by her sign off.

Amore mio. My love, Italian style. *Russo style*, he thought with a strangled laugh.

Did she mean it or is it just a nod to my sign-off? Do I mean it? he wondered but had no doubt about it.

In just a little over a week, he might have fallen in love with Jessica Russo.

While he didn't believe in love at first sight, his world had definitely tilted on its axis the moment he had set eyes on her in her paint-stained overalls and raggedy T-shirt, a sprinkle of sanding dust in her hair.

And in the time since then, that world had kept on spinning, almost out of control, as he got to know her better. Emotionally intimate. As for physically...

No, this is so not good. In a couple of days, Jessica was going home, and he had no doubt she'd be taking a piece of him with her unless...

He wouldn't think about the *unless.*

Unable to sleep after the call, he returned to his home office and stared at the business plan he'd been putting together for months. Now more than ever, he had to finish it and show it to Carmen, and then...

He forced himself not to think about the *then* which was on a par with the *unless.* He had to focus on the present, so he could think about his future.

The one big question that loomed large: Could it be a future that included Jessica Russo?

Jessica was lounging by the pool, listening intently for the sound of Luis's car pulling up, when she heard the purr of engines down by the water.

She popped up and peered toward the water's edge as a sleek red-and-white catamaran navigated to the dock at the edge of the property, Luis at the helm. He waved at her to come over, and she hurried toward the boat as he killed the engines and hopped from his seat. He tossed her ropes that she grabbed and, with his help, tied them to cleats on the dock.

He jumped onto the dock and brushed a kiss across her cheek, but she rose on tiptoes and turned the chaste kiss into more, laying her mouth full on his, savoring his pleased sigh that mingled with her breath as the kiss continued until a soft cough drew them apart.

Consuelo stood there, a broad smile on her face, holding a picnic basket. "La Viejita thought you might want some lunch for your boat ride."

"*Gracias,* Consuelo. That was very thoughtful. Please thank my *abuela,*" Jessica said, but Luis waved his hand in the direction of the pool.

"You can thank her yourself," he said.

Her grandmother hurried toward the dock, a broad smile on her face, making Jessica wonder if she had seen their earlier kiss. She wanted to kick herself for not being more discreet, but Luis's smile as he'd seen her had been just too tempting. She wished that he hadn't been wearing sunglasses, so she could have seen that smile reach up into his hazel eyes.

"*Buenos dias, mi'jito. Mi'jita,*" her grandmother said and took hold of Jessica's hand while pecking Luis on the cheek.

"*Buenos dias, viejita.* How are you today?" Luis said.

"I'm fine. More than fine," Carmen said with a big smile and looked at the two of them with undue interest, confirming to Jessica that her grandmother had seen the kiss.

"Thank you for the lunch, Abuela," Jessica said, and her grandmother's smile grew impossibly broader now that she'd called her *abuela.*

Carmen squeezed her hand. "My pleasure. You two have a nice day, and don't worry about rushing back for dinner. We'll make *arroz con pollo.* That'll keep no matter when you get back."

"We won't be too late," Luis said, stepped back onto the boat, and offered a hand to help Jessica onto the deck of the powerboat.

The boat rocked a bit from the wake of another boat going by, but Luis had a firm grip on her and eased her into the cushioned bucket seat. It enveloped her in plush comfort much the way she imagined a race car would protect a driver.

Luis undid the ropes holding the boat and tossed them onto the dock. He jumped down and settled himself behind the helm.

"Hang on," he said, started up the engines, and the thrum of their power surged through her body.

Luis maneuvered away from the dock and, at a measured pace, navigated under the causeway and past a nearby island with luxury homes. "That's Fisher Island. It's one of the most expensive zip codes in the country."

"More expensive than Star Island?" Jessica said in disbelief.

Luis laughed and shook his head. "No way."

They had cleared Fisher Island and the southern point of Miami Beach and reached open ocean.

Luis smiled, a dimpled and mischievous grin. "Ready to race?"

Boys and their toys, she thought, but didn't get to answer as he gunned the engines, pushing her back into the cushioned leather seat. The intense vibrations of the engines thrummed through her as the boat rocketed across the waves, dragging laughter from her as it bounced across some rougher spots and sent water splashing up over the bow.

They traveled northward, past the art deco area of South Beach, with its colorful buildings and his hotel. Upward toward the larger resort hotels in the center of Miami Beach, their tall spires rising along the shore. A sudden splash of green in an open space park broke up the buildings before they started up again as they sped ever northward along Miami Beach, until Luis slowed and turned inward.

He kept a more sedate pace in the waters of the bay as they powered past islands on one side, the mainland on the other, and beneath the causeway joining them.

The sun beat down, warming her against the chill of the breeze as they moved along the calmer waters of the bay until Luis pulled eastward once again and toward a southward facing point on an island off Miami Beach. He powered down substantially and navigated beside a dock where he cut the engines and hopped onto it to secure the boat.

She got to her feet, slightly shaky from the thrill of the ride and the roll and rock of the deck thanks to the wake from a passing boat. Luis leaned down, offered a helping hand, and boosted her up onto the dock.

"No sea legs," she said, still feeling the movement beneath her feet, but then she caught sight of the home in front of her.

A wide stone walkway surrounded by lush, manicured lawns led up to a patio with a pool and an outdoor sitting area off to the side. Beyond that a large two-story contemporary home boasted windows along every wall and balconies to enjoy the million-dollar views of Biscayne Bay and the carefully tended gardens all around.

"Wow, this is beautiful," she said, appreciating the thoughtful lines and layout of the structure and landscaping.

"*Gracias*. I'm quite happy with it," he said, but she sensed some hesitation there and wondered at the reason for it. "We can take a dip to wash off the salt before lunch," he said and grabbed the picnic basket from the boat.

He took hold of her hand and drew her toward a covered patio, and at her questioning look, he tapped the end of her nose. "You're getting burned."

She covered her face with her hands and heat greeted her despite the suntan lotion she'd put on earlier. "I do feel baked," she admitted.

"Dip. Dry off. Lunch before we head back," he said and laid the picnic basket on a table on the covered patio.

"So demanding," she teased, but was eager to get the salt off her skin. She quickly pulled off her T-shirt and board shorts and rushed to the edge of the pool. She dipped in a toe, testing the water, which turned out to be a waste as he cannonballed into the pool and sent a shock of chill water up to drench her.

"Thanks," she said with a roll of her eyes, brushing back wet strands of hair from her face.

He grinned devilishly and slicked back his hair, the movement displaying his toned arms and chest.

To avoid the too-irresistible sight of him, she dove into the water.

Cool slipped all across her body before she rose up to the surface. Luis was just a few feet away, drops of water glistening on his tanned skin. He was still grinning happily, drawing her like a moth to a flame.

She laid a hand on his shoulder, using his greater height and strength to keep her afloat.

He placed a hand at her waist to steady her, but in those seconds, the moment changed. Became charged with the tension that had sprung up between them and she couldn't resist.

When he applied gentle pressure to draw her close, she went, bringing her body full against him. Skin against skin as he shifted them until he was sitting on the bottom steps of the pool and she was lying along him.

"Luis," she began, but stopped abruptly, not sure of what to say. Only sure of what she wanted to do.

She shifted upward to kiss the hollow just beneath his ear and the edge of his jaw. She followed the straight line of it to the dimple by his lips, deep now thanks to the smile on his face. Moved to that smile, so happy and relaxed. *Welcoming*, she thought as she covered his smile with hers.

"This is crazy," she said, but didn't stop kissing him.

"*Sí, es loco*," he said, but didn't pull away. Didn't stop touching her, running his hands to her sides. Shifting one to the small of her back while he moved the other up to caress her.

"*Dios, mi amor*. This is so hard," he said, his voice rough. His body tensed beneath her. "I'm not sure I can hold back."

"Do you want me?" she asked, although she had no doubt about it.

"I do, but not just for now, *mi amor*. I want so much more."

It was like pouring cold water over them because she wasn't sure there could be more. She cupped his jaw and with a tender swipe of her thumb across his lips, she said, "I'm sorry, Luis. This just isn't the right time for this."

The boyish grin evaporated like dew beneath the morning sun and was replaced by a knife-sharp slash. "*Lo se*. I'm sorry too, Jessica. If you can give me just a few minutes—"

"I'll get lunch set up," she said, pushed off him, and raced up the steps of the pool and back to the patio where she began to lay out the lunch that Consuelo had packed for them.

Some kind of pâté, large Cuban crackers, slices of Cuban bread, manchego cheese, wine, and a bowl filled with fruit salad. She finished by taking out the cutlery, plates, and glasses that had also been carefully packed into the picnic basket and setting two places at the table.

Luis approached, a towel wrapped around his waist, and he handed her a towel for her to dry off. His gaze was penetrating, and she used the towel as a defense against that intensity.

"Consuelo packed a wonderful lunch," she said with a sweep of her hand in the direction of the food she'd placed on the table.

"It looks delicious. *Carne fría* is one of my favorites," he said and rubbed his two hands together in delight.

"The pâté?" she asked as she sat and served him several slices of the meat along with crackers, cheese, and bread.

"More like cold meatloaf. It's baked ham but mixed with raw pork and beef that you cook. Try it on a Cuban cracker."

The cracker wasn't like the typical flaky one, but rather hard, almost bland, and thick, with a not quite flat top. But with the slight saltiness of the cold meatloaf, it was the perfect carrier. Topped with the slightly nutty manchego, it made a tasty variation on ham and cheese. Hungry after the boat ride, she devoured slice after slice and then served them the fruit salad.

The fruit salad was packed with mango, papaya, and passion fruit in addition to more pedestrian strawberries and melons.

By the time they finished eating, she could swear her stomach was bulging and after-meal lethargy was hitting her hard. She yawned unexpectedly and quickly covered her mouth with her hand.

"Tired?" he asked with the lift of a brow.

She had to admit a nap would be heavenly. "I am."

"There's a hammock just around the corner, beneath some palm trees," he said.

The thought of lying beneath the palms, swaying in the breeze, was way too tempting. Especially if he was part of the package, danger notwithstanding.

"I may need some help getting into the hammock," she said, and he jutted his eyebrow higher, in surprise and question.

"Are you sure?"

"No," she immediately said. "But I'd like to do it anyway."

He'd like to do it as well, although it would be sheer torture to lie beside her, but with their time being limited, he wanted to experience as much as he could with her.

Rising, he reached out to her and she slipped her hand into his. With a gentle tug, he brought her around the corner of the patio to a wide swath of grass tucked between thick hedges and the house. A bright orange hammock swung from the thick trunks of two palms and a slight breeze rocked it back and forth.

He released her hand to sit in the hammock, centering himself before he swept his legs up and invited her to join him. She copied his actions, sitting carefully before tucking herself against his side. He slipped his arm beneath her head and around to draw her near, and she came willingly.

"This is nice," she said and rubbed her hand across his chest, the gesture soothing.

"It is," he admitted. "I don't get to do this often."

She rose up on an elbow and peered at him. "Because you work too much," she teased.

He smiled and nodded. "Because I work too much, although I have been thinking about some things that might change that."

"Care to share?" she asked.

He shook his head. "Not at the moment," he said and at her disappointed look, he added, "But I will when I can. What about you? I gather you're as much of a workaholic as I am."

She lay back down, pillowing her head in the crook of his arm and shoulder. "I am. That's why this is so nice."

"Relax, then," he said.

She murmured a sleepy "Mmm."

It didn't take long to feel the change in her body as her muscles grew lax and her breathing lengthened in sleep.

He stared upward, watching the play of the palm fronds in the breeze against the azure sky. Enjoying the feel of Jessica tucked against him, trusting in sleep. Peaceful.

It was odd that a woman who could rouse the kind of need that she had in the pool earlier could also bring him the peace he was feeling as they lay there together.

He imagined what it would be like if that was a regular thing with them. If it could become something more permanent and not just with the two of them. It was too easy to picture little ones with Jessica's green eyes and the Guerreiro dimple in their chins. His darker hair. Toys strewn all across the tiled floor of his sterile living room, finally giving it life.

Too easy to imagine, but infinitely harder to accomplish, he reminded himself.

But he didn't let that dim the joy of the moment.

Nothing worthwhile is easy, he thought, recalling something Carmen had told him on more than one occasion.

A life with Jessica...definitely worthwhile, he thought and let himself imagine it as they swayed in the hammock together, enjoying the spring day. Their time together ticking away with each breath.

Chapter Twenty-Three

JESSICA SMOOTHED HER HANDS down the skirt of the little black dress she'd decided to wear to meet the family. She'd bought it at the last minute at a friend's shop just a few doors down from her own business. Made of raw silk, it was dressy enough for evening, especially when paired with the elegant wrap she'd also bought at the shop.

With a deep breath, she took a last look in the mirror, tucked a stray tendril of hair back into her french braid, and hurried from the closet. Sounds of activity filtered upstairs from down below, announcing that family had already begun to arrive for the big event.

Butterflies didn't just flit in her stomach. They scrambled and bounced around like a flurry of bats chased from their cave. She laid a hand there and told herself she could do this. After all, it was the reason she'd come to Miami: to meet the family.

At the base of the stairs, she ran into Carmen as she hurried from her wing of the house.

"You look lovely. Just like your mother," she said and clapped her hands over her mouth, tears shimmering in her gaze.

"No tears today, Abuela. Only happy thoughts," she said and embraced her grandmother. Her body seemed so slight in Jessica's arms, but just like her Bisnonna Russo, the steel of her character was what made her indomitable.

Carmen nodded and echoed the sentiment, "Only happy

thoughts," although Jessica was sure that her grandmother was thinking the gathering wasn't complete without the presence of her eldest daughter.

Determined to keep the spirit upbeat, Jessica eased her arm through her grandmother's and together they walked outside to where family was gathered across the covered dining patio, pool, dance floor, and bayside areas.

As they exited, two women rose, almost in unison, from the patio table and came to stand before them.

Gloria and Anna. Jessica would have recognized them anywhere, the Guerreiro look was so strong in them. Their green gazes settled on her above high cheekbones, Roman noses, full lips, and the thumbprint dimple in their chins.

Carmen held out her hand to them in invitation. "Jessica, meet your Aunt Gloria and Aunt Anna."

"So nice to meet you," she said and wasn't quite sure what would be right. A handshake? A hug?

But the two women took the decision from her, heartily embracing her at the same time, their voices filled with joy. Arms wrapped tight around her as they swayed together.

"You look so much like Lara!" her aunt Gloria said.

"We're so glad you're here," Aunt Anna added.

Jessica looked between them and her grandmother. "I'm glad to be here. Thank you for the warm welcome."

"*¡Niños, ven aquí!*" Aunt Gloria said and waved to Carlos and David to come over from poolside.

More hugs and greetings followed from the men she had already met during her time in Miami. They had no sooner stepped away when Angelica and her brother, Esteban, came over. Angelica's greeting was, as expected, cooler than that of her other cousins, including Esteban, who was a strapping, movie-star handsome man sure to break hearts.

But she had no eyes for any man other than Luis and searched the property for any sign of him.

"He's not here yet," her grandmother whispered in her ear, and her face flamed at how transparent she was.

Intending to forestall her grandmother's matchmaking, she threw herself into learning more about her aunts and cousins, especially her aunts with their stories about growing up with her mother.

"Lara was always so serious," Anna said and mimicked her mother's stern face, looking so much like Lara that Jessica had to laugh and shake her head.

"I've gotten that hairy eyeball more than once," she admitted.

"But so bright and daring too," Gloria added and recounted a story about how the two of them had been inspired by a show they'd seen to use the family's turntable to make pottery.

"No, really?" Jessica said, trying to understand how her by-the-book mother would have ever decided to do something so unexpected.

"Really," Carmen said and playfully glared at her daughters.

"We were a handful until Anna came along," Gloria said, prompting a loud chuckle from her younger sister.

"And then I took over the getting in trouble," Anna admitted, but quickly tacked on, "We were a handful, the three of us, although Lara tried to keep us in line as the oldest one. We were the Three Musketeers."

Her sister Gloria mimicked lifting a sword and Anna joined her, laughter in both their voices as together they said, "All for one, one for all."

Only that hadn't happened, Jessica thought, and apparently so did the other women as their earlier exuberance dimmed.

"We had fun," Gloria said, sadness slipping into her tone.

"You did and maybe one day you will again," Carmen said and laid a hand on each of her daughters' knees.

Gloria nodded and sniffled. "We will." She turned her attention to Jessica and said, "Please tell us about yourself. Your shop."

"I flip furniture," she began and at their questioning gazes, explained. "I find older pieces that need some love and fix them up. Resell them. Sometimes someone will commission me to find a piece for them and upcycle it or they have a piece that needs to be restored."

"Very hands-on," Gloria said.

With a nod and a smile, Jessica said, "I learned from my dad. I used to go with him on jobs, and he taught me so many things."

The two women shared a questioning look, but then Anna quickly said, "It sounds like you have a wonderful dad. Does he make Lara happy?"

Jessica enthusiastically nodded. "Very much so. He's very supportive and he makes her laugh."

"She needs that," Anna said and made her sister's stern face again, rousing laughter from all of them.

The stories continued, tale after tale of the three girls' adventures and how their grandparents had kept them in line during the day and Carmen at night when she got home from work.

"It sounds like you had a wonderful time together," Jessica said, but sadness filtered in once again.

"Lara...she had more to deal with. We were too young to really understand what was happening at times," Gloria said.

As interesting and heartwarming as the earlier stories had been, it was these other stories that might unlock the pain her mother had kept hidden away for so long.

"Like what? What did she have to deal with?" Jessica asked.

Gloria peered at Carmen, who dipped her head as if to confirm she should go on.

"Like something as simple as going to school," Gloria said.

Miami, August 1962

Her *abuela* and *mami* had dressed her and Gloria as if they were getting them ready for church on Sunday. A simple dark blue skirt with a decorative brass safety pin just above the hem. A starched white shirt whose collar was so stiff it was starting to rub her neck a little raw. Beside her, Gloria was in a similar outfit but with a red skirt.

Only it wasn't Sunday and there was something about the way Abuela and Mami kept on looking at each other and then at her that made her stomach feel funny.

She held Gloria's hand tightly as they were bundled into the family's sedan for the ride. Gloria, who was normally antsy, likewise seemed to sense this ride was different and was unusually still. Her sister huddled close to her, as if needing comfort, and she wrapped an arm around her shoulders.

Her *abuela* kept checking on them in the back seat, wearing the face Lara knew as her bad face. Every time something bad happened, like Papi leaving or not having enough money at the grocery store, she saw that face.

Her *abuela* leaned close to her *mami* and whispered to her, increasing that funny feeling in her stomach. Making her clutch Gloria ever tighter, but her sister squirmed against her, unhappy with the harsh embrace.

The car slowed and Lara leaned up to peer out the window as the car came to a stop.

A big gray building sat up on a rise, looking like one of the prisons she'd seen in her *abuelos'* television shows. But it didn't have bars, just a lot of windows. It didn't make it look any friendlier and the flutters in her stomach increased, almost to the point of pain.

Her *mami* shut off the car, laid her arm across the top of the bench seat, and peered at her, wearing her *mami's* version of the bad face.

She clutched Gloria even tighter, making her sister cry and struggle against her.

"It's time to go, Lara," her *mami* said.

Go? What did her mami mean by that?

"No," she said, shook her head, and shot a quick glance at the big gray building again, her stomach flipping and clenching at the sight of it.

"It's school, *mi'jita*. It's where you go to learn," her *mami* said, stepped out of the car, and opened the back door.

Her *mami* held her hand out to her, but Lara cringed and shuffled away toward the other door, dragging her sister with her. Gloria's crying grew ever louder as tension built.

"No, Mami, no!" Lara screamed and avoided her mother as she reached for her.

"Lara, por favor. You'll like school," her *mami* pleaded, but Lara didn't believe it.

They were going to leave her again in the big ugly gray building. Leave her just like her mother had left her in Cuba, but this time, she wouldn't even have her *abuelos* with her.

"No, no, no," she screamed and kicked at her *mami*'s hands.

I won't go, she thought. *I won't let them leave me again.*

Jessica's eyes widened as Carmen said, "It took nearly an hour to convince her to leave the car. I held her hand all the way up the steps and had to sit with her in the classroom for nearly half an hour before she finally relaxed."

Jessica couldn't imagine the fear her mother must have had inside her. Fear that had been lurking there since being left in Cuba. Fear that she suspected had never really left her mother. At times she'd sensed it but hadn't really understood it and had been too afraid to ask.

"I always wondered why my mother seemed so...insecure at times," Jessica said, but also held back, not wanting to betray any of her mother's confidences.

Gloria nodded. "I think it was why she always worked so hard to be the best at everything."

Anna playfully elbowed her sister. "Well, that and Mami always pushing us. We couldn't embarrass the family."

Gloria rolled her eyes and wagged her head. "Or our fellow Cubans. No one was ever going to say we didn't deserve to be here."

"Very true, *niñas*. We had to prove that we were worthy of this amazing country," Carmen said, her voice filled with certainty.

"My dad always teases my mom that she's more American than most Americans, and now I can see why," Jessica said.

"Am I interrupting anything?" Luis said as he sauntered over to drop a kiss on her cheek before embracing her aunts and grandmother.

"We were just reminiscing," Carmen said and swiped a finger beneath her eye, skimming away an errant tear.

Luis skipped his gaze across all of them. "Seems like it was mostly good," he said, but his tone had a note of hesitation.

To reassure him, Jessica smiled and said, "Mostly good and quite enlightening."

"I'm glad to hear that," he said and took a spot beside Jessica. He reached beneath the table and took hold of her hand. Squeezing it reassuringly, he said, "I'd love to know more about your *mami*."

"I would too. I was sixteen when she came back from college, and then poof, she was gone," Anna said, emphasizing her words with a magician-like flourish of her hands.

Gloria nodded and said, "And I'd just finished my first year at U of M. I was so looking forward to spending the summer with her, only..."

My mother decided to marry my father and stay in New York, Jessica thought.

"Mom worked her way through law school and stayed at that firm through everything, including me," she said.

"That must not have been easy, being a mother and a lawyer," Luis offered and squeezed her hand again.

"She was lucky to have my dad. He was very supportive. I know you worried about that," she said, peering across the way at the three women, who all shared a look and nodded.

It was Gloria who said, "Mami was worried about him. We were too, but for different reasons. He was taking away our *hermanita*."

Anna's head bopped up and down vigorously. "Like I said, poof she was gone, and she never came back. Not even when we begged her to reconsider."

Reconsider my dad? Jessica thought and stiffened her spine against that suggestion.

"My father is the best. He's made her very happy," she said in defense.

Gloria waved her hands to stop her, and Carmen held her hands up as well.

"No, *mi'jita*. We just wanted your mother to not stay away," her grandmother explained.

Only emotions would have been riding so high that any communication could have been misinterpreted, Jessica thought. *But for thirty years?* the little voice in her head challenged.

"Please understand that it's hard for me to wrap my head around that," Jessica said, caught between her love for her mother and the sentiments she'd begun to feel for her grandmother as well as the almost-instant connection she'd felt with her aunts. They were so like her mother physically, and she could tell from their stories that they truly loved Lara.

The women shared another look again and almost in unison nodded as Luis laced his fingers with hers, offering additional comfort.

"*Comprendemos*," her grandmother said and turned her attention to Luis. "I imagine you don't want to sit here all night with *las viejitas*. Why don't you go and spend some time with your *primos*. Get to know them better."

Luis shot her a sidelong glance. "Would you like that, *mi...* Jessica?" he said, barely catching himself with the endearment she'd come to love hearing.

She nodded and rose. "I'd like that, but would love to chat with you more later."

"We'd like that as well, *mi'jita*," Gloria said and shooed her off. "Go meet your *primos*."

Luis had taken her hand to offer comfort, but as they'd left the aunts and Carmen, Jessica had latched on to it the way a drowning sailor might grasp a lifesaver. For the rest of the night, she'd held on to him as they'd strolled around and chatted up the cousins before dinner. The only time she let go was when they'd eaten in the large formal dining room inside the home. The table easily sat at least thirty and was more than enough for the dozen family members gathered there.

The meal was a traditional Cuban Noche Buena offering with hearty slices of citrus-and-spice-marinated roast pork, rice, and black beans. An assortment of side dishes complemented the main meal. Ripe maduro and green tostone plantains. An avocado salad. Boiled yucca topped with tasty sour orange juice and sweet fried onions.

It was the kind of meal he'd eaten with them many a Christmas Eve after sharing a similar meal with his own family, only...

I'm family here too, he thought. It was why there'd been no doubt that he'd be here tonight on such an important night for the family. A night that would keep the healing going, he hoped.

After the meal they'd scattered back outside for after-dinner drinks and bite-size desserts that the waitstaff passed around. Cigars for the men down by the water, Jessica still by his side, prompting the female cousins to also join them for the normally male ritual, sans cigars for them except Angelica who was always up for any challenge.

After the cigars, it was time to dance, but Jessica held back along the edge of the dance floor, seemingly content to watch instead of participating. As Esteban danced with Angelica, their movements were fluid, graceful to the beat of the Cuban music.

"They're so beautiful," Jessica murmured and sighed. "I wish I could dance like that. I've got two left feet."

"Impossible. You're part Cuban," he teased and at that moment, Esteban peeled away from Angelica and stood before Jessica, hand outstretched.

"*Vamos, Prima,*" he said, a welcoming smile on his face.

Jessica shot him a hesitant look, but at Esteban's additional prompting, she slipped her hand into his and followed him onto the dance floor.

Luis told himself not to be jealous, but Esteban was almost too smooth and too handsome for his own good since women usually fell at his feet.

In this case, Jessica literally almost did that since, as she'd warned, she had two left feet.

As she stomped on Esteban's toe, he winced and backed away from her, unbalancing her with the tug of his hand.

Luis rushed over and asked Esteban's permission to take over, and Esteban gave him a grateful glance.

"I warned you I couldn't dance," she almost hissed at him.

"Relax, *mi amor,*" he said, then slipped a hand to her waist and took hold of her hand. "It's just one-two-three and a pause. Like this," he said, and she looked down to see what he was doing.

When she tried to repeat it, he helped her by saying, "One-two-three, pause."

"One-two-three, pause," she repeated and managed it without stepping on him.

"*Así*, that's it. You can do it," he encouraged, but she shushed him.

"Quiet. I can't count if you keep on talking," she said, determination evident in her tone and the way she worried her lower lip with her teeth.

He smiled as he heard her counting beneath her breath, but little by little, she let herself relax and the beat of the music enveloped her. Her movements became more fluid, less mechanical, and as her comfort grew, he urged her close and let himself relax.

As the salsa song ended and a slow bolero began, they drifted toward each other and swayed to the romantic music. He brushed a kiss across her temple, and she whispered, "I did it."

"You did," he said and couldn't resist adding, "Sometimes it just takes the right partner."

She chuckled and said, "Humble, aren't you?"

"Determined," he shot back playfully, dragging another chuckle from her, but then let silence reign as they gave themselves over to the music. When another salsa song came on, Jessica surprised him by staying on the dance floor and joining him in the dance, her steps growing more and more fluid with each new song.

As the night grew late, the cousins excused themselves, since some of them had work the next day. The aunts and their husbands lingered a little longer, shared a few more stories, but then likewise bid them good night, leaving Carmen, Jessica, and him alone in the living room.

Carmen rose from the sofa with a slight hitch and Luis jumped to his feet to help her up. "Are you okay, *viejita*?"

She nodded and passed a hand across his cheek. "Just a little stiff, *mi'jito*. I'll be fine."

He returned to Jessica's side, and she rose, took hold of his hand again, drawing Carmen's attention.

"I hope you had a nice time, Jessica," Carmen said, rubbing her hands against the skirt of her black dress, clearly anxious.

"I did, Abuela. It was lovely," Jessica said, obviously wanting to ease any concerns her grandmother might have.

Carmen smiled and bounced her gaze between them again. "Easter is just weeks away. Maybe you can think about joining us again for that holiday?"

Jessica tensed beside him, and he braced himself for a rejection of that invitation.

"I think that would be lovely. I always close for Good Friday anyway, which would make for a nice long weekend," Jessica said, and her words filled him with pleasure since it opened the door to a different future for the family. One which included Jessica and maybe even in time Lara.

"Wonderful. You've made me very happy, *mi'jita*. I'll leave you two alone, then," Carmen said and hurried from the room, but with a decided stiffness in her step.

Luis glanced at Jessica and cradled her cheek. "You have made her very happy. *Gracias*."

"I'm glad. I only wish…" She dipped her head down and shook it.

He cupped her jaw and applied gentle pressure to urge her gaze upward. "You wish your mom could be a part of this."

She nodded. "It's obvious Gloria and Anna love her. Miss her. So many years apart. Wasted years."

Luis nodded and strummed her cheek with his thumb. "A great deal of hurt, for everyone, including your mother."

"Maybe in time… When I get home, I want to talk to her again. Try to wrap my head around her side of the story and what I know from Carmen and my aunts." She hesitated, looked away for a second. In a soft voice, she said, "What about our maybe, Luis?"

His hand shook against her cheek, and he drew it away and

shoved both hands into his pockets to keep from reaching for her. "I won't lie. I want there to be more between us."

"I want more as well. I think I'm falling in love with you," she said and laid a hand on his chest. She smoothed her hand back and forth and said, "I'm willing to take a chance. Are you?"

Chapter Twenty-Four

HER BREATH TRAPPED IN her chest and her heart pounding in her ears, Jessica waited, anticipation twisting her gut into a knot.

Luis rocked back and forth on his heels and looked away before nailing her with his gaze. "I am. I think I'm falling in love with you too."

He grasped her hand and she took the lead, tugging him toward the stairs and up to her room.

At her door she hesitated, but then pushed through, eager for what would follow.

As she turned to face him, he was immediately there, moving his hands to her back to cradle her close. Her body was flush against his and she shifted against him, but he stilled her motion.

"Shh, *mi amor*. There's no need to rush. We have all night," he whispered and kissed her again.

He tasted of rum and cigars and Luis, and she took it all in. Took all of him in. The press of his body. The way his muscles shifted beneath her hands as he tightened his hold on her and walked her back toward the bed.

As her knees bumped the edge of the bed, he stopped, sat, and urged her in between the V of his thighs.

With his help, she quickly undressed, baring herself to him.

"*Dios*, you're beautiful," he said, encircled her waist with his hands, and drew her near.

Luis splayed his hand across the smooth skin of her back as he caressed her.

She kissed his forehead and whispered his name. "Luis. Please."

As much as he wanted to wait and make this first time special, he needed her too badly.

In a flurry of action, he ripped off his clothes with her assistance, and they fell onto the bed together, kissing and caressing and laughing. Joyful in anticipation of what was about to happen.

She lay beneath him, gazing at him as she skimmed her hand across his face and then up to brush away a stray lock of hair. She seemed about to say something, but then held back and instead leaned up to kiss him. She shifted her hand to his shoulder and urged him down.

He went willingly, eager to be with her. Eager to taste her lips again and her breasts and her skin and everything that was Jessica.

He didn't think he could ever get enough of her.

His heavy weight pressed her into the mattress and a maelstrom of emotions filled her. Comfort. Peace. Need. Such intense need.

She spread her legs and reached down to guide him to her, but he shook and whispered, "Protection."

He shifted off her only long enough to rummage through his pants and wallet and hastily ease on the condom. And then he was back, staring down at her, his hazel eyes burnished gold with passion.

The earlier rush to this moment was forgotten as he joined with her.

Her breath caught in her chest at the perfection of it. At the feel of his power above her, inside her. He was so big, so strong, but he was hers in that moment. Totally hers as she laid her hands on his shoulders and joined him in the rhythm of their lovemaking until they both slipped over together.

She urged him onto her, but he protested and said, "I'm too heavy."

"No, you're not," she said and dug her fingers into his back to pull him to her. She gentled him, stroking her hands across his sweat-slick skin. Savoring the connection with him.

"Give me a second," he said and hurried to the bathroom.

She eased under the sheets to wait for him, and he returned quickly and joined her. He tucked her into his side, and she nestled her head on his shoulder, laid her hand on his chest, and tossed a thigh over his. Contentment and satisfaction filled her, but slowly, other emotions crept in no matter how hard she tried to keep them from surfacing.

He must have sensed the tension in her since he said, "Penny for your thoughts."

"I'm not sure a penny would be enough," she said and leaned on her elbow to peer at him.

"Sometimes you can think too much," he said and skimmed a hand across her upper arm to press her back down.

"Avoidance mode much?" she challenged, but truth be told, maybe avoidance was what was needed right now because she wanted to enjoy this night with him. She wanted to explore the feelings that had sprung up so suddenly. So powerfully. She shut down her thoughts, not wanting them to go to the next stage. A stage that would only bring separation and pain.

She didn't want separation now. She wanted him. Again, and maybe again after that.

She wanted to make the most of their time together.

She'd think about everything else tomorrow.

Luis stroked his hand along her back and held her close, as if by doing so he could keep her with him, but he knew that in a little over twenty-four hours, she'd be on a plane back to New York. A contented sigh slipped from her and she murmured, "That was... amazing."

He couldn't disagree. Waking up with her ready to make love again had been the best wake-up call of his life. But so had making love with her just after midnight and of course their first time together the night before.

"It was," he said and rolled to his side so they were face-to-face because he needed to see her reaction. "I'd like to do it again."

She drew her brows together, puzzled. "But we just—"

"Yes, we just did, but I meant like tonight. And tomorrow," he said and watched sadness slip into her features as her smile faded into a frown.

"I'm leaving on Saturday morning," she reminded him, looked down, and stroked her hand across his chest as if trying to soothe the pain she caused with her reminder.

"I know you're leaving, but you'll be back in just over a month. And I can fly to New York. And there's video calls."

She met his gaze, hers assessing and not quite convinced. "A long-distance relationship?"

"I'm willing to try if you are," he said, no hesitation in his voice despite the concern in his heart that it could bring them both a great deal of pain. Maybe even hurt others caught in the blowback, like Carmen, if it kept Jessica from coming back more regularly.

"I'm willing to try," she said and shifted upward on the bed to kiss him, sealing the promise with a kiss.

He deepened the kiss, opening his mouth on hers and pressing her into the mattress, needing more despite the fact that they'd made love just a short while ago. But then the insistent blare of his phone alarm intruded, reminding him their time this morning was over.

Shifting away, he shut it off and said, "I'm sorry. I have a meeting and have to go."

"I understand," she said and lay in bed, watching him get up and dress.

When he bent to drop a quick peck on her lips, she grabbed hold of his tie and held him there for a longer, more demanding kiss.

"Tonight," she whispered against his lips when she finally released him, and he hurried from her room, hoping to make an exit without being seen.

Unfortunately, Consuelo was an early bird and caught him as he tiptoed across the living room, but as she saw him, she smiled and made a motion with her fingers that she was locking her lips. He was grateful for that, even as he acknowledged that one of the first things he had to do after his meeting was speak to Carmen about his relationship with Jessica.

My relationship with Jessica, he thought with a smile and walked out the door, determined that he was going to make it work no matter what it took.

What have I done? Jessica asked herself barely minutes after Luis had left her bedroom.

Are you crazy? Are you insane? the little voice in her head added. A little voice that oftentimes sounded too much like her uber-responsible mother.

Not insane, possibly crazy in love, she shot back while again questioning the wisdom of her decision. She was leaving in just over twenty-four hours, and while she might come back to Miami on occasion to see her newfound family, Brooklyn was her home. And Luis was her grandmother's right-hand man, almost like a son to her. And they were so, so different. The furniture flipper and the CEO. She had no doubt Carmen would be supportive of the relationship, but likely because she thought it might mean Jessica would stay in Miami, only that wasn't going to happen. *Brooklyn is my home*, she repeated to herself.

That became almost a mantra for her as she got out of bed and prepped for her last full day in Miami and what was bound to be an emotional time with her grandmother.

She wasn't surprised when she got to the kitchen to grab her cup of coffee to hear Consuelo say, "Your *abuelita* is waiting for you on the patio."

But she was a little confused by Consuelo's sly smile until it occurred to her that the older woman must have seen Luis escaping the house that morning.

"Consuelo—" she began.

"I won't say a thing. That is up to you and Luis to share with La Viejita," Consuelo said.

She was grateful for the other woman's understanding even as guilt and possibly shame dimmed the joy of what she'd shared with him just hours earlier.

"*Gracias*," she said, grabbed the mug of *café con leche* that Consuelo thrust at her, and headed outside to find her grandmother.

She was sitting on the bayside patio beneath the shade of the large umbrella, sipping her coffee and staring out across the waters of Biscayne Bay.

"Good morning, Abuela," she said and brushed a kiss across her cheek before sitting catercorner to her at the table.

"Good morning, *mi'jita*. Did you have a good night's sleep?" Carmen asked innocently enough from over the rim of her cup of coffee.

Jessica had never been good at lying, a fact proven by the heat that flooded her face and warned that her grandmother was sure to notice.

"I did have a good night," she said, carefully parsing her words, but her too-wise grandmother was clearly aware of what she wasn't saying. It had been especially nice to sleep tucked against Luis. To make love to him.

Carmen finished her last bit of coffee and reached for the carafe sitting nearby. As she poured herself a fresh cup, she said, "Luis is a good man. You'd be hard-pressed to find someone better."

There was a slight tremble in Jessica's hand as she set her mug down and reached for the toasted Cuban bread piled high on a plate set before them. She grabbed a piece and dunked it, paying undue attention to the way it soaked up the coffee and the butter melted into the liquid.

After a quick bite of the sopping wet bread and a thoughtful chew, she said, "I know he is. We just have to see what happens."

She dunked again, fixing her gaze on the coffee and bread once more to avoid her grandmother's keen perusal and the inquisition she was certain would follow.

To her surprise, Carmen said, "You're both quite intelligent adults. I'm sure you will figure it out."

And that was that, apparently, surprising Jessica as her grandmother turned the conversation to how they would spend their day together.

But even as they chatted about going through the last of the family photo albums, Luis was on her mind.

"Are you up for a shopping trip?" she asked, recalling the conversation she'd had with Luis days earlier.

"Chica, I love to shop! There are some wonderful shops in Bal Harbour—"

"I was thinking the Design District. I'd like to pick out something for Luis's office," she said.

Carmen dipped her head thoughtfully at her request. "I've been telling him for months that he needs to redecorate. Every time I go in there, I feel like it's a shrine to me, only I'm not dead yet," she said with a bold, almost bark of a laugh.

Jessica joined in her laughter, laid a hand over her grandmother's, and gave it a squeeze. "No, you're not, and we had talked about me helping him make it his own. Are you game for that?"

"I am. Luis is like a son to me, Jessica. I want only the best for him and for you. I hope you know that," Carmen said, her tone way too serious.

"I do, Abuela. It will be a lot of fun to go shopping with you," Jessica said, her tone bright to head off the moment growing maudlin.

"Well, let's get going. I know a few places where we can find some nice pieces and maybe we can even have them delivered this afternoon and surprise Luis," Carmen said, and her gaze glittered with happiness.

"That sounds wonderful, Abuela," she said, and together they rose and hurried off to shop for something for the man they both loved.

Chapter Twenty-Five

JESSICA PAUSED IN FRONT of the executive desk, admiring the clean lines of it. A large writing surface in gleaming ebony was supported by slabs of ebony in front and along the sides, but the austereness of that black was broken up by thin horizontal inlays of stainless steel. To one side of the desk, a low console was built into the slab, allowing for more surface area for papers, but also drawers for storage. Stainless steel handles complemented and provided relief from all the dark wood.

"What do you think?" Jessica asked her grandmother.

"It's very different from the desk that's there, but it will fit in nicely with the mid-century pieces in the reception area."

"And it reminds me of what he has in his home," she said, but that prompted a nose wiggle and frown from her grandmother. "He doesn't like that?" Jessica asked.

With a shrug, Carmen said, "I've gotten the sense from him that he feels it's sterile, but sometimes it's not the furniture that makes it that way, but the lack of life in a home."

Armed with that view, Jessica changed her tack as they breezed through the first wing and moved into a second one that had more traditional pieces. Unfortunately, the various offerings struck her as too boring for a man like Luis, and as she was getting ready to ask her grandmother to try another store, she caught sight of Carmen staring at a typewriter that had been used to stage one of the desks.

She walked over to her, puzzled by her delay. "Abuela, is something wrong?"

Tears glistened in her grandmother's gaze as she gestured to the old Underwood typewriter. "I used to have one just like this. Your mother would spend hours pounding out her stories on it."

The manual typewriter would have been hard to use and had likely prompted the request for a more modern typewriter as a high school graduation gift, Jessica thought, recalling what her grandmother had told her.

Jessica laid a hand on her shoulder, offering comfort, and Carmen dashed away a tear and said, "Did you see anything you like here?"

Jessica shook her head, and Carmen said, "I have another place for us to try." She led Jessica to a second store just a few doors down from the first. This store was filled with pieces more like those that graced Carmen's home and the reception area of the business.

She spotted the dark walnut desk almost as soon as they walked in.

The front had an inches-wide band of floral carving along the topmost edge and columns that split the face of the desk in threes. In the center of each section was an inlay in a slightly lighter color, edged with gilt. The desktop had a central inset of leather whose edges were gilded with gold. Golden handles graced the fronts of the drawers, three on each side.

"This is beautiful," she said and ran her hands across the leather writing surface.

"It is, and it would fit in with the other furniture in the reception area, but still be unique," Carmen said as she examined the piece.

"Carmen, so good to see you. It's been a long time," a salesman said as he approached them.

Carmen hugged the man. "Good to see you as well, Victor. What can you tell us about this desk?"

"Rococo style made in the early 1800s in England. Walnut with various gilded elements and a leather inset. It's quite a nice piece," Victor said.

Jessica and Carmen shared a look and Jessica nodded. "I'd like to buy it."

"*Mija*, let me. I should have thought to do something like this long ago," Carmen said and then turned to the salesman. "Please put it on my account, but more important, could you deliver it to the office by this afternoon?"

"I can have it there in the next couple of hours. Is that acceptable?" Victor asked as he jotted down the information on a notepad.

"It is. We'll be waiting for you," Carmen said.

Jessica hadn't expected it to all go so quickly, but then again in the days she'd been in Miami, she'd come to realize that Carmen was a determined woman who usually got what she wanted. A trait that could have both good and bad outcomes. Her resolve had guaranteed her family's future, but also its heartbreak by driving away her mother.

Since the Design District wasn't all that far from the Guerreiro Enterprises building, they arrived in no time, but Luis wasn't available. According to his assistant, Luis was at a meeting with some prospective distributors and was then taking them out to lunch. He wouldn't return until early afternoon, which meant they would have hours to prepare his office for the new arrival.

"Perfect," Carmen said and clapped her hands. "We'll be able to move things around and surprise him."

Luis is definitely going to be surprised, Jessica thought and what had once seemed like a good idea was suddenly not feeling all that good. *Is this how my mother felt? Like a steamroller running her flat? Or am I seeing the negative in it because of my mother's anger and pain?*

"Would you like to get some lunch in the cafeteria?" Carmen asked.

"That would be nice," she said, trying to fight the growing sense that they were making a big mistake with the gift of the desk.

After instructing Luis's administrative assistant to call them when the desk was delivered, they walked down the stairs to the cafeteria on the lower level.

In the cafeteria, Carmen was warmly welcomed by various employees, from the lunch counter girl who took their order to those workers at the nearby tables, where they sat on the outdoor patio to eat. Everyone smiled and asked Carmen how she was doing, and she took the time to chat with each one and inquire about how they were.

It delayed their meal but relieved Jessica's uneasiness about Luis's new desk.

When one of the security guards came up to their table, it was to announce that the furniture had arrived and the delivery people needed instructions on what to do.

They hurried back to Luis's office and in a flurry of activity, workers from her grandmother's business and the furniture shop had muscled the old desk out and the new desk in.

Luis's assistant, a quick-thinking young woman, had carefully packed up the contents of Luis's desk. With Jessica's assistance while Carmen sat nearby, the two of them returned everything to the drawers and laid out his items on the desktop.

They had just finished putting things to rights when Luis returned to the office.

His pleased look at seeing her quickly faded when he caught sight of the desk. "*Viejita.* Jessica. This is a surprise."

He walked over and trailed his fingers across the gilded leather inset. "Beautiful," he said, but it was obvious his pleasure was guarded. Almost cautious in its praise.

Carmen immediately picked up on it. "*Perdoname*, Luis. We wanted you to have something of your own in your office."

He held his hands up to stop any additional apology. "*Lo se, viejita.* I'm just... *Gracias.* It's a wonderful gift. I love it."

Jessica went to his side and twined her fingers with his. Leaned into him and said, "We meant well, Luis."

He met her gaze, but his was shuttered, hiding his true emotions from her. "I know you did, *mi amor*. I do love it," he said and dropped a kiss on her cheek. But then he pushed on, obviously wanting to change the subject. "I know we had planned on dinner later, but I'm done for the day. Is there anything you want to do before you go home?"

Jessica thought back to the Underwood typewriter her grandmother had spotted in one of the furniture stores. "Actually, there is. I want to pick up something for my mother."

"I'd be delighted to take you, but let me drive Carmen home first," Luis said, but her grandmother quickly demurred.

"No need, *mi'jito*. We brought the Range Rover, and I can drive myself home. I'm not feeble, *sabes*."

"Are you sure, Abuela?" Jessica asked.

Carmen's shrewd gaze skipped from her to Luis and back. "Never more sure. I'll see you two later for dinner."

With that, she used the arms of the chair to push up, and with quick kisses for both of them, she hurried from Luis's office, leaving the two of them there in silence.

In a soft whisper, Jessica said, "I'm sorry you didn't like the desk."

Luis turned, cupped her cheek, and said, "I love the desk, only… it's complicated, *mi amor*, and I can't explain right now. Just trust me."

Surprisingly, she did, a decided change from her impression of him from just a couple of weeks ago.

"I do," she said and rose on tiptoes to kiss him, wanting to reassure him.

He deepened the kiss and splayed his hand across her back to draw her near. But reality intruded as his assistant discreetly coughed.

"*Perdoname*, Luis. You have a call from one of the distributors you met with earlier."

With a sigh, Luis said, "Do you mind?"

Jessica shook her head. "Not at all. I'll be waiting for you outside."

"*Gracias*," he said, and after she walked out of his office, he closed the door to take the call.

She sat outside, waiting. Wondering at his reaction and hoping it would be possible to set things right later that night.

Their last night together for weeks.

To distract herself from those thoughts, she skimmed through her emails, pleased to see two new commission requests from one of the interior decorators with whom she worked, as well as an email from Sandy, reassuring her that everything was just fine in the shop and with a quick list of the pieces they'd sold in the last week.

It all looked good, relieving some of Jessica's concerns about her absence from home. The major outstanding issue being her mother and how she would respond to Jessica's intention to reestablish a connection to the Miami branch of the family.

When Luis sauntered out of his office, a broad smile graced his features, and she was grateful the earlier tension she had sensed was gone.

He took hold of her hand and helped her rise from the low-slung chair.

His Jaguar was parked just a few doors down from the front of the building, and he ensconced her in the passenger seat before pulling away to drive them to the Design District, which was only about four miles away. The area was more crowded than it had been earlier, with many people shopping in the high-end retailers along the streets in addition to the restaurants and furniture and art galleries in the area.

It took a few tries for Luis to find a parking spot, but when Jessica returned to the shop where she had seen the typewriter, it was gone.

"I'm so sorry, but we sold it just a short time ago," the salesperson said.

Jessica craned her neck, searching for another one, but couldn't spy anything similar. Still, she had to ask, "Do you have another one?"

The salesperson shook his head. "I'm sorry, but we don't even normally carry anything like that. We were just using it for staging."

Her shoulders sagged with disappointment, and Luis stroked his hand across her back. "We can look for another typewriter," he said, but she shook her head.

"It's okay. We should probably head back home."

Home. Funny how easy it was to think of her grandmother's place in that way. Maybe too easy.

The loss of the typewriter and Luis's tepid response to the desk cast a pall over their trip to her grandmother's home. When they arrived, Carmen had arranged to have cocktails in the living room, since the weather had started to turn and rain seemed imminent. In addition to the cocktails, she had a collection of family photos laid out on the coffee table for one last viewing.

Viewing, like at a funeral, which was how Jessica was feeling inside even though she thought she hid it well so as to not dim her grandmother's happy mood. But as her gaze met her grandmother's, so much like her own and her mother's, she realized that Carmen was putting on a show as well. The sadness was there in the deep green of her eyes. In the slight downward tilt of her mouth at times.

Luis, who was sitting at her side, obviously sensed it. He rested his hand on her shoulder, providing comfort. Stability. Support. Love. Acceptance.

"I pulled these out because I thought you might want to take them with you for your mother," Carmen said and lovingly passed a hand across the photos. "That is, if you would like to take them."

Jessica thought about the photos, mostly ones which included her mother. If she shared them with her mom…it would be a less-than-subtle reminder of the family she'd left behind. Maybe it was what was needed to open her mother's eyes and heart to the possibility of a reconciliation.

"I'd like to take them. Show them to Mom."

And although she was sure the pressure to do that was what Carmen had intended, Jessica was certain that would be the right thing to do for her family, despite Carmen's obvious manipulation. That action, as well as some of Carmen's other machinations, made it easier to understand her mother's upset with Carmen. Especially considering the turmoil her mother had been experiencing at the time. The roller-coaster ride of emotions created by her exile from Cuba.

But were they enough to justify a thirty-year exile from her family?

A soft squeeze on her shoulder pulled her from those thoughts and she met Luis's worried gaze.

"Are you okay?"

She nodded. "I am. Just thinking about…things."

––––––––––––––––❖––––––––––––––––

Luis had no doubt which things Jessica was thinking about. Her mother. Grandmother. Maybe him.

So many things for her to consider. For him to think about as well.

It was why, despite the happy tone of the meal, tension simmered beneath the surface, much like the storm building outside. It would be a hard storm, unlike the usual daytime tropical soaks that occurred. Dark clouds had been building for the last couple of hours, and as they sat for dinner in the formal dining room, the heavens opened up with a deluge of rain that rattled against the glass panes of the french doors, sounding like gunshots. The reverberating rumble of cannon fire thunder joined in as lightning erupted, slashing through the night sky.

Beside him, Jessica jumped at the sound. "That's some storm."

"It's going to rain all night," Carmen said, peering out the windows at the almost horizontal sheets of rain pelting the house. "I hope it won't interfere with your flight tomorrow morning."

"I hope not too," she said, but as the storm of the emotions gathering inside them grew like the tempest outside, silence settled over the table. It was broken only by the clatter of cutlery against china or the clink of crystal on the tabletop.

"Would you like coffee?" Manny asked after he and his staff had cleared off the dinner dishes.

"I'm a little tired, Manny. I think I'll make it an early night," Carmen said and slowly, almost painfully, pushed to her feet.

Jessica was immediately at her side, helping steady her. "Are you okay, Abuela?" she asked.

"*Estoy bien*. This weather is tough on my arthritis," she said and passed a hand across Jessica's cheek before gazing at Luis.

"Let us walk you to your room," he said, and together he and Jessica strolled with her, Carmen's gait a bit stilted.

At her door, Carmen turned and smiled at them. Kissed them both on the cheek and said, "*Gracias*. I'm so sorry the storm has made our last night together so…sad."

Trying to lighten the mood, Luis said with a laugh, "There are some things that not even you can control, *viejita*."

"*Fresco*," she teased and tapped his chest playfully. "*Buenas noches*."

Carmen entered her room and left them standing in the hallway, staring at each other. Tension building between them that matched the intensity of the storm raging outside.

"Would you like a drink?" he asked.

"I think I need one," she answered and walked back to the living room and the bar tucked into an alcove at one side of the room.

She picked up a bottle of the same rum her grandmother had poured the other day and held it up for him to see. He nodded, and she added ice to two glasses and poured a couple of fingers of rum.

Raising the glass up, she said, "I don't really know what to toast to."

Chapter Twenty-Six

LUIS SMILED WRYLY, CLINKED his glass against hers, and said, "Neither do I."

With a shrug, she said, "To family. I guess that's as good a toast as any."

"To family," he said and tapped his glass to hers again. After he had taken a sip, he said, "Have you thought about what you'll say to your mother?"

She shook her head, walked to the couch, and sat. He took a spot beside her, rested his arm across her shoulders, and drew her near. "I haven't thought about it. So much has happened so fast."

She shot him a side glance, but her gaze was intense, watching to see how he'd respond.

His downcast features, the way he stared at his glass as he swirled the rum around, told her he agreed that it was all too much so very quickly.

"It has," he said and hesitated. "But I'm not sorry, Jessica. The last week...it's been amazing. I'm looking forward to it continuing."

She released a pent-up breath and took a sip of her rum. "I am too, Luis. I'm so very grateful you convinced me to come."

He raised his rum. "I guess that's one thing we can toast to. Your coming to Miami."

She lifted her glass. "To my coming to Miami."

After a sip, he set his glass down, leaned into her, and cupped her cheek. "I...I want to spend the night with you again. I want to remember every minute, every second of our time together to keep with me until you're back in Miami."

Her heart pounded in her chest so powerfully, she was sure he could feel it against his, as close as he was. It echoed in her ears so loudly it drowned out the tempest raging outside. She licked lips that were suddenly dry and said, "I'd like that, Luis. I want to remember too."

In a rush they abandoned their drinks and hurried to her room, eager to be together. Aware that after tonight they'd be separated by thousands of miles and possibly more.

As happy as he made her, there was no escaping the thoughts in the back of her mind that she'd have to deal with her mother on her return, and that if that didn't go well...

She blanked that from her brain, intent on enjoying this moment with him. This night. This man. An unexpected man, but one who had already changed her life.

In her bedroom, she took her time removing his clothes, wanting to explore his beauty. She ran her hands across the powerful slope of his shoulders and down to his muscled chest.

"I want to make love with you."

"I want that also," she said and helped him remove her clothes, each piece dropping away until she stood naked before him.

"You are so beautiful," he said and touched her, his caress gentle until she leaned into him.

That broke loose his restraint and they fell onto the bed, savoring the pleasure of their togetherness and the peace that followed while the storm raged outside.

Jessica had no question that he would stay the night.

She wanted to spend every last minute with him until she packed and got on the plane to New York.

"Don't think about it," he said, seemingly aware of where her thoughts had gone as they lay there together, limbs entwined. Hearts beating in unison. Skin against skin.

"I'm trying, but it's hard, and it's even harder to think about what my mother will say. How she'll react to how I feel about my grandmother now. That I plan on coming back to Miami."

Luis heard her words and couldn't help but wonder at the meaning behind them. "How do you feel about Carmen?"

Jessica sucked in a long inhalation and held it before expelling her words in a rush. "Proud. Angry. Confused. Worried. Happy."

"Complicated," he offered.

She leaned up on an elbow to peer at him. "That sounds accurate. I know you had hoped that by my coming here, it would set things to rights."

"That was one of my hopes. My other one was that Carmen wouldn't get hurt if this all went south."

She raised her eyebrows in question. "And now?"

He shook his head and blew out a breath. "So many more hopes. For your mother. For us."

Jessica smiled, but it didn't chase the sadness from her eyes. Cradling his jaw, she leaned over and kissed him. Then whispered against his lips, "I have the same hopes, Luis."

"Then let's hope together," he said and deepened the kiss, sealing that promise. Optimistic that they could make things right between them.

Jessica hauled her suitcase up the two flights of stairs to her loft apartment. The suitcase bumped loudly on each stair and dragged on her arm, almost as if to chastise her for being home.

Home, she thought and opened the door.

The slight chill and damp of a New York spring welcomed her as she entered. She'd set the thermostat to an away setting to conserve energy and money but regretted it now. The chill matched the emptiness she'd been feeling since leaving Luis and Carmen by the TSA entrance at the airport early that morning.

Even now, a few hours later, the image of the two of them standing there, optimism forced onto their faces, was tattooed on her brain.

She drove herself to feel that optimism as well since she was sure the next couple of days would be difficult. As if to remind her of that, her phone chirped to warn of an incoming text.

You home? her father wrote.

Just got here, she texted back.

You still coming over later?

That had been the plan just a little over a week earlier when she had left for Miami. It was almost as if making that plan had cemented for her parents that she would be returning. That she wouldn't be seduced into staying in Miami by her grandmother.

I am. Is 6 good? she asked. That would give her plenty of time to unpack and prepare herself for seeing her mother again. For answering any questions she might have, and for sharing what her grandmother had given her.

6 is good. See you then, her dad responded.

See you, she texted back and smiled. Her dad always complained that she was the last texter and she wanted him to know that some things hadn't changed.

She had barely put her phone away when it chirped again with another message, this one from Luis.

U get home ok?

She smiled and hit the dial button on the message. As he answered, his deep voice filled her with calm. "I miss you already."

"I miss you too."

"How was the flight?"

"Uneventful. Taxi ride, not so much. I think my guy thought he was a Formula One race car driver," she said with a laugh.

"I'm glad you got there safely…" He paused and she pictured him in her mind. How his eyebrows would draw together as he considered his next words. When they came, he said, "I hope tonight goes easily. I know you're worried."

"I am, thank you. It's going to be rough, no doubt about it, but I'm hopeful," she said and plopped on her sofa, already tired even though it was just barely past lunch.

"I am too, and if you need me, I'm here, Jessica. I'll always be here for you no matter what," he said.

She'd known that even without his saying so. "*Gracias.*"

"Take care," he said and ended the call.

Her suitcase sat a few feet away, a reminder that she had to unpack. But she was tired and wired at the same time, dreading dinner with her parents and what would follow if she decided to talk to her mother about her grandmother.

She pushed off the couch and headed down to her shop, where Barbara, another of her part-time managers, was at work. The shop was busy for a Saturday, with several customers strolling around looking at furniture while Barbara handled a sale at the front counter.

Jessica walked over to each of the customers to ask if they needed assistance. While most were just looking, one young couple had questions about another table she had finished just before leaving for Miami. She explained the history of the piece and how she had cut it down so it would be a better fit in a smaller space.

"That's amazing, and you did such a fabulous job on the restoration," the woman said and ran her hand across the surface of the table.

"Thank you. It's a unique piece and so perfect for a typical New York apartment," Jessica said, talking up the piece although she suspected that wasn't necessary, judging from their reaction.

"It is perfect for our place. We'll take it," the husband said with a broad smile and hugged his wife.

"Let's go ring you up. Do you need delivery?" Jessica said and guided them toward the counter, where her manager was just finishing up with the other couple.

"No, thanks. We have our SUV just up the block and it'll fit in there," the man said.

"Wonderful. Barbara will help you with anything else you might need," Jessica said, and seeing that everything else seemed in order, she headed to her workshop to inventory the pieces she had there ready to be worked on. Satisfied that she had enough work to keep her busy until next week when she'd planned a trip to one of the local flea markets, she triaged which pieces she would restore first. She removed them from inventory and brought them closer to the counter, where she normally did sanding before taking the pieces to a clean counter for stain or paint.

She inspected each of the pieces, seeing if they also needed any repairs, and if they did she set them to the side, writing quick notes on a scrap of paper that she taped on each piece of furniture.

With her week's work laid out for her, the earlier tension she'd been feeling receded a bit. Work always did that for her, just like it had for her grandmother and just like it did for her mother. So similar and yet still so far apart.

Tension returned, building in Jessica's shoulders and neck. She worked her head back and forth then around in a small circle to ease the kinks, but it did little.

Instead, she grabbed one of the smaller pieces she'd chosen and got to work, taking apart the Windsor-style chair just like her father had taught her years earlier, his voice in her brain soothing. Calming as she disassembled the piece with the intent to put it back together stronger than it had been before.

A couple of hours passed as she labored, cleaning and sanding all the joints. Checking one spindle that had a split in the wood. Luckily, it was a surface crack that she could easily repair with some sawdust and wood glue.

Her phone chirped to signal that it was time to get ready for the visit to her parents' house. She often set an alarm because it wasn't uncommon for her to get so caught up in her work that she failed to realize just how much time had passed.

She set aside the spindle and after a short conversation with Barbara, mostly about her kids since the shop seemed under control, she returned to her loft, showered, and prepared for the visit to her parents.

Her grandmother had gifted her with a lovely leather portfolio for the photos she had pulled aside for Jessica. Photos Jessica intended to give to her mom in the hopes of opening a fresh dialogue about what had happened with Carmen.

She hopped into her pickup and drove from her Fourth Street location to the expressway, hands tight on the wheel in expectation of what might happen at dinner. The road took her past the Williamsburg Bridge and then the DUMBO section and Manhattan Bridge. Traffic zipped and swerved in front of her on the BQE and grew heavier on the Belt Parkway, slowing as she wound her way past the Verrazano Bridge and Coney Island until she reached her parents' home in Sheepshead Bay.

Originally two attached single-family homes, her parents had bought both parts of the structure to make it into a larger home and double the backyard that was her father's pride and joy. In the summer months, the double lot boasted flowers, vegetables, and fig trees surrounding a small patch of carefully manicured lawn. The front yard was as beautiful, with a weeping Japanese cherry tree, azaleas, and hydrangeas. Beneath the bushes, her father had already set out colorful pansies that he would swap out for hardier vinca when the weather got warmer.

Home, she thought as she pulled into the driveway. Her parents always parked on the street so she would have a spot when she visited, which was often.

The front door opened almost as soon as she killed her engine and stepped out. Her father stood waiting with a smile behind the screen door.

Sucking a deep breath in through her nostrils, she walked up the path to the front door, trying not to feel like a death row prisoner on her way to the gas chamber.

Chapter Twenty-Seven

"HI, SWEETIE. WE'VE MISSED you," her dad said as she stepped through the door.

She laughed and kissed his cheek. "I've only been gone a week, Dad," she chastised.

"Jessica," her mother said with a disciplined dip of her head and a forced smile.

Jessica took it to mean that her mother was still unhappy that she'd gone to Miami, but she wasn't about to get into it the moment she walked through the door.

"Mom," she replied with as much control.

"We're happy you're home," Lara said although there was nothing about her demeanor that hinted at that happiness.

Her father's comforting touch came at her shoulder. "Made your favorites. Antipasto with fresh mozzarella. Gnocchi with meatballs and sauce meat. Pastries and cheesecake for dessert. Your mom made the cheesecake herself."

"Sounds delicious. Thank you," she said, and with his gentle pressure on her shoulder guiding her, they went into the dining room. Her parents had gone all-out, setting the table with the china and crystal that only came out on special occasions. A bottle of red wine had been opened to allow the wine to breathe.

Her father quickly poured glasses for all of them but didn't do a toast. She sensed that both her parents were uncomfortable, so she tried to get them past it. Raising her glass, she said, "To being home. I missed you guys."

With a sharp exhale, as if he'd been holding his breath, her father said, "To being home."

Her mother joined in, her voice husky with suppressed emotion. "We missed you too."

They sipped the wine and immediately sat at the dining room table to eat, but unlike one of the typical Sunday gatherings where voices were loud with talk and laughter, silence dominated as Jessica served them all antipasto from the large plate brimming with the fresh mozzarella, chopped celery, olives, roasted peppers, marinated mushrooms, and artichokes.

"Delicious, Mom," she said. Her mother had been handed down the antipasto recipe and preparation from Bisnonna Russo. A family recipe which made Jessica wonder what kinds of Cuban recipes her mother still harbored in her head and might share if she asked.

"Thank you, Jess. I'm glad you like it," her mother said and forked up some of the mozzarella and roasted red pepper.

"I do. Thanks for making one of my faves," she said, wanting to keep moving the dinner in the right direction so that when they got to talking later something positive might happen.

"Our pleasure, Jess," her father said with a broad smile and, reading her mood, continued with a relatively neutral topic. "I dropped by the shop midweek, and it seemed like everything was going well."

Jessica nodded and swallowed. "I talked to Sandy regularly, and we had a good amount of business, and some new commissions came in. This afternoon was quite busy as well."

"That's good to hear. You should be proud of the business you've built," he said.

"I couldn't have done it without you guys and all your support." Her parents had been there with advice, elbow grease, and a small investment, making her dream possible. Her Abuela Carmen as well, she now knew, but kept that to herself for the moment.

As they finished the antipasto, her mother excused herself to cook the gnocchi while she and her father cleaned up the plates and put away what remained of their appetizer.

Her parents had premade a salad that her father dressed as her mother dumped the gnocchi in the boiling water and then fished out the meatballs and stew meat from the sauce.

In a ballet that was as well-rehearsed as *The Nutcracker*, her mother served the pasta, her father finished the salad, and she sliced bread and refilled wineglasses.

Once they were all seated again, hunger took over as they dug into the meal.

Jessica savored the hearty flavor of the sauce over the creamy and light potato gnocchi. After she swallowed, she said, "Did you make these yourself, Mom?"

Her mother chuckled and shook her head. "I wish I could say that I did, although I was able to make some sweet potato ones a few weeks ago."

"She cooked them with a brown butter sage sauce, and it was delicious," her father said, smiled, and tenderly laid a hand over her mother's as it rested on the table.

The love and support between her parents were palpable, which only again made her wonder how her mother could just say goodbye to her family and never go back. How she had seemingly given up everything Cuban to become part of her father's big Italian family.

Even with all the upset her mother had experienced in her young life, it was almost like cutting off a piece of yourself. But then again, didn't surgeons cut off limbs that threatened a patient's life?

A drastic action because it had not only cut her mother off from her family, but it had severed Jessica's connection to her family's history and the Cuban culture she had found so intriguing during the last week.

But she held back from saying so, at least until they'd finished dinner and had coffee and dessert. In her humble opinion, a full belly always made for a calmer discussion.

With that driving her, she stuck to neutral things and loved that the meal finished without any upset. As they sipped coffee and assorted liqueurs, ate cannolis from the local Italian bakery and slices of her mom's cheesecake, Jessica finally shifted the topic to the Miami family.

She excused herself to get the leather portfolio with the photos from where she'd left it on the living room sofa when she'd first come in. She shifted her seat to sit next to her mother and said, "Your mother, my grandmother, sent some photos for you."

She didn't give her mother time to protest, depositing the stack of photos in a free spot in the middle of the table. "You probably haven't seen these in a long time," she said to hopefully break the ice even though she knew her mother hadn't seen them in nearly thirty years.

Her mother said nothing. Did nothing as she stared at the photos, her body tense beside Jessica's.

"Is that you?" her father asked, puzzled, and pointed to her mother in the photo.

"It is. My hair was curlier then and lighter," she said in barely a whisper, her voice so tight with emotion it was almost inaudible.

"That must be your sister next to you. You look so much alike," her father said, surprise in his voice, and Jessica understood. Like her, he knew little to nothing about her Miami family.

"It's Gloria, and they still do look alike," Jessica said, hoping to elicit some kind of reaction from her mother.

Lara said nothing but took hold of the photos with trembling hands and flipped to the next photo that showed the three young girls in their Easter finery. Matching pale-yellow dresses and hats, except for the different-colored glittering Easter egg on each hat. They were all smiling happily in contrast to the three adults who stood behind them, looking way too serious.

"Lara?" her father said, clearly trying to prompt a response from his wife.

"We had so much fun this Easter, even though my dad…" She choked up then and tears came to her eyes, but she didn't swipe them away. She let them flow down her face and said, "That's my *abuelo* and *abuela*. My mom's parents. They watched us while my mom worked. She was always working."

"She told me as much, Mom. She also said she was sorry she didn't do more to help you when you came from Cuba." Jessica held her breath after she said it, waiting for an explosion, but it didn't come, surprising her.

Her mother flipped to another photo and then another of her sitting at a small secretary painted a salmon-y orange. With a loving pass over the photo, her mother said, "I used to sit here to write. I always thought I'd write a book one day, but when you're the child of immigrant parents, they want you to have a 'profession.'"

"Italian or Cuban, not much different," her father said with an indifferent shrug.

"Yes and no, Sal," her mother said, her tone slightly brusque, surprising her husband.

"I didn't mean anything by it," he said, apologetic.

"It's just that…I know it was tough when your grandparents got here. Lots of people didn't want them here. Or the Irish for that matter, only…they came here for a better life."

"And you didn't?" he challenged, obviously surprised by her demeanor.

Sensing the growing tension, Jessica jumped in to try and ease it. "When I was talking to Luis, he mentioned that many Cubans had better lives in Cuba."

With a shrug, Lara said, "We did. My father was a police officer and my mother was working at an import/export company and going to law school when they shut down the university due to the political unrest."

Sal sat back in his chair, a puzzled look on his face. "I didn't know that."

Lara bit her lip and shook her head. "That's on me, not you, Sal. It was just all caught up with what happened with my mother and why bring up old hurts?"

Her father relaxed a little and laid a hand on her mother's shoulder. "I'm sorry. I don't want to bring up the past if it will hurt you."

"I know, only it's hard sometimes to think about it. To know I can't go home, and I don't just mean Miami. We've been to Italy how many times?" she asked, and even though it was rhetoric, Sal answered.

"Two or three times."

Her mother huffed out a laugh but said, "I love you, Sal, but you don't understand. I can't go to Cuba, as much as I might want to go and see my family's home. Where I was born. Where my grandparents lived. Because of that, there's a hole here," she said and gestured to her heart. "It's here and there's no way to fill it."

"We can go if you want," he said, still slightly clueless, but Jessica understood. She had been as clueless as well until Luis had explained.

She laid a hand on her mother's to offer comfort and said, "It's not that easy, Dad. The Cuban government has all kinds of requirements, and why would Mom want to go somewhere that was so hard to leave?"

Her father was silent for a moment, obviously considering what she'd said, and nodded. "I'm sorry you feel that way, Lara. I wish I had known. I wish there's something I could do to change it."

Lara smiled, a sad half smile, and cupped her husband's cheek. "You have given me so much, Sal. Your love, your laughter, and your family. I don't know how I would have survived without that. I love you."

Her father grinned and dropped a kiss on her cheek. "And I love you. I'd do anything for you or Jessica," he said, drawing her back into the discussion.

Lara smiled and glanced at her. "Thank you for understanding."

"I wish I knew more, Mom, but it's a start," she said, smoothed her hands over the portfolio her grandmother had given her, and pushed on. "We had a big family gathering a couple of nights ago. I got to meet Aunt Gloria and Aunt Anna. It sounds like the three of you were quite a handful at times."

Her mother laughed, sniffled, and flipped to another photo of the three girls with their mother. They all had parrots of varying sizes and hues on their arms, although Anna and Gloria were both cringing.

"We were. My poor *abuelos* were always after us, but it wasn't ever anything dangerous or bad, just…creative," her mother said and moved on to another photo, this time one of her father in an army uniform. Her grandmother was off to one side, her eyes shattered and sad. Her grandfather cradled a baby Anna in his arms while Gloria and Lara stood in front of him.

"He was so handsome. Strong," her mother said, worship in her voice.

"It must have been hard for all of you when he was gone. First the Bay of Pigs and then Vietnam."

"He must have been gone a lot," her father said, wading into the discussion. Unprepared yet again for the vehemence of Lara's response.

"He was a hero, Sal. He fought for what he thought was right," she snapped at him and then glared at Jessica as she repeated, "He was a hero."

Despite her passionate response, Jessica got the sense it was almost like her mother was trying to convince herself of the truth of her statement. Trying to keep the lines of discussion open, she said, "He was a hero, but it's a hard life being with someone who's gone a lot. Especially with three babies."

"It is, but we didn't want for love. My *abuelos* saw to that," her mother said and flipped to another photo, this one of the entire family in front of the first tiny location for Guerreiro Enterprises.

"And your mother saw to it you had a roof over your heads and food on the table," Jessica reminded and gestured to the photo. "She gave you a future."

"One that I didn't want, Jess," her mother shot back and glared at her, green eyes spitting emerald fire. "I wanted to follow my own path, but my mother wouldn't let me."

"I think she's realized that. Too late, unfortunately. Your sisters each have their own professions. Only two of the cousins work at the family business," she explained.

"And that lawyer who came here, I suppose," her mother said and frowned. "Has he turned you against me as well?"

Jessica shook her head and laid her arm across her mother's shoulders, but she shrugged it off and pushed away the photos. Taking the hint, Jessica backed off, but not before clarifying one thing.

"It's not about choosing sides, Mom. It's about making peace. Being the bigger person. That's something you've taught me my whole life." She took the discarded photos and gently tucked them back into the leather portfolio, which she left in the center of the table.

"I think it's time for me to go. I guess I'll see you tomorrow at Grandma's." She didn't wait for a reply, hopped up, and dropped kisses on each of their cheeks before bolting out the door. Hoping as she did so that her father could, as he always did, smooth things over and have her mother maybe finally reconsider her exile from her family.

After Jessica had left, Lara sat there, anger melting into regret. "I'm sorry, Sal. I wanted this to be a happy night, only…"

Her husband squeezed her hand gently. "It's okay, Lara. I

understand this is difficult for you, but Jessica seems to be handling this quite well. She seems sympathetic to what your mother may have told her. To your sisters."

"Jessica always had a kind heart. She always wants to see the best in people," Lara said. As upset as she was with the situation, she didn't want it to affect her relationship with her daughter any more than it already had.

"She does, and what if you tried to do the same? What if you tried to imagine what it might have been like to have three young babies, a new business, and a husband who was always leaving you?" Sal said, his tone almost condemning which surprised her.

"You think I haven't done that? That I haven't thought about it?" she said, recalling the many times over the years that they'd had this discussion, since Sal had always been uncomfortable with her break with her family. He had always felt guilty that he had precipitated the rift and she realized now how unfair that had been to him.

She tenderly cupped his jaw, which was rough beneath her hand from the start of his evening beard. When they were younger, he would sometimes shave before going to bed to keep her from getting beard rash when they made love. He was always the considerate one. Always the one who kept the ship sailing straight, but sometimes not even his strong hand on the tiller had made that possible.

Brooklyn, 1993

The phone calls from her friends in the law office had started while she was in the hospital. Phone calls filled with warning and concern for her more than questions about her new baby.

The colleague who was supposed to be working with her during her maternity leave had started totally taking over her responsibilities.

Her cases. Her boss seemed quite taken with him so Lara should hurry back before things got too out of control. By the time she'd returned to the office a month later, things were beyond different. The smooth partnership path she had thought she'd been on had suddenly become like the ascent to Everest.

And all because she'd dared to do the unthinkable.

Lara had dared to have a baby. Jessica. A beautiful little girl. One she'd give all her love and attention, unlike the way her mother had abandoned her.

But back at the office, before she even had time to deal with her colleague's actions, she'd been tapped to conduct due diligence in a complicated divestiture.

Her hours had been difficult even before Jessica's birth. Now they were impossible, leaving Sal and an au pair who they had brought in to help to basically raise her child. A child that she usually only saw asleep thanks to the demands of her career.

The pace and responsibility of the due diligence, twelve-hour days and intense pressure, together with the absence from her family, pushed her to the brink until one day she snapped.

Knees tucked to her chest, Lara buried her head against them and wrapped her arms tight to silence the sobs bursting from the depths of her soul, the bathroom floor cold against her skin. She rocked back and forth, keening. Praying for relief from the nightmare her life had become. Despair filling her that everything that had ever meant anything to her was disappearing like smoke blown away on the wind.

She was lost and she had no idea how to find herself again.

But she wasn't a quitter, she was a warrior. For the last year, she'd let others decide her path and she was done doing that.

You are your mother's daughter, the little voice in her head reminded, and she couldn't argue with that. Her mother had not let anything stop her and Lara wouldn't either.

She wouldn't let them force her out at the firm, no matter what it took.

And she wouldn't let them take her from her family because she didn't want her daughter to feel the way she felt about her mother. That she'd been absent. Missing.

That Jessica wasn't loved, because more than anything, she loved her daughter. And her husband.

Wiping away the tears, she pushed to her feet and drew in a deep breath.

Facing herself in the mirror, she said, "You can do this."

Because you are your mother's daughter, the little voice said.

And as much as Lara wanted to deny it, she couldn't. But she wouldn't make the same mistakes her mother had.

She'd get through this divestiture and she'd get her place back at the firm. She wouldn't let them push her out. If she left, it would be on her own terms, but she had no intention of leaving.

She would be a partner one day, and her family would be standing beside her to celebrate that career achievement. Because family came first no matter what.

Then why haven't you talked to your mother or your sisters? the little voice in her head chastised.

She shut it down because she had her priorities here in New York. Her husband. Her daughter. Her career. Nothing was going to get in the way of those priorities.

Chapter Twenty-Eight

SUNDAY DINNER WAS WELL underway when Jessica arrived at her grandparents' the next day.

Grandmother Rosa was at the stove, stirring the giant pot of sauce when Jessica let herself in through the back door of her grandparents' home. The front door was reserved for company and family knew better than to come in that way.

She laid an arm across her grandmother's shoulders and bent to kiss her cheek. Her grandmother was several inches shorter than she was and growing shorter the older she got.

Inside the dining room, assorted members of the Russo family were gathered around the table and involved in a heated discussion about the Mets' chances for the World Series that year, including Bisnonna Russo who was a diehard Dodgers fan despite their abandonment of Brooklyn in 1957. She embraced her great-grandmother who passed a papery smooth, arthritis-gnarled hand across her cheek.

"*Benvenuti*, Jessica. *Come è* Miami?" Bisnonna Russo asked.

"Nice. Very nice," she said.

Her uncle Vinny, her father's younger brother, eyed her up and down. "Didn't get much color, Jess. Guess it was cold there."

Vinny's son Sal shook his head and said, "She went there to see family, not go sunbathing. How was that family?"

"Not as nosy as you, Cuz," she said playfully and hugged him before continuing to her spot at the table. Every Russo member had their own place at Sunday dinner, which made the empty seats for her parents all the more glaring. But it was still early, and she hoped that yesterday's argument wouldn't keep them from attending.

Much like the dinner from last night, an antipasto was already on the table along with slices of hearty Italian bread, a big plate of fresh mozzarella, and even more roasted red peppers.

As soon as she sat beside her cousin Sal, he snatched up her empty plate and piled on some of the antipasto as he said, "Spill, Cuz. I heard they're loaded. Got some fancy place on one of those private islands."

She should have known that the Russo grapevine would be hard at work while she was away. She also knew they wouldn't give up until she'd given them some kind of rundown about her trip.

She was about to begin when her parents walked in and the conversation was disrupted by greetings. But as soon as her parents sat, Cousin Sal said, "Jessica was just about to tell us all about the family in Miami."

Her mother physically tensed, and her father laid a hand on her mother's shoulder to soothe her. He also glanced at Jessica in a way that said *Go easy*.

"From what I can see, they're a lot like you guys," Jessica said, her head downturned as she gave undue attention to her plate.

"Except they're loaded, right?" Cousin Sal pressed.

"*Silenzio*, Salvatore," Nonna Rosa said with a quieting wave of her hand in her cousin's direction as she entered the dining room with a fresh basket of bread and laid it at the head of the table near her husband, Salvatore.

"Come on, Grandma. Don't tell me you don't want to know," her cousin pleaded and reached for a slice of bread, which earned him a sharp slap on the hand from his grandfather.

"Wait for your grandmother to sit," he said, and once she had, her cousin took a slice of bread and ate his antipasto silently but shot Jessica a look that warned he wouldn't give up until he got his answers.

But as her gaze met her father's, he wordlessly warned once again that silence would be appreciated.

Conversation picked up around them, returning to the upcoming baseball season with all in agreement that this was the year the Mets might do it, except for Bisnonna Russo who held on to her dedication to the Dodgers.

When her grandmother rose, it was a signal for anyone who wanted to help to clear off the remains of the antipasto and assist with the service of the pasta, salad, and meats.

Almost in a choreographed dance, the antipasto remnants were packed away by her while her mother took a spot by the pot of water heating on the stove and her grandmother scooped sausages and meatballs out of the sauce.

Wanting to make today just like any other Sunday, she walked to her mother's side, laid a hand on her shoulder, and leaned forward to check the water. "Still not ready."

"Just a little longer," her mother answered, almost mechanically.

"Jessica," her grandmother called out and handed her the bowl with the sausages and meatballs. "Please take this to the table."

Jessica did, only to reignite Sal's interest in her Miami visit. "Spill the beans, Cuz. *Mucho dinero*, right?" he said and skimmed his thumb and fingers together as if he was rubbing money.

It earned him a slap across the back of his head from his father and a sharp "*Basta*" from her father.

Likewise exasperated, Jessica said, "It's about more than money, and I'd appreciate you dropping this discussion."

"Says someone who's got money," Sal said with a shrug, but finally shut up after a glare from his mother as she came in with a large salad and placed the bowl next to the sausages and meatballs.

Her cousin held his hands up in surrender. "Got it. *Silenzio*."

"Thank you," Jessica said and returned to the kitchen to assist with the rest of dinner.

The water had come to a boil and her grandmother tossed in a handful of salt, and after a stir, her mother added the ziti. The three of them stood for long minutes there in silence, waiting for the water to re-boil. Inside she was much like the water, seemingly calm on the outside while below the surface it was churning, just waiting to bubble up and spill over.

It was her grandmother's simple words that caused the eruption.

"You had a good time in Miami?"

"Rosa!" her mother said sharply at the same time that Jessica said, "Nonna!"

Much like Sal had done before, Rosa raised her hands in surrender and possibly apology. "Sorry. I know it's a touchy subject."

"Ma! *Basta!*" her father Sal called out from the dining room, obviously having overheard.

"Sometimes it's better to get it all out. Just saying," Rosa replied and shifted Lara out of the way to pull the lid off the pot to check the water. She stirred the pasta and then faced the two of them. Gesturing between them with the spoon, she said, "You and you. You're two of a kind. It's why you bump heads so often."

"We don't," they said at the same time, prompting both of them to stare at each other, but then Jessica chuckled, and her mother shook her head.

"We might be a little alike," Lara said, stepped toward Jessica, and hugged her. "I love you, Jess. It's just that there's so much hurt there."

She returned the embrace, even tighter, and said, "I know, Mom, but she's hurting too. So are your sisters. They miss you."

With a sniffle, her mother said, "I'll try, Jess. I'll try. I promise."

Jessica wanted to press. Wanted to know more about what her mother meant with those words, but Rosa shooed them away from the pasta pot. Her grandmother's eyes were a little watery as she pulled off the lid, gave a stir, and scooped out a little of the pasta to test its doneness. Seemingly satisfied, she grabbed the pot to drain the pasta.

Jessica and Lara waited nearby, knowing the next steps in the dance that was Sunday dinner.

After a shake of the colander to remove the last of the water, Rosa dumped it back in the pot, added a few spoonfuls of sauce, stirred, and started plating the ziti. "You ladies ready?" Rosa asked, eyebrows raised in challenge.

"Are we ready?" Jessica asked her mom, but the question wasn't just about the pasta.

"I think we are," Lara said.

The call came much later that night.

Jessica was already in bed, watching a rom-com on a streaming service and trying to make sense of what had happened at today's Sunday dinner.

"How are you, *mi amor*?" Luis said.

"Dealing. I had dinner with my parents last night and our big Sunday dinner today. It was tense at times," she admitted since he would understand.

"I can only imagine. Any progress?" he asked, but then muttered a curse. "*Perdoname*. I don't want to add to any upset you might be feeling."

"I appreciate that. Honestly, maybe some progress. A big maybe." *A big maybe much like our relationship*, she thought, but to head off going there, she said, "How's my *abuela*?"

"Hanging in there. I had dinner with her yesterday. She went to Gloria's for dinner today. I don't think she was ready to handle being alone this weekend," he said and followed with a heavy sigh. "She misses you. I miss you. I didn't think that was possible after only a week together."

A week together that already seemed like an eternity ago. "I miss you too."

"Easter's not so far away. I'm looking forward to seeing you again, *mi amor.*"

"Me too, Luis. I…can't wait," she said instead of what she really wanted to say.

"I love you, Jessica. I will find a way to make this work," he said, braver than she was.

"I believe you, Luis. I have to go. I'm kind of tired. It's been an emotional few days." Kind of tired being an understatement. She was exhausted from the roller-coaster ride of emotions she'd been on over the last week and since coming home.

A hesitant pause drifted across the line. "Get some rest. I'll talk to you again soon," he said.

And just before he ended the call, she whispered, "I love you too."

Chapter Twenty-Nine

IT HAD BEEN ANOTHER trying day at the office.

Another day of dealing with bullshit office politics when all she wanted to do was her work so she could best represent her clients and go home to her family. But a meeting about a possible new partner and health insurance costs had delayed her review of a brief for an overseas litigation. The meeting had been bullshit because all the existing partners, including her, had known that the equity holders had already made their decisions on both issues and the rest of the partners were expected to just rubber-stamp them.

When she arrived at home, Sal was at the stove, busy preparing tacos, one of her favorite foods even though their homemade versions were nowhere near as good as the ones she'd had on her many trips to Mexico City for business. But Sal's love added something special to the meal.

"Smells delish," she said and kissed him on the cheek.

He slipped his arms around her and drew her in for a real kiss. She relaxed into him, his touch offering the peace and comfort that she needed way too often lately after a day at work.

As he drew away and returned his attention to the meat cooking on the stove, he said, "After we talked today, it sounded like you could use some comfort food."

"Just another day in paradise," she said, sarcasm heavy in her tones.

Sal set aside his wooden spoon, turned, and leaned on the edge of the counter. "I don't want to add to your misery, but you got a box today. From Miami. I put it in your office."

"A box?" Lara asked, both puzzled and worried.

"Big," he said and used his rough workman's hands to demonstrate the size of the package.

"Big, huh? I guess I'll go see what it is." After all, what did it matter if the day got any shittier?

She pushed into the small ground floor room she used as her home office. Sitting beside her desk was a large box with her name and address printed on the label. The return address said the package wasn't from Star Island, where Jessica had said Carmen was living. She wondered for a moment if the box could be from either of her sisters, and if so, what could be inside.

She scrounged around her desk drawer for a utility knife and handed it to Sal as he came to stand beside her. "Would you do the honors?" she said, almost afraid to open the box and see what was inside.

Sal slit open the packing tape and opened the cardboard flaps of the box to reveal heavy foam packing beneath. He lifted the foam and the first hint of the contents peeked out from a sea of foam peanuts. A black plastic handle on a fake marbleized, gold-colored case.

"Oh, shit," Lara said, immediately recognizing what it was.

Sal pulled on the handle to remove the case from the box and lay it on her desktop.

"Is that what I think it is?" he asked and shifted away the packaging so they could both stand in front of her desk to stare at the vintage case.

Lara's heart skittered in her chest and her hands shook as the locks on the case opened with satisfying *thunk*s. She lifted the top to reveal the antique-gray-and-black Underwood typewriter inside. An envelope was tucked beneath the paper bail just above the gap where the keys rested beneath the ribbon spool cover.

Her name was written on the face of the envelope, the script more spidery than it had been over thirty years ago, but still familiar.

"Lara?" Sal asked as she picked up the envelope and slipped it open.

"It's from my mother," she said and pulled the note out from the plain white linen envelope.

The words on the paper struck her so hard, she had to pull out her desk chair and sit. After she did so, she handed Sal the note and laid her hands on the keys. They felt familiar, like the face of a long-ago lover.

Sal read the note aloud. "It is never too late to reach for your dreams, *mija*. I am truly sorry I didn't support you. *Amor y un fuerte abrazo, Mamacita.*"

Sal laid a hand on her shoulder and squeezed it tenderly. "This is from your mother? An old typewriter?"

"I used to call her *Mamacita* when I was little. It was a thing between us. And yes, an old typewriter. It's just like the one I wrote my first book on." She passed her fingers over the keys again, almost a caress. They were smooth beneath her fingers and cold, but despite that, she felt the energy in them. The life they helped create, and her husband didn't fail to notice her fascination with the typewriter. With what it represented.

"It's been a while since you thought about your writing."

It had been a very long time. Too long. Since before Jessica's birth, although afterward her writing had become a catharsis for the pain she'd been feeling. A release from the frustration of smashing into a glass ceiling before being able to shatter it with the force of her determination. The power of her stubbornness to not be marginalized.

"Maybe it's time, Lara," Sal said and squeezed her shoulder.

"Maybe it is," she replied, agreeing. She'd paid her dues over and over at the law firm. Her family was financially comfortable. Jessica was well-established. There were only a few missing pieces in her life at this point. Her writing set aside so long ago. Her Miami family set aside nearly thirty years ago.

Maybe it's time, Lara thought, grabbed a piece of paper off her desk, and slipped it beneath the platen. She rolled the paper around until she could engage the paper bail to hold it down.

Smiling, she hit the first key, but without enough force, and the strike barely made a mark. She backspaced, hit the key again harder and the first letter appeared. She kept on typing until she had pounded out the first words.

Chapter One.

Luis breathed in deeply and launched the presentation he had prepared for Carmen and the other members of the board. Carefully he went over the facts and figures he had assembled over months of research, pointing out what the benefits were to the company in his opinion as well as the possible downsides to what he was proposing. From slide to slide, he presented the data and plan he'd prepared, hoping the board would be receptive, expectant—because if they were, it might mean a major change for his future.

He finished the presentation and said, "There are additional details and financials in the reports for your review. I appreciate that you'll need time to look them over and consider what to do. I understand that it's a big change and not just for today. If it works, Guerreiro Enterprises will be an even bigger player in the Latino food market."

"If it works, Luis," said one of the board members, a man who was usually the Debbie Downer in most discussions.

"You're right to be concerned, Benjamin. There is a risk to going forward with what I've laid out in my presentation and in the reports before you. But with risk comes reward, and I believe the reward will be to keep the company growing and viable for the future."

An awkward silence followed, worrying him that the proposal hadn't been well-received.

Carmen must have sensed it also, since she rose and came to stand beside him, saying more with that action than any words.

"Thank you for a very well-prepared presentation, Luis. We appreciate all the time and effort you put into it, but I know that I need more time to consider it and suspect that you all do as well. Because of that, I suggest we adjourn the meeting to give us all an opportunity to review the materials and reconvene in the future," Carmen said.

"I second that," said Benjamin and he was joined by a chorus of agreement from the other board members. But as they rose and filtered out of the room, several of the board members stopped to personally thank him for his work, which left him feeling slightly more positive about their reception of his plan.

Once everyone had filed out, he released a breath and slid Carmen a look from the corner of his eye. Slowly she lifted her gaze to his and grabbed one of the reports.

He gave her his full attention, waiting for her impressions of his work.

"Are you sure about this, *mi'jo*?" she asked and held up the papers.

He nodded. "I am, *viejita*. I've been researching this intensely for nearly a year, watching the trends and markets. Looking at the major players who would be our competition. I think this is the right thing to do."

She tilted her head to the side, but her gaze never wavered as she said, "It will take quite an investment and a lot of time. A lot of *your* time."

Luis nodded again, more emphatically. "*Lo se*. It will take a great deal of effort, but in my opinion it's worth the payback."

Carmen laid the report back down on the table. "I trust you, *sabes*. But to be fair to everyone, I have to review this proposal impartially."

He'd heard more than once the phrase about a person's heart sinking. He'd never ever really thought about what that felt like, but now he knew. His heart seemed to drop out of his chest and down to his toes because he had somehow thought he'd have Carmen's unwavering support.

She must have sensed his disappointment since she laid a hand on the sleeve of his suit jacket. "*Mi'jo*, have faith. You put a lot of work into this, and it shows. I'm sure the other board members will see that as well as they consider what you've laid out."

He forced a smile he wasn't feeling. "I hope they do. I hope you do, *viejita*."

She slipped her arm through his, the gesture supportive and personal as she shed her role as chairwoman of the board. "I think it's time for lunch and an interrogation."

"Interrogation? About?"

"Jessica."

Miami, 1970

It was rare for Carmen to have a day off, but the girls had a big dance recital that night and she had wanted to be home to help them get ready. She was truly looking forward to watching her girls perform.

Her mother and she were at work on some last-minute adjustments to their costumes, sewing sagging hems and loose sequins, when the doorbell rang.

Midday visits were also rare since most in the neighborhood were working folk just like her and normally at their jobs. It made her wonder who might be at their door.

Carmen set aside the skirt she'd been sewing and answered. She was shocked to find a familiar face on her front step. A little more aged and weathered, but still recognizable. "Juancho. *Que bueno verte de nuevo. Por favor*," she said and invited their old Havana neighbor into their home.

He held his hand up and said, "I don't want to be a bother. I just had something to return to you."

Since he wasn't holding anything, Carmen was puzzled until he reached into his pocket and handed over something neatly wrapped in tissue.

She accepted the tiny bundle and unwrapped the tissue to reveal her mother's engagement ring. It had been lost during their escape from Cuba, and they had all supposed it was long gone. Surprised and puzzled, she said, "I don't understand."

"When Nieves was leaving, she gave my wife some things, including a robe. The ring was in the pocket. Since your family was so kind to us, we hoped that one day we could return it to her," Juancho answered with a negligent shrug.

"Please, come in and give it to her yourself. Have a coffee with us," she said, wanting to hear more about it as well as his escape from Cuba. He finally relented.

Carmen walked him in to where her mother worked at the sewing machine, but as soon as Nieves saw him, she rushed over to greet their old neighbor, tears in her eyes.

They embraced, hugging each other hard and for long moments. After they broke apart, Carmen presented her mother with the missing engagement ring.

The joy on her mother's face was radiant, adding to the happiness of the reunion. But as Juancho sat and told of their family's recent flight from Cuba, Carmen was floored. They had only been able to leave a few short months earlier. It meant that through a decade of the deprivation his family must have suffered under the Castro regime, Juancho had held on to a ring that could have been sold or bartered for food for his family. He had honored the bonds of friendship and kindness her family had shown him and his family by returning something precious to her mother.

It only further cemented her desire to help her fellow exiles in any way she could. As Juancho finished his story and Nieves asked him what he was doing now that he was in Miami, their old neighbor grew uncomfortable. Obviously, he still wasn't on his feet, prompting Carmen to say, "I could use some help over at my place. That is if you're interested."

Juancho hesitated, wringing his hands together with worry. "Are you sure? I don't want to impose. But I'll work hard."

Carmen laid her hand over his, no doubt about what Juancho said. The younger man and her father had often spent time together working on their homes, and her father had always said Juancho was *listo*. Intelligent and eager to work.

"I would be delighted to have you. I could use someone like you to help me," she said and squeezed his hand in reassurance.

Juancho beamed, eyes wide. "*Gracias*. I'd be honored to work with you."

If anyone is going to be honored, it's me, she thought as she watched Nieves hold up her hand and stare at the long-lost ring.

Only it was lost no more.

———————— ◇ ————————

Hand sweaty on the handle of her rolling luggage, Jessica walked beside her parents through the airport terminal. She kept on glancing at them from the corner of her eye, still unable to believe that they were really here with her in Miami. Even more, that they were on the way with her to Carmen's house.

She shot another look at them, worried. Unsure of how this would all turn out.

Her mother had surprised her when she had said that she had

reached out to Carmen and the two had discussed this Easter visit. Since Easter was a time of rebirth, Jessica hoped that maybe this would be the start of a new life for all of them with the Miami family.

A buzz and vibration in her pocket warned that she had a text message, and she had no doubt who it was. She stopped only long enough to pull the phone from her pocket to confirm it was Luis, advising her that he was waiting in the pickup area for them.

Her heart pounded in anticipation of seeing him. Being with him. It had been weeks and weeks of only sporadic calls, since they'd both been occupied with work, especially Luis. He'd been exceptionally busy, although he hadn't said why. The rushed calls had been unsatisfying, making her look forward to seeing him even more. Making her worry that their newfound and long-distance relationship was unsustainable.

"Something wrong?" her father asked.

She shook her head. "No, not at all. It's just Luis texting to say he's waiting for us outside."

"Just Luis?" her father teased with the arch of a hairy eyebrow.

"Don't tease her, Sal," her mother said and elbowed him playfully, relieving some of Jessica's anxiety about how her mother would handle this visit. So far, Lara had been far more relaxed than she'd expected.

Jessica pushed ahead, weaving her way through the slow-moving, luggage-laden tourists slogging their way toward the hotel shuttle buses and taxis.

As she popped out of the terminal, her parents steps behind her, she saw Luis and her heart stopped for a moment. *Is it possible he's even more handsome than I remembered?* she asked herself and picked up her pace even more, almost running to reach him.

Luis immediately saw her, rushed toward her, and swept her up in his arms. "Dios, I've missed you," he said and kissed her.

Any fears she'd had that what they'd experienced weeks earlier had been a fluke vanished with the kiss. A kiss of welcome and promise.

A rough cough pulled them apart, although Luis kept his arm around her waist as she settled back to earth after the kiss.

"Mom. Dad. This is Luis Torres."

Luis held out his hand and shook her parents' hands and said, "It's a pleasure to meet you. *Bienvenida a* Miami."

"Thank you, Luis. We're…" Her father looked toward her mother, as if uncertain of how they felt about being here.

"We're happy to be in Miami," Lara said, her tone one that Jessica had heard on many an occasion. It was a neutral tone Jessica thought was the equivalent of a poker face, revealing nothing about how her mother was truly feeling, despite the words.

"Carmen is likewise happy that you're coming. So are Gloria and Anna," Luis said and gestured in the direction of a white Range Rover sitting at the curb. The family Rover instead of his classic Chevy or sexy Jaguar. A family car for her family and because he was family.

She slipped her hand into his as she walked with him to the cargo area of the Rover but released his hand so he could load up all their luggage.

Her parents sat in the back seat while she took the front passenger spot.

When Luis slipped behind the wheel, he paused to look at her again and smiled. The smile warmed her heart, which skittered in her chest at the thought of being with him that night. She had no doubt about that. About what she felt for him and that it hadn't been an aberration.

But as Luis pulled away from the curb, reality slammed back into her.

This trip wasn't just about her and Luis. About her and her Miami family.

It was about her mother and *her* family. It was about healing the exile that had kept them apart for the last thirty years, maybe even longer, she had realized after hearing the stories about their past.

As Luis drove, he pointed out some of the sights visible from the highway since Miami had changed quite a bit since her mother had left the city. But some things hadn't changed all that much, and as they got on the causeway heading toward Star Island, the tension in the car seemed to grow and become an almost physical thing.

She risked a quick look at the back seat. Her mother held her father's hand, knuckles white with pressure. Her father's lips were a tight slash and not his usual smile. His gaze met hers, almost pleading, but Jessica didn't know how to help. What to do to make the upcoming moment any easier.

The tension only grew as they passed the security guard and drove the short distance to the entrance for her grandmother's home.

Luis steered down the driveway to the front door. As he parked the car, he said, "Please go ahead. I'll have your things brought in."

"Luis," Jessica said and gripped his hand. "Please come in with us. The luggage can wait."

"Are you sure, *mi amor*?" he asked with an arch of a brow.

She squeezed his hand and smiled at him. "You're family too. Please."

With a smile, he nodded and opened his door, prompting all of them to leave the car and walk the short distance to the front door. There, Jessica took hold of his hand again and looked over her shoulder at her parents.

"You guys ready?" she asked.

Her mother and father were likewise holding hands again, and at her father's questioning look, her mother slowly nodded.

Luis must have seen the exchange since he opened the door and they all walked in together.

Chapter Thirty

AN ALMOST SICKLY COLD settled in the pit of Lara's stomach and her hands were wet with sweat. So wet she almost lost her death grip on Sal's hand, and she tightened her hold on him even more. He was her rock and had been for the last thirty years. He had given her the love and support she'd been missing for most of her life.

Jessica and her Luis—Lara had no doubt her daughter's heart belonged to that man—entered. It worried her that her normally responsible daughter had become involved so quickly with this man. And that it was clearly more than an infatuation.

But that worry had to wait as Jessica and Luis stepped aside and she saw them.

Carmen. Gloria. Anna.

She would have known them anywhere. It was like staring into a mirror with Gloria and Anna. They had always looked alike and that hadn't changed in thirty years. Sure, there were a few more lines around their mouths and creases at their eyes. But they were smiling, and their eyes were wet with tears. Happy tears.

Her mother…her mother had aged so much. It wasn't just lines and creases. Her hair, which had been almost seal-black and down to mid-back, was now a shock of carefully tended white, cut in a stylish bob. Carmen seemed shorter also. Inches shorter and thinner. Maybe too thin, almost frail. Guilt swept through her, but Carmen pulled her shoulders back in a gesture that roused years of unhappy memories.

Lara drew herself upright as well, girding herself for what normally followed that posture.

"*Mi'ja*. Mr. Russo—"

"Sal, please," her husband said.

With a dip of her head, Carmen said, "Sal. *Bienvenida*. We are so very happy to have you with us. So very, very happy."

Her mother's voice was husky. Choked with emotion much like her own throat was almost strangled closed. Closed off like she had been closed off from her family. But she'd vowed to keep an open mind for this Easter visit.

"Mami. Thank you for having us." She took a step toward her mother and suddenly they were in each other's arms, holding each other in an awkward embrace. Not quite a hug, but far more than just a casual clinch you'd use with a friend.

"*Mi'jita*. Sal. *Bienvenida*," Carmen repeated and stepped away. She gestured to Gloria and Anna, and Lara moved toward them with a clumsy stutter step, but suddenly her sisters flew to her, hugging her tight. Laughing and swaying with her and the years slipped away, reminding Lara of how they'd banded together as children. Of how they'd always had one another's backs until she'd fallen in love with Sal and moved away.

That cooled the embrace somewhat, and she pulled back and motioned for Sal to come over. When he did, he shook their hands as Lara formally introduced them. "This is Gloria, the middle child. She'll tell you how that always made her life difficult, but don't believe her," she said with a chuckle. "Anna is the baby, which means she almost always got her way unless Gloria and I ganged up on her," she said, humor surprisingly alive in her tone.

Gloria wagged her head and said, "And Lara was always the bossy one, trying to tell us what to do."

Lara had been forced to be that way because Carmen was never around, and when she was, Gloria and Anna had been the ones who had garnered most of the attention. She'd never blamed her sisters for that, or at least she didn't think she had, but Carmen…

Lara forced away the anger. The hurt.

This visit was about coming together again. Possibly. It had taken a great deal for her to visit. It would take even more for her to come to grips with all that had happened to her—to them—as children.

"Why don't we all get settled outside? It's a lovely day, and I've asked Manny and Consuelo to prepare a light lunch for us," Carmen said and held her hand out in invitation.

Sal laid a comforting hand at Lara's back. "We'd love that, Carmen. Thank you so much."

Lara peered at him from the corner of her eye, trying to judge what he was thinking, feeling, but it was impossible. His face was a stilted mask of his normally open and welcoming features. Ahead of her, Jessica stared at her expectantly, Luis by her side. Like Sal, Luis's face was set in stone, as if he were afraid of revealing too much emotion.

Emotion that all were carefully curbing. Maybe too carefully, and she worried their emotions were churning inside, like molten lava beneath a volcano, waiting to erupt.

At the gentle pressure of Sal's hand at her back, Lara followed her sisters to an outside dining area just beyond the walls of the massive home. Several Brooklyn homes would have fit inside Carmen's mansion, but then again success had been very important to her mother.

She had clearly succeeded.

At the table, Carmen sat at the head and Luis directly opposite her, cementing Lara's impression that he was as good as a son in this family. Maybe even more of a family member than she was, but then, he had been here when she hadn't. Because of that, she stifled her unreasonable anger at that realization.

Gloria and Anna sat side by side to Carmen's right, with an empty spot next to them.

Lara could have sat beside them, but she couldn't force herself to do it. It wasn't the three of them against the world the way it had been at one time. Not yet anyway.

Jessica took a place at Luis's right, leaving Lara and Sal no choice but to sit at Carmen's left. The left, which had so many negative connotations. Sinister in English. Gauche in French. The Book of Matthew detailing how those on the left would be condemned to eternal hellfire on Judgment Day.

But she sat to the left anyway, beside Sal and Jessica. A united front even if her daughter was in love with Carmen's right-hand man. She had no doubt about that now the way she had when Jessica had first come home from Miami. Her question now, her fear now, was what Jessica would do about the long-distance relationship. Whether it would stay long distance.

In her many years as an attorney, she'd learned when it was best to keep quiet and let others talk and she did just that, encouraging her sisters to share. "*Por favor, cuéntame más sobre tus familias,*" she said, slipping into the Spanish of her childhood the way she put on a comfortable pair of shoes.

Her sisters, ever the chatterboxes, obliged, regaling her with stories about their families as if thirty years of pain and separation hadn't happened. In a way, she was grateful for that. Gloria spoke lovingly and filled with pride about Carlos and David, her two sons. Anna's eldest, Esteban, was in medical school, while Angelica wanted to go into the family business.

With a moue, Anna said, "But Angelica's got a lot to learn. She's used to just getting everything she wants. She can be a brat at times."

Lara chuckled. "The apple didn't fall far from that tree," she teased.

A momentary silence filled with surprise followed, but then laughter rippled across everyone at the table.

Luis nodded, but said, "She's got a good head on her shoulders. She'll come around."

"*Gracias,* Luis. She thinks the world of you," Anna said, clearly misreading the signals if Lara was any judge of the look that Jessica and Luis shared. Angelica was obviously attracted to the handsome man who only seemed to have eyes for Jessica. That hadn't changed during the weeks of separation since Jessica's last visit.

She pulled her mind from those troubling thoughts and focused on her sisters and Carmen, who so far had been sitting by silently, letting her girls—*las niñas*—get reacquainted.

Maybe that had been her goal all along: a reunion of the sisters.

And so far it's going fairly well, Lara thought as Gloria and Anna continued sharing stories about their children as well as about the recent reunion they had and how happy they were that Lara was now there.

Lara had thought it would be harder to say, but the words fell from her lips easily. "I'm glad I came as well." She glanced at her husband and took his hand. "That Sal is here with me so you can get to know him and what a wonderful man he is."

Guilt flashed across her sisters' faces with the reminder of one of the reasons, a big reason, they had been apart.

"From what Jessica has told us, Salvatore is a wonderful man," Gloria said and peered toward Sal.

"We're happy he's here so we can get to know him better. Now and in the future," Anna added, making it clear that she hoped this would not be their only trip to Miami.

"I'm very glad we're here and I want to thank you for the warm welcome," Sal said and squeezed Lara's hand to reassure her that all was okay.

"Mami?" Lara said, because so far her mother had said little, making her wonder and worry about what was going on in her head. What machination she was planning.

"I'm very happy that you're here. If I've been silent, it's just that I'm so very excited and words fail me, *mija*," Carmen said.

It was impossible not to hear the suppressed emotion in her voice and see the shimmer of unshed tears in her gaze. The truthfulness in her words. Because of that, Lara said, "I understand, Mami. I have to be honest and say that I wasn't sure about coming, but I'm glad Jessica and Sal convinced me to try."

"We're glad too, Lara. We've missed you. We've wanted to do this for so long—" Gloria began, but Lara raised her hand to stop her.

"Let's not rehash the past, Gloria. Let's move forward," Lara said, fearing that reminders of why they were there would only cause problems.

"*Sí*, you are very right, Lara. The past is something we cannot change, but the future…the future is ours," her mother said and held her hand out to Lara.

A hand of peace? Lara wondered, but to refuse it would be rude and hurtful. No matter how much pain still resided in her heart, it was time to change the future, if only for Jessica's sake. Her daughter had clearly taken to the Miami family, and Luis, of course. Lara didn't want her daughter to live with the kind of hurt she'd carried with her for so long.

As a mother, she'd do whatever she had to in order to secure her daughter's happiness—while she hated to admit it, much like her mother had tried to do. Lara took her mother's hand and said, "To the future."

Chapter Thirty-One

JESSICA LAY NEXT TO Luis in bed, stroking his chest absentmindedly as she thought about all that had happened that day, from the trip to Miami to all the talking and meals that had followed.

"I think it went well. What do you think?" Jessica said, leaning up on an elbow to peer at Luis, who lay there, a muscled arm upraised, hand tucked under his head.

"I have to confess that I was worried—"

"So was I. So worried that I was making a mistake by convincing them to come," Jessica admitted.

Luis shifted slightly to meet her gaze and cupped her jaw. "You did the right thing, *mi amor*. As concerned as I was about the hurt this reunion might cause everyone, I think it's going well, especially with the sisters."

"*Las niñas*, Abuela called them."

"'The girls…only they're all successful women now. Carmen is very proud of them, including your mother," Luis said and tenderly ran his thumb across the slight dip in her chin.

Jessica nodded. "Abuela told me she created news alerts so she could keep up with what my mother was doing."

"She did, but…can we talk about us for a second?" he said, his tone so serious it made her tense in anticipation and her heartbeat hitched in her chest.

"Sure," she said, but reluctantly, worried about what he would say next.

He sat up and draped the sheet across his lap and she did the same, hiding herself from his gaze by holding the sheet to her body. The sheet was a shield, creating a barrier between them that concerned her, especially as Luis looked away from her as he said, "In the next few days Carmen is going to be making a big announcement about the business."

Jessica tilted her head to the side and peered at him, puzzled by what that announcement would be and, more important, what it meant for them. "I don't understand."

"I want you to understand, Jessica," he said so earnestly her heart picked up speed, racing in her chest with fear and anticipation. "I'd been working on something for nearly a year, but after meeting you…I knew I had to do it, but I also knew the business might not want to," Luis said and wagged his head, as if chastising himself. "I'm sorry, I don't mean to be so cryptic."

"So say it," Jessica challenged, wanting to hear his news already.

"*Amorcita*, don't worry. It's all good. Very good, or at least I hope you will think so," he said and leaned over, reached into the nightstand, and removed something that he hid inside his large hand.

"I've been reviewing the possibility of expanding the business into the Northeast. Of turning Guerreiro Enterprises into a national player in the Latino food market, like Goya, Iberia, or La Costeña. The demographics support the expansion and also diversifying to include other brands from the Caribbean and Latin America," he said, optimism and excitement in his voice. But there was one word that had caught her attention within all that he'd said.

"If you expand to the Northeast—"

"We'll need an office there and someone to run it," he said and held out his hand, opened it to reveal the diamond ring within. "This belonged to your Bisabuela Nieves. She thought she had lost it when your family escaped Cuba, but a neighbor returned it to her a decade later. When I told Carmen that I planned to ask you—"

"To marry you?" she squeaked, air barely making it out of her throat as her heart beat an almost violent tattoo in her chest.

Luis chuckled and shook his head. "Are you always so impatient?"

"Well, do you? Want to marry me?" she pressed.

He moved to kneel before her and held out the ring. "Jessica Russo, will you marry me? Be my wife? I promise to help you flip any furniture you want if you promise to keep me sane during this expansion."

She came to her knees, the shield coming down as she cupped the hand that held the ring. "I will, Luis. I love you," she said, but quickly added, "but what about my parents?"

"My mother always told me that you don't just marry a woman, you marry her family, so I hope the entire Russo family will become part of mine," he said, took hold of the ring, and gently placed it on Jessica's finger. It was a little large, but despite that, it looked beautiful sitting on her finger.

"Did you ask them? My dad is kind of old-world, you know."

Luis muttered a curse. "I didn't, but I'll make it right first thing in the morning. I promise."

Jessica smiled and cradled his cheek. "I promise too, Luis. I will be at your side. I will become part of your family the way you're already a big part of mine."

He grinned, that boyish grin that did all kinds of things to her heart and her body, which prompted her to say, "I guess we should celebrate."

"I guess we should," he said and moved toward her, pressed her down into the mattress, and kissed the crook of her neck, yanking a giggle from her.

She pushed him off a bit and said, "I was thinking champagne was in order."

"Later," he said and bent his head to kiss her.

"Later," she said with a laugh and welcomed him home.

Carmen couldn't sleep. Her mind refused to shut down and kept on replaying all that had happened that day. A good day, she had to admit. It had gone far better than she had expected. Las niñas had seemed to get along as if the many years had not passed. Even the upset that Carmen had sensed at times from Lara, namely that Gloria and Anna got all the attention, hadn't reared its ugly head.

Las niñas seemed to be on the road to finding their friendship again, their sisterhood, and if that was all this reunion accomplished, Carmen would be happy with that. Her time on this earth might be short, but *las niñas* still had the possibility of a great deal of time together.

Because she was so awake, Carmen escaped her bedroom to go to her office to review tomorrow's big announcement, another thing that had kept boomeranging through her brain.

But as she stepped from her wing of the house, she noticed Lara was sitting in the living room, staring at the embers of the fire that Manny had started earlier to chase away the damp and slight chill of the April night.

"Lara," Carmen said softly, not wanting to startle her daughter who seemed deep in thought.

Lara slowly lifted her gaze from the fire to meet Carmen's gaze. "Mami. You're up late."

"So are you, *mija*," she said, walked to the sofa where her daughter sat, and gestured to the spot beside her. "May I?"

"It's your home," Lara said with a flippant wave of her hand.

"*Y tu casa tambien, mija*," Carmen said, and despite the dismissiveness in her daughter's voice, she sat beside her.

"*Mi casa*," Lara said with disbelief and swiveled her head to peer about the space. "You really did it, Mami. This is the American Dream on steroids."

Carmen tracked her daughter's gaze, viewing her home the way Lara might. "It is, but it's also a wise investment for the family's future."

A long pause followed her statement. "You were always so concerned about the future. So worried about it that you forgot there was a present to deal with."

Carmen had hoped to avoid unpleasantness during this reunion, but given Lara's words and the tension she had sensed from the moment of her arrival, that might be impossible. But she also didn't want a rupture of the seeming truce that had arisen because she wanted her girls to have a future together.

"I know that I wasn't always there for you, Lara. That I was too busy with other things."

"The business. Gloria. Anna. Strangers even. And if it wasn't them, it was something else, Mami. It was always something else," Lara said, the last words so low and strangled they were barely audible, but Carmen didn't fail to hear. The pain laced through them cut through the air like a sharp knife.

"I'm sorry, Lara. I've said that to you so many times, and I know that's not enough. But everything I did was for you and your sisters. For the family."

"And for you," Lara said and gestured to the wealth surrounding them.

She couldn't deny it. "For me and for others. I'd like to think I've made the world better for others as well."

A harsh breath exploded from her lips. "Like Luis. The man who is now upstairs in bed with my daughter. My only daughter. Are you going to take her away also?"

There was something behind that question. Something that Carmen had always suspected but had never voiced. Until now. "You think I took your father away."

Another rough breath escaped her daughter, and the firelight made the trails of tears down her cheeks glisten before Lara wiped them off her face. "Not exactly," Lara admitted.

The shock of it, of what she'd only imagined for so long now confirmed, rocked Carmen, but before she could utter a word Lara plowed on.

"You were always so busy. Always running from one thing to another. What reason did he have to stay home? You were never there."

The years fell away, and Lara sounded like that lost little child again, questioning her father's absence. Wanting her *papi* home again.

Miami, January 1964

Carmen cradled Anna close as she finished reading *las niñas* one of their favorite books, a ritual she kept no matter how busy she might be. It was one of the best parts of the day and she cherished the time with her daughters.

Anna was so sound asleep in her arms, she didn't move as Carmen shifted to tuck the blanket in around Lara and Gloria, who was also dead to the world. But Lara sleepily opened her eyes and said, "Why is Papi leaving again?"

She wished she had an answer to the question she'd asked Carlos multiple times in the days following his announcement that he was enlisting to go fight in Vietnam. But she didn't have an answer, and even if he had provided one, it could never justify his abandoning his family. Again.

But Lara adored her father. That much was clear. She followed her father around with puppy-dog eyes, reveling in his presence. There was no way Carmen was going to tarnish the reverence Lara had for her father.

"Your father is a hero and there are bad people who want to hurt others. Communists like those that stole Cuba from us," she said.

"Com-mmoo-nistsss," Lara repeated sleepily.

"Communists," Carmen repeated. "Horrible people like Fidel. People who want to control others. Silence any opinion that isn't theirs. Steal the hard work of their people," she said, trying her best to explain to her seven-year-old. She intended to repeat that lesson over and over so that her daughter would never fall prey to the lies she'd believed and which had cost her family their beloved Cuba. So that Lara would never let that happen here, in America, a country that had blessed millions with freedom and liberty.

"I don't want him to go fight commoonists. I want him to stay home," Lara said as tears leaked from her eyes and ran down to the pillow beneath her head.

Even if Lara was only seven, Carmen often butted heads with her daughter, but on this they agreed.

"I don't want him to leave either."

But that wasn't enough for Lara. "Will you talk to him? Ask him not to go?"

Ask him again, as she had too many times to count, but she nodded and said, "I'll ask him again."

"If I could have stopped him, I would have, but I think that would only have made both of us miserable," Carmen admitted with a heavy sigh.

"But he'd be alive," Lara shot back.

"But unhappy that he hadn't done what he wanted. Resentful."

"Resentful? Why would he possibly be resentful?" Lara pressed.

Carmen paused, trying to imagine how to discuss such a delicate topic without setting back whatever progress they'd made so far during the visit. Carefully, as if she were walking through a minefield, she proceeded.

"I pushed you to have a profession even though I knew you wanted to do something else," Carmen began.

"I wanted to be a writer," Lara began, but hesitated before a rush of words spilled from her. "But that profession you pushed on me gave me opportunities I wouldn't have otherwise had, and it let my family prosper. My family is everything for me."

Carmen wanted to lighten the mood a little, so she said, "I think there might be a thank you there."

Lara chuckled, as she'd intended, and shook her head. "I guess there is. And thank you for the typewriter, although I have to confess I'm not using it to type. Just for inspiration."

"You're writing again?" Carmen asked.

"I am. Getting down some ideas for a story."

"About?" Carmen pressed.

Lara shot her a glance from the corner of her eye. "About regrets, like those you think my father might have had."

"Like he would have definitely had, I think. He truly believed he was doing the right thing and if I'd held him back—"

"He'd wonder *what if* for the rest of his life," Lara said.

Carmen shook her head and peered at her daughter. "Worse, I think. He'd come to hate himself and me for keeping him at home," she explained, even though Lara was old enough and wise enough to understand.

"Like you tried to keep me from doing what I wanted to do. First with the writing and then with Sal," her daughter challenged, raising a brow, but her words had little bite.

"Yes, like I tried to do, and for that I am eternally sorry. You were right to be angry with me and maybe even with your sisters, but we were only trying to protect you. Believe that. We only had your well-being at heart," Carmen said and laid a hand over her heart to stress that.

"If I had listened, you would have kept me from the love of my life, Mami. From an amazing man and his family."

"A family we'd love to meet and get to know, Lara," she said, wanting with all her heart to keep her family moving forward rather than looking back.

"This house is certainly big enough for all of them if they want to visit," Lara said, a hint of laughter in her voice, giving Carmen hope.

"It is. Maybe they could join us in the future. Memorial Day isn't all that far away and it won't be that hot and humid then."

Lara frowned. "Summer in Miami was always tough, but I imagine you get some nice breezes here from the bay. It must be lovely," she said with a wistful smile.

"I'd love for you to come and find out for yourself."

A long pause followed, causing Carmen to hold her breath, but then Lara said, "I think I'd like that, Mami."

And with those words, hope continued to grow.

Chapter Thirty-Two

A PLEASANT LETHARGY FILLED her bones after her early morning shower and lovemaking with Luis. But that pleasure was short-lived as they came down the stairs holding hands and found her parents and Carmen huddled together in the living room, voices low but insistent.

With her peace shattered, she gripped Luis's hand tightly, preparing herself, but as they entered, her parents and grandmother looked in their direction, broad smiles on their faces.

Her grandmother rose and invited them to join the gathering. "We've been up for some time talking about having the Russos come and visit."

Well, that's a major step in just a hot second, Jessica thought.

"That sounds…nice," she replied hesitantly and glanced up at Luis.

"It would be nice, especially before…"

He held back because he had yet to do what he'd promised, but there was no avoiding it as her mother said, "Before what, Mr. Torres?"

"Luis, *por favor*," he insisted yet again. With a gentle tug, he urged Jessica forward until they were standing before her parents and Carmen. Carmen was smiling, but her parents were obviously confused, and beside her, Luis was tense. He clearly anticipated this might not go well, especially since Carmen had been aware of Luis's intentions before her parents.

"Mom. Dad. I think Luis has something to say to you," Jessica said, trying to ease the moment forward.

Both her parents' eyes widened in surprise, and then her mother's gaze shifted to their joined hands and then back to her husband, but she remained silent.

"Mr. and Mrs. Russo—"

"Sal and Lara, please," her father said.

With a nod, Luis continued. "Sal. Lara. I never expected love when I first came to Brooklyn, but that's what happened. I love Jessica. She's an amazing woman and I want to spend the rest of my life with her. I'm asking you for your permission and blessing to marry her."

Her parents exchanged looks of concern, prompting Jessica to say "I know this is sudden."

"That's an understatement, Jess," her mother said. "Sal?"

Her father stared at them, the earlier surprise and concern fading to a face made of stone. "As you can imagine, Luis, this is quite a shock. You've only known Jessica for a few weeks. Her life is in Brooklyn and your home is here in Miami."

Luis nodded and shot a glance at Carmen, who dipped her head as if to confirm he could go on. "My home is here for now, and I hope you can understand that what I'm about to tell you is confidential at this time."

Jessica's mom had not failed to see the interaction between Luis and Carmen. "You knew about this? About what he planned?"

"I did, and I also urged him to speak to you two before this announcement," Carmen said in response to the very accusatory tone in her daughter's voice.

"Please don't blame Carmen. It's all on me because I couldn't wait to ask Jessica to be my wife," Luis said and splayed a hand across his chest to emphasize he was responsible.

Jessica held her breath, waiting for a reaction from her mother, who she thought would be quick to assign guilt to Carmen. But it didn't happen, shocking her. It gave her hope that things might change for the better. Instead, her father said in a controlled voice, "Please go on, Luis."

Luis acknowledged the request with a tilt of his head. "As I said, this is confidential, at least for another few hours, until the rest of the family gets here. But you'll know first, besides Carmen, the board, and Jessica, that the company plans to expand into the Northeast, which means we'll need an office there and someone to oversee the expansion."

"You," Lara said. "You're going to oversee the expansion and move to New York?"

"I am. I wouldn't dream of taking Jessica from you or from her business. You can't start a life together with regrets," he said.

Bright color flooded her mother's cheeks, causing Jessica to wonder about that, but in a rough voice, Lara said, "No, you can't have a marriage filled with regrets."

Her father, still in protective mode, said, "Will you regret leaving Miami? Your family and life here?"

With an unassuming shrug, he said, "My life is with Jessica. As for my family and yours…I expect we're going to be visiting Miami a lot. What about you?"

Her father exchanged a look with her mother but remained silent. That silence hung there, almost physical, tangible, until her mother said, "I think we'll be visiting."

Jessica released a breath she didn't even remember holding as Luis said, "Good. I'd love for you to meet my family. They'll actually be here tonight for dinner."

Her mother and father exchanged a look. One she'd seen more than once when her mother and she had butted heads. But as they remained silent and returned their gazes to where Luis and she stood, relief slipped through her.

"We look forward to that very much, Luis," her mother said.

Sal and Lara stood surrounded by Gloria, Anna, and their children, who seemed fascinated with the newly reunited members of the family. Luis's parents and siblings were also nearby, trying to get comfortable with the family.

Lara smiled as David, the oldest of her nieces and nephews, introduced his very pregnant wife, Sophie. She shook the young woman's hand and said, "So nice to meet you. When are you due?"

Sophie laughed and peered at her watch playfully, yanking a laugh from Lara. "Any day now. I'm actually a little overdue."

"I was that way also," she commiserated and searched through the crowd for Jessica.

She found her daughter, standing by Luis and chatting with Carmen.

Carmen—her mother—who had orchestrated this whole thing, much like she had controlled most of Lara's life until she had rebelled and fled to New York to marry Sal.

Sal, she thought and judged his reaction from the corner of her eye.

He wasn't overwhelmed by the sometimes loud and brash crowd as they peppered them with questions intermixed with stories about growing up with their parents and Abuela Carmen.

The Russo clan was as noisy and boisterous as her Gonzalez family. *My Gonzalez family,* she thought, examining her sisters and each of their children. There could be no denying they were family since they all looked so much alike.

All my family, she thought yet again, and regret filled her for the years lost with them.

Luis's words from earlier that morning came to her again. *You can't start a life together with regrets.*

She peered at Sal again and he caught her look, turned to meet her gaze, and smiled. "I'm sorry," she said, causing him to start with surprise.

"What? I don't understand," he said, his gaze intense, worried as he guided her away to a quieter spot to talk. When they stood alone by the edge of the outside dining room, he said, "What's wrong, Lara?"

She looked away, tears blurring her gaze as she choked out, "All these years...I've kept you and Jessica from this. I forced this exile on you."

"But it's over now, isn't it? We have a new beginning here," Sal urged and wiped the tears from her face.

"It is, but...I realize now that I kept all that pain and regret hidden because I thought it was the right thing to do."

"Like your mother did what she thought was right?" he said gently, the tone one he used often as the family mediator.

Lara risked a quick glance to where her mother sat with Luis and Jessica. Lara had no doubt Carmen had her regrets about what she had done. Lara had her regrets as well, but it was time to set it all aside and begin anew as Sal had said.

"No more regrets, Sal. It's time for a life without any regrets," she said and kissed him to seal that promise.

***

Carmen sat to the side of the gathering with Jessica and Luis, watching the interactions between Sal and Lara and the various family members. The welcome to Luis's family, soon to be a more permanent part of their lives.

Carmen had been grateful that yesterday's reunion had gone well, and so far, tonight was filled with happiness from what she could see. But as Sal and Lara drifted off to the side, it was impossible to miss her daughter's upset. She wanted to go over, but Jessica laid a hand on her knee.

"Let Dad handle it, Abuela. He'll know what to do," her granddaughter said.

"But she's upset," Carmen said, worry eating away at her earlier satisfaction.

"That's only natural, *viejita*," Luis said, also trying to reassure her.

There had been so many times when Carmen hadn't been there for Lara as a child. No matter what, she wouldn't start this new part of their lives that way.

"I'm going over, Jessica. Luis. Lara needs me," she said and slowly got to her feet. Her arthritis had been acting up today, more than usual, but even if each step brought pain, she'd make her way to her daughter to ease her anguish.

"I'll go with you, Abuela," Jessica said.

Jessica slipped her arm through her grandmother's, offering support since she had noticed the hitch as her grandmother had stood and taken a stuttering step toward her mother.

Together they slowly walked the short distance and as her father noticed them approaching, he said something to her mother who nodded and offered him a hesitant smile.

He kissed her and walked away to join the rest of the family by the pool.

With that, Lara hurried toward them, her head tilted at a determined angle and her shoulders pulled back. Her attorney face was on, giving no hint of what she was feeling. But when she stopped before them, her manner softened.

"Are you okay, Mami?" she asked, her concern transparent.

Carmen laid a shaky hand on Lara's arm. "I am. And you, *mi'ja*. Are you okay?"

Lara took Carmen's hand in hers and then reached for Jessica's.

"From this day on, we move forward. No more regrets about the past."

Jessica bit back tears, but of joy this time as she drew her mother and grandmother together and the three hugged each other. "No regrets," Jessica said.

The long separation from one another was over, but there was still one exile in their lives.

"*Volveremos*," she said, dragging the word from the memory that was only weeks old but had made such an impression on her.

Lara shook her head vehemently. "No, *mi'jita*. America is our home. The future is here and not in the past."

There was no doubt in her mother's gaze and tone, but Jessica worried about what her grandmother might think until she met Carmen's gaze, a mirror of Lara's.

"As long as we're together, we are home, Jessica," Carmen said and drew them in together for another tight hug.

Enveloped in their arms, Jessica knew.

Their long exile was finally over.

Epilogue

JESSICA STOOD BEFORE LUIS as his desk was wheeled into his office at the company's new Manhattan headquarters in the Seaport District. It had taken several months to find the right location, namely one that would provide a short commute to her Williamsburg building which they were busy renovating to give them room to grow. She loved overseeing the changes which had begun almost immediately after the wedding they'd had only a few months earlier.

As she peered at the desk she'd selected with her *abuela*, she wondered why Luis had brought it from Miami, since he hadn't seemed so pleased when they'd placed it in Carmen's old office. But it looked wonderful against the walls of windows that offered spectacular views of the East River and Brooklyn Bridge from one side and the new World Trade Center and Financial District from the other.

When Luis walked in with one of the boxes packed with other belongings from the Miami office, he smiled at her and laid the box on the desk. He ran a hand across the surface, almost lovingly, which confused her even more. Especially as he said, "I want to thank you again for finding this for me. It's a beautiful piece."

She narrowed her gaze and peered at him, searching for any signs that he was only trying to spare her feelings but found none. Still, she asked, "You really like it? You're not just saying that?"

He seemed to understand her upset since he walked over, took hold of her hand, and gave a reassuring squeeze. "I do. Why do you ask?"

Sucking in a breath, she blurted out, "You didn't seem so in love with it in Miami."

"Ah," he said and looked away. But then he met her gaze again. "I was…surprised by it. I felt like it almost said to me, 'Your place is in Miami' at a time when I thought there was something growing between us," he explained.

She cupped his jaw and ran her thumb across his cheek. "You thought I was pushing you away?"

He shrugged, that all-too-familiar shrug, and said, "I did. I know it was a reach, but so much was happening at that time. So many emotions I was trying to sort out. I'm sorry I didn't seem happier when you gifted it, but I do love it. I love you."

"I love you too," Jessica said, rose on tiptoes, and kissed him.

He answered her kiss, splaying his hand across her back and drawing her close. Holding here there, tight against him, as the kiss deepened until a knock on the doorjamb drew them slowly apart.

Jessica turned and found her mother, father, and grandmother at the door, smiles wreathing their faces. Although a hint of pink colored her father's cheeks, as if he was embarrassed to realize she was no longer his little girl.

She was happy to see all of them together. Her *abuela* Carmen, as well as Gloria and Anna and assorted family members, had all traveled to New York City to celebrate the grand opening of the new offices, which would occur in a few days.

The Miami clan had finally come to Brooklyn, and judging from the look on her mother's face, she was totally happy with everything that was happening. And because of that, she knew it was the perfect time to share some news with them. But first, she gazed at Luis who smiled and wrapped his arm around her waist, confirming her unspoken decision.

"Please come in and sit down. We have something to tell you," Jessica said and gestured to the leather sofa at one side of the office.

The earlier looks of happiness turned to ones of puzzlement, but the three did as she asked, and to her surprise, her mother reached for Carmen's and Sal's hands.

"Something good, we hope," Lara said.

"Good news," Luis said and moved his hand down and around, to rest on her still-flat belly.

It was a move that, while subtle, was noticed by one and all. A whispered "*Dios mio*" escaped her mother and grandmother, but her father remained silent.

"Dad?" she asked, worried about that telling silence.

But then he smiled, that broad grin that had always communicated his joy. And his acceptance.

When the baby arrived in several months, she would be surrounded by the love of her family in both Miami and Brooklyn. While Jessica wasn't certain it was a girl, Luis had told her that he'd had a dream where the Virgencita had come to him and told him he'd have a daughter.

A daughter they'd decided to name after Carmen.

But that's news for another day, she thought as Luis and she accepted the warm hugs and congratulations from her family. In that moment, she once again knew what she had realized so many months ago.

Her family's pain was now firmly part of the past. And the future...

The future was theirs to build together.

Discover Caridad Piñeiro's Latinx love story *One Summer Night*, available now wherever books are sold.

Sea Kiss, New Jersey

TRACY PARKER WAS IN love with being in love.

That worried her best friend and maid of honor, Maggie Sinclair, more than she cared to admit.

In the middle of the temporary dance floor, Tracy waltzed with her new husband in a satin-and-lace designer gown, gleaming with seed pearls and twinkling sequins. But the sparkle dimmed in comparison to the dreamy glow in Tracy's eyes.

The sounds of wedding music competed with the gentle rustle of seagrass in the dunes and the crash of the waves down on the beach. The fragrance from centerpiece flowers and bouquets battled with the kiss of fresh sea air.

Connie and Emma, Tracy's two other best friends and members of the bridal party, were standing beside Maggie on the edge of the dance floor that had been set up on the great lawn of Maggie's family's beachfront mansion on the Jersey Shore. Huddled together, Maggie and her friends watched the happy couple do a final whirl.

"She's got it *so* bad," Maggie said, eyeing Connie and Emma with concern past the rim of her rapidly disappearing glass of champagne.

"Do you think that this time he really is *The One?*" Connie asked.

"Doubt it," Emma replied without hesitation.

As the DJ requested that other couples join the happy newly-weds, Maggie and her friends returned to the bridal party dais set out on the patio. Grabbing another glass of champagne, Maggie craned her neck around the gigantic centerpiece piled with an almost obscene mound of white roses, ice-blue hydrangea, lisianthus, sheer tulle, and twinkling fairy lights and examined the assorted guests mingling around the great lawn and down by the boardwalk leading to the beach.

She recognized Tracy's family from their various meetings over the years, as well as some of Tracy's sorority sisters, like Toni Van Houten, who in the six years since graduation had managed to pop out a trio of boys who now circled her like sharks around a swimmer. Although the wedding invite had indicated *No Children,* Toni had done as she pleased. Since Tracy had not wanted a scene at her dream beachfront wedding, Emma, who was doing double duty as the wedding planner for the event, had scrambled to find space for the children at the dinner tables.

"Is that Toni 'I'll never ruin my body with babies' Toni?" Connie asked, a perplexed look on her features. At Maggie's nod, Connie's eyes widened in surprise, and she said, "She looks…happy."

A cynical laugh erupted from Emma. "She looks *crazed.*"

Maggie couldn't argue with either of their assessments. But as put-upon as their old acquaintance seemed, the indulgent smile she gave her youngest child was positively radiant.

Maggie skipped her gaze across the gathering to take note of all the other married folk. It was easy enough to pick them out from her vantage point on the dais, where she and her friends sat on display like days' old cakes in the bakery. They were the last three unmarried women in an extended circle of business and college acquaintances.

"How many times do you suppose we've been bridesmaids now?" Maggie wondered aloud. She finished off her glass and motioned for the waiter to bring another.

"Jointly or severally?" asked Connie, ever the lawyer.

"Way too many," replied Emma, who, for a wedding planner, was the most ardent disbeliever in the possibility of happily ever afters.

Maggie hadn't given marriage a first thought, much less a second, in a very long time. She'd had too many things going on in her life. Not that there hadn't been a few memorable moments, most of which revolved around the absolutely worst man for her: Owen Pierce.

But for years now, she'd been dealing with her family's business and its money problems, which had spilled over into her personal finances. As she gazed at the beauty of the manicured grounds and then back toward her family's summer home, it occurred to her that this might be the last time she hosted a celebration like this here. She had mortgaged the property that she had inherited to funnel money into the family's struggling retail store division.

Unfortunately, thanks to her father's stubborn refusal to make changes to help the business, she spent way too much time at work, which left little time for romance. Not to mention that none of her casual dates had piqued her interest in that direction. Looking down from her perch, however, and seeing the happiness on so many faces suddenly had her reconsidering the merits of married life.

"Always a bridesmaid and never a bride," she muttered, surprising herself with the hint of wistfulness in her tone.

"That's because the three of us are all too busy working to search for Prince Charming," Connie said, her defense as swift and impassioned as if she were arguing a case in court.

"Who even believes in that fairy-tale crap?" Emma's gaze grew distracted, and she rose from her chair. "Excuse me for a moment. Carlo needs to see me about something."

Emma rushed off to the side of the dance floor, where her caterer extraordinaire, Carlo da Costa, raked a hand through his thick, brown hair in clear frustration. He wore a pristine white chef's jacket and pants that enhanced his dark good looks.

Emma laid a hand on Carlo's forearm and leaned close to speak to him, apparently trying to resolve a problem.

"She doesn't believe in fairy tales, but her Prince Charming is standing right in front of her," Connie said with a sad shake of her head.

Maggie took another sip of her champagne and viewed the inter-action between Carlo and Emma. Definitely major sparkage going on, she thought.

"You're totally right," she said with an assertive nod.

Connie smiled like the proverbial cat, her exotic green-gold eyes gleaming with mischief. "That's why you hired me to represent your company as soon as I finished law school. Nothing gets past me."

"Really? So what else do you think you've seen tonight?"

Raising her glass, her friend gestured toward the right of the mansion's great lawn, where some of the fraternity brothers from their alma mater had gathered. One of the men slowly turned to sneak a peek at them.

"Owen has been watching you all night long," Connie said with a shrewd smile.

"Totally impossible, and you of all people should know it. Owen Pierce has absolutely no interest in me."

She set her glass on the table to hide the nervous tremble of her hand as her gaze connected with his for the briefest of moments. Even that fleeting link was enough to raise her core temperature a few degrees. But what woman *wouldn't* respond like that?

In his designer tuxedo, Owen was the epitome of male perfection—raven-black hair, a sexy gleam in his charcoal-gray eyes, broad shoulders, and not an ounce of fat on him, which made her recall seeing him in much, much less on a hot summer night on Sea

Kiss Beach. She had been staying in the quaint seaside town on the Jersey Shore with her grandmother that summer, much as she had all her life. As they also had for so many years, the Pierce boys had been residing next door for the entire season.

The two beachfront mansions had been built side by side decades earlier, before the start of the Pierce and Sinclair rift. The cost of waterfront real estate had escalated so drastically since their construction that neither family was willing to sell their beloved home to put some distance between the warring clans.

Well, make that the warring fathers, because as far as Maggie was concerned, she had no beef with Owen. They had played together down on the beach as kids. She couldn't count the many sand castles they'd built or the time they'd spent out in the surf.

But after her mother had died, things had changed, and the care-free spirit of those halcyon days had disappeared. The Pierce boys had stopped coming down to the Shore for the next few years, and combined with the loss of her mom, it had created an emptiness inside her that hadn't really gone away.

By the time the Pierce brothers returned years later, the feud had gotten worse, and Owen and Jonathan had been instructed to stay away. But an ill-timed and half-drunk kiss with Owen on a moonlit summer night had proved that staying away was impossible. It had also helped the emptiness recede for a bit. Since then, Fate had seemed to toss them together time and time again in both their business and personal lives, keeping alive her fascination with him. She felt not quite so alone when he was around, not that she should get used to that.

Owen Pierce had left her once before when she'd needed his friendship the most: right after her mother's death. His on-again, off-again presence in her life proved that she couldn't count on him.

Owen stood next to his younger brother, Jonathan, who couldn't be more different. While Owen was clean-cut and corporate,

Jonathan had the scruffy hipster look going on. It was appealing in its own way, but not to her.

"Trust me, Maggie. Your families might be at war, but Owen would clearly love to sleep with the enemy," Connie said.

She blew out a frustrated sigh. "More reason to avoid him. You know I'm not the kind to sleep around."

Emma returned, color riding high on her cheeks, but not in a good way.

"Something wrong?" Maggie asked.

Emma kneeled between the two of them and whispered, "It seems the groom had a bit too much to drink and Tracy caught him being hands-on with an old flame."

"Not Amy? Tracy always lost it if she spotted him with Amy," Maggie whispered.

"Definitely Amy. Now Tracy is refusing to come out and cut the cake. I have to say, this takes the cake, literally. Married a few hours, and already there's trouble."

"Ever the hopeful romantic, Em," she kidded.

"If you think you can do better, why don't the two of you come help me talk Tracy off the ledge?"

With keen interest, Owen Pierce took note of the three women as they hurried away from the dais and into the Sinclair mansion.

"Put your eyes back in your head, Bro. She's nothing but trouble," Jonathan warned in low tones.

Owen bit back the retort that if anyone knew about trouble, it was his brother. Jonathan had always marched to a different drummer and had set out on his own as a teenager to explore what he wanted out of life. Now a successful entrepreneur, he had captured the media's attention with his innovative designs and daring adventures. That left Owen to shoulder most of the burden of the family's real estate business, as well as deal with his father's anger over Jonathan's latest newsworthy escapade.

He envied his brother's carefree spirit and determination, especially as Maggie Sinclair marched back onto the patio with her friends, an angry bride, and an obviously inebriated groom. Both the bride and groom looked far from happy as they approached the elaborate, multitiered wedding cake that had been wheeled out to the middle of the makeshift dance floor.

He worried the bride might plunge the long knife she held into her new husband, but luckily for the newlyweds, Maggie directed the blade toward the cake.

Jonathan playfully elbowed him. "Seriously, Owen. She's not for you. Father declared the Sinclairs off-limits ages ago. He would have a stroke if he thought the two of you were involved."

Involved with Maggie Sinclair, Owen thought and sighed with regret.

In a way, he'd been involved with her forever. He'd like to chalk it all up to a sloppy, hurried, and stolen kiss at eighteen and the allure of forbidden fruit. But since that kiss, he'd watched her mature into a smart, beautiful woman. One who was willing to work hard for the town and business she cared about as well as friends and family. With every encounter, he'd grown more intrigued with the person Maggie had become.

But his father had come down hard on them about mingling with the Sinclairs right after Maggie's mother's death. For years, they'd been unable to come to their Sea Kiss home, and even when they'd returned, they'd done so without their father, who refused to be so close to the family he thought had wronged him.

Not that Owen expected that Jonathan would kowtow to such rules, since his brother was the kind of man who didn't hesitate to take what he wanted.

He arched a brow and met his brother's blue-eyed gaze, which glittered with a mix of undisguised challenge and amusement. "Do you think you're the only one entitled to a little adventure in your life?" he said.

Jonathan chuckled. "My kind of adventure is way safer than what you may be considering."

"Why's that, Li'l Bro?" he asked, appreciating the sight of Maggie in a dusty-rose gown that hugged dangerous curves. Her chestnut-brown hair fell to her shoulders in soft waves and framed ice-blue eyes and a sassy, sexy face that snared his attention every time he saw her.

Jonathan took a last sip of his champagne and barely stifled another laugh. With a shake of his head, he replied, "Because all I risk is an occasional broken bone, but that..." He jerked his head in Maggie's direction as she stepped back beside Connie and Emma. "*That* will break your heart."

Chapter 2

THE BRIDE AND GROOM had departed hours earlier for their honeymoon. The guests had lingered to enjoy the beautiful midsummer day at the beach but had cleared out shortly before midnight. Connie and Emma were staying for the weekend, as they had so many times before. The two of them and Maggie had sat on the patio, sharing a final glass of champagne and listening to the peaceful lullaby of the ocean. The sweet noise of the sea had swept away the tension and stress of the day. One by one, with a simple wave and smile, they'd gone their separate ways to their bedrooms.

Maggie was finding it hard to sleep with all the thoughts rampaging through her brain. Image after image of profit and loss statements raced through her mind followed by scenes of out-of-business signs on their storefronts.

She cursed, threw back the covers, and slipped out of bed, intending to walk off the disturbing thoughts. Jerking on jeans, a T-shirt, deck shoes, and a hoodie to fight the chill that sometimes swept in along the shore, she stole out of the house like a thief in the night. Outside, the susurrus of the ocean beckoned to her.

At the end of the great lawn, she strode across the short boardwalk and down to the beach, pulling the hoodie closed against a strong ocean breeze and a misty fog that had settled all along the beachfront. She paused to look back at the home she loved so well. The fog had shrouded the mansion, making it nearly disappear. For a moment, it was almost as if she had already lost the place she loved so well.

Swiping at an errant tear, she tucked her head down and walked the familiar way southward, but as she did so, the faint scent of cigar smoke caught her attention. She glanced around and, in the dim light of an almost moonless night, saw the glowing tip of the cigar and the shadow of a man sitting on the steps of the boardwalk leading to the Pierce family mansion.

"Owen," she sighed as the man rose and she recognized his silhouette. She stopped, unsure whether he would acknowledge her, but he smiled and walked toward her. She noticed that he had changed into casual clothes, not that they lessened the sense of power that always seemed to surround him.

"Maggie," he said with a dip of his head as he sidled up to her. "You're up late."

"You too." She started walking again, alternately worried and excited that he would join her for her walk.

"Too many thoughts in my head." He matched his pace to hers, taking an occasional puff on his cigar as they strolled down the beach.

"Me too," she said, but then they fell silent. They had known each other all their lives and had been friends at one time, but in recent years, they'd kept an awkward distance. Even with the silence, there was something comforting about his presence beside her during the walk. Maybe it was that aura of innate strength and assurance in the way he carried himself. Maybe it was that she felt not so lonely with him. Regardless of the why of it, the quiet as they walked side by side along the beach soothed the riot of thoughts that had kept her from sleep.

With a half glance in his direction, she noticed that he seemed more relaxed as well, and a part of her wondered what it would be like if they could be more than just distant acquaintances. Deciding to breach that distance, she said, "Will you be at the lighthouse re-dedication at the end of the month?"

She and Owen had worked on their town's committee to repair

the destruction done by Hurricane Sandy years earlier. Federal and state funding had helped to rebuild most of the public areas, like the boardwalk. Their fundraising efforts had gone toward fixing the damage to the Main Street business area in time for the first summer season after the horrific storm, but it had taken much longer to raise the funds to fix the lighthouse and a nearby pier. The committee was still working on how to help repair the many private homes and cottages not covered by insurance and that still languished years later.

"I hope to be there. It all depends on some business items that need to be wrapped up." He paused as they neared the long rock jetty that marked the end of Sea Kiss and the start of the next town. She hadn't realized that they'd walked nearly a mile together in companionable silence. With a wry smile and a wave of his hand, they turned and started the walk back up the beach. Every now and again, he would meet her gaze and hold it, almost as if to reassure himself she was still there.

"Is that what kept you from sleep?"

"Possibly. What about you? Will you be there? Seems like we should attend, considering how much time we put into the committee."

"I've got some things I need to do as well, but it would be nice to be there to celebrate. It took so long to reach this point."

"But we did it. The town was ready for the first season. We helped a lot of people get back into their homes, even if we still have a long way to go to set everything right."

"You led most of that, Owen. I was hard-pressed to know one end of the hammer from the other," she said with a laugh, recalling her tortured efforts when they had volunteered to do some construction work on one of the damaged homes.

Owen chuckled. With a sexy grin, he said, "You did okay, and more importantly, you were there to help. People appreciated that, and they won't forget it anytime soon."

"That's not why I did it," she said.

He nodded. "I know."

His easy reply and the warmth of his gaze confirmed that he understood what had motivated her to volunteer, and in truth, she'd always known that he'd helped for the same reason. They both loved Sea Kiss and considered it home, even though they both worked and had residences in New York City.

They fell quiet again until they reached the boardwalk for the Pierce mansion. Maggie waited for him to head there, but Owen kept on walking beside her.

"No need for you to see me home," she said.

He rolled his eyes and shook his head. "I always see a lady home," he replied and did just that, going so far as to walk her up the boardwalk and across the great lawn. When they reached the patio, he looked back toward the dunes and jerked his head in the direction of the corner of the lot.

"I see you rebuilt the gazebo that Sandy took out."

"I couldn't imagine not putting it back up." When the storm surge had gouged away huge pieces of the protective dunes behind the house, it had swept the old boardwalk and gazebo out to sea.

"You always spent a lot of time there reading," he said, surprising her.

"I didn't realize you'd noticed," she replied, but as she glanced toward the Pierce mansion, she recalled that he would often sit on the second-story balcony where he would have a clear view of the gazebo.

"I've noticed a lot about you, Maggie," he said and then walked with her again until they reached the french doors to her home.

Maggie faced him and stood there awkwardly, wondering how to end the night. A handshake was way too formal given the situation. A hug way too friendly. A kiss was…unfathomable.

That Owen was feeling the same way was obvious as he rocked

back and forth on his heels and then shoved his hands into his jeans pockets. With a very masculine head nod, he said, "I guess I'll see you around."

She dipped her head in agreement and said, "See you around."

He forced a smile, pivoted on his heel, and walked away, but as he did so, she called out to him.

"Owen."

Turning, he stared at her, a perplexed look on his face.

"This was nice. Thank you."

His smile was brilliant in the dark of the night. "It *was* nice. Get some sleep, Maggie."

"You too, Owen." As she headed through the french doors and up to her bedroom, she suspected her thoughts would once again keep her from a restful slumber. Only this time, those thoughts wouldn't be about her family's business problems and losing the home she loved. They would be about something much more pleasurable.

Maggie Sinclair had been on Owen's mind a lot in the weeks since the wedding and their unexpected, enjoyable walk along the beach. He had been looking forward to seeing her at the lighthouse rededication this past weekend, only he hadn't been able to make it due to a surprise strike at one of the Pierce company's construction sites.

Owen had just settled that issue after a meeting at the union's offices, and the summer day was too nice not to take the time for the crosstown walk to his office. As he strolled up Fifth Avenue, it occurred to him that he would walk right past Maxwell's, the Sinclair family store, and he did need a birthday gift for his administrative assistant.

It was a long shot that he'd run into Maggie there, but he was willing to take the risk.

He rushed past the smaller retail stores and restaurants on Fifth

Avenue in the Twenties but slowed as he neared the Empire State Building and the Maxwell's store diagonally opposite the New York City landmark. As he stood on the corner, he appreciated the elegant look of the big, shiny windows with their displays and the graceful blue awnings above them. The navy blue was as true as it had been years earlier. At each entrance, a uniformed doorman in Maxwell blue and gold greeted shoppers and assisted them with hailing taxis and managing their bigger packages.

The building itself looked like it had been recently cleaned, the stone a pale gray that shone in the bright summer sun. Planters with flowers in a riot of colors were placed at various spots all around the building, which stood tall against most of its neighbors.

Prime real estate, he thought, although he knew that for Maggie and her family, Maxwell's was way more than that.

He crossed the street, nodded at the doorman, and pushed through the entrance and onto the main floor. He paused there for a moment as he was transported back in time. Suddenly, he was eight again, and he and his brother were in the store with their mother to visit Santa. It had been one of the last times with his mother before she left them, never to return. It wasn't difficult to picture the store as it had been back then, all done up for the holidays. He remembered seeing Maggie there with her mother during that visit, waiting in line like everyone else for her turn at Santa. She'd peeked around her mother's skirts and waved at him, a friendly smile on her face. Even at eight, her smile and bright blue-eyes had made his heart beat a little faster.

Christmas was still months away, however, and the store was bedecked in flowers and bright colors in honor of the summer season. While the decor might be lively, the activity on the main floor was nothing like it had been twenty years earlier during the holiday season. Far fewer patrons were strolling through the aisles, but Maxwell's still gleamed.

Ambling through the store, he peered at one display case after another, telling himself it was because he was in search of his assistant's gift and not because he was hoping to see Maggie. Luck wasn't on his side as he finished perusing the various items in the first aisle and doubled back along the second where some scarves caught his attention.

He was fingering one lightweight scarf, considering whether his assistant would like it, when, from the corner of his eye, he saw Maggie coming down the aisle with an older woman. Maggie was clearly in work mode, the sleeves of her pristine white shirt tidily rolled up and her hair done in some kind of fancy braid. Wisps of hair had escaped confinement and curled around her face, highlighting eyes the color of the ocean by Sea Kiss and the creamy skin along the straight line of her jaw.

Maggie walked behind the counter, moved some of the items on the display, and spoke to the woman, earning a smile and a nod. She grinned at the woman and turned to walk away when she noticed him. Her smile dimmed, and the happy look on her face turned to one of puzzlement. She strode toward him, her movements brisk, efficient, and totally businesslike, and yet no less enticing. She stopped a foot away from him and, with a slow nod, said, "Owen. It's a surprise to see you here."

"Because of the feud?" he asked. He shifted his gaze back to the scarf, because the sight of her beautiful face was just too distracting.

"In the women's section," she clarified. "I didn't realize you were seeing someone," she replied but then murmured a sharp curse beneath her breath as a becoming stain of color blossomed on her cheeks.

He was secretly pleased she might be keeping track of whether he was involved, not that he was. In fact, being a type A workaholic, he hadn't been involved in some time. He couldn't resist teasing her and said, "Actually, we see each other almost every day, and I can't imagine not having her in my life."

"Oh, that's nice," she said.

It pleased him even more that he detected a hint of disappointment in her tone. Despite that, he couldn't keep up the deception. "She's my administrative assistant and a very lovely lady. Her birthday is coming up, and I wanted to get her a gift, but I'm not sure this is right."

Maggie blew out an obvious sigh of relief and skimmed her hand along the scarf he had been examining. "This is nice for an older woman, but if she's younger—"

"She's a grandmother but quite a fashionista."

With a nod, Maggie picked through the other scarves and pulled out one in a light-taupe color with alternating bars of metallic gold and navy blue. She handed it to him, and their hands brushed, causing her to jump back a bit.

Stammering, she looked down and said, "It's raw silk, and the fabric and colors will work well with either a suit or jeans."

He placed his thumb under her chin and applied gentle pressure to urge her gaze upward. "It's lovely. Thank you," he said. When she locked her gaze with his, he hoped it was clear he was referring to something other than the scarf.

"You're welcome. If you don't mind, I have to finish my walk-through," she said and pointed toward the far side of the floor.

"Not at all," he said and held out his hand for a handshake.

She looked at it and then back up at him before finally placing her hand in his. As he closed his fingers around hers and held her hand for way too long, he decided to take another gamble. He leaned forward, brushed a fleeting kiss across her cheek, and whispered, "It was nice to see you again, Maggie."

Before she could respond or he totally embarrassed himself, he hurried away, smiling, pleased both with the gift and with himself. He might work way too much and his father might have a ridiculous hatred of the Sinclairs, but he didn't have to be shaped from the same mold. Especially when the reward was a possible relationship with Maggie.

Chapter 3

Maggie always enjoyed the peacefulness of early morning in her mother's old office in the Chrysler Building, now her main workplace. Her father hadn't changed a thing since her mother's death over twenty years earlier, which made it easy for Maggie to remember how she'd come and visited her mom as a child. She would play on the mahogany coffee table in front of the silk-upholstered settee while her mother sat across the way, working at her Victorian pedestal desk.

She could feel her mom's presence here as well as at their Sea Kiss home and the store. It was why she would do almost anything to keep from losing them. Even though her mother had been gone from Maggie's life for more years than she'd been in it, she knew that her mother would have wanted her to fight to keep the business alive and to safeguard the jobs of the many employees who had been loyal to them for years. Plus, she had her own dream to put her stamp on the upscale stores her mother's family had founded nearly a century ago.

A job made harder by the fact that her father not only hadn't changed a thing in the office, but he also refused to consider modifying any aspect of how the stores operated.

With a heartfelt sigh, Maggie rose from her mother's desk and walked to the windows. From their location fifty-some floors up, she could see all the way downtown to the new World Trade Center and the Verrazano Bridge at the mouth of the harbor. The eastern-facing windows brought a view of the United Nations and, stretching beyond that, Queens and Long Island. From her father's office on the opposite side of the floor, the vistas of the New Jersey Palisades and Hudson River were equally spectacular.

Prime real estate, her father would say, and if there was one thing her father knew about, it was real estate. His wedding gift to his new bride had been six fabulous locations in upcoming suburban areas that his wife had used to expand the reach of her family's signature Fifth Avenue department store. That real estate was one of the few things left to bargain with to help keep the stores afloat and to help her make the modifications necessary to compete in a world filled with cheap fast-fashion establishments, big-box stores, and the internet.

Returning to her desk, she sat down and opened the file folder with the earnings report that had been unofficially released, probably by a disgruntled board member and minority shareholder. As a closely held corporation where she and her father owned over fifty percent of the shares, they had far fewer reporting regulations to worry about, but they still had to have audits and reports on their financial status. She had gotten a tip from a friendly reporter that the information would be made public later that morning.

Her stomach clenched at the sight of the losses stemming from the retail division. The numbers had caused her many a sleepless night the last few weeks. Especially since she had mortgaged the family's Jersey Shore mansion for money to keep the stores running for the next few months. She was already in talks with another bank for a loan against the New York City town house she'd also inherited and lived in when she wasn't in Sea Kiss. If she couldn't turn the stores around...

For months, the other half dozen or so shareholders had been pressing for them to close the retail division, add the valuable properties to their real estate holdings, and focus solely on the real estate division in order to cut their losses. But Maggie was determined to save that part of the company for her mother, herself, and their many employees.

Closing the folder, she opened a bottom drawer in the pedestal desk and took out another portfolio, thicker by far than the earnings report. Flipping open the file, she skimmed through her notes and the collection of photos and rough designs she'd sketched to transform their signature Fifth Avenue store.

Little by little, a smile crept onto her face as she ran through her idea file and sipped the latte she had picked up on her way to the office. By the time she flipped the last sheet of paper, her latte was done, and the first sounds of activity were filtering in from the outside work space.

A knock at the door had her collecting her papers and closing the file before she called out, "Come in."

Her administrative assistant entered, a wary smile on her face and another cup of coffee in her hand, because she knew Maggie fueled her mornings with nonstop doses of caffeine.

"Good morning?" her assistant said with some trepidation, aware of what would happen that day.

Maggie smiled and accepted the large mug the young woman offered her. "You're a godsend, Sheila, and yes, it's a good morning for now."

She checked her watch. The morning business shows would soon be turning their attention to various earnings reports, and she had no doubt that the Sinclair Corporation would be a topic of discussion. Whoever had released the report without authorization had likely done so to publicly embarrass her father in the hopes of getting him to take some kind of action regarding the stores.

"Do we have to worry, Maggie?" Sheila asked while wringing her hands.

Her assistant was a single mom, loyal, smart, and highly responsible. It was why Maggie had chosen her for the job as her right-hand woman. She wouldn't violate Sheila's trust by sugarcoating what was happening. If they had to sell the stores to pay off the debt they had accumulated, many people would lose their jobs, including those in the office area, since they wouldn't need as much staff to run only the real estate division.

"It's going to be a rough day, Sheila. The numbers aren't good, but I really believe we can still turn things around."

The hand wringing stopped, and Sheila smiled. With a nod, she said, "If anyone can do it, you can, Maggie."

The weight of such unfailing belief was a difficult burden, but as Sheila left the room, Maggie stiffened her spine and flipped on one of the morning business shows. The commentary from the talking heads was harsh, but it could have been worse. One reporter even made a positive mention of some of the cost savings Maggie had accomplished by renegotiating one of their union contracts and another with a delivery firm. As they finished with their discussion about the Sinclair Corporation, Maggie shut off the television and prepared herself for what would follow now that people knew that the grand old lady of Fifth Avenue was in trouble.

The first email hit her inbox seconds after the financial reporters ended their talk. She muted her computer speakers in an effort to ignore the *bing-bing-bing* as a deluge of messages flooded her mailbox, and she phoned Sheila to warn her that she didn't want to be disturbed in case anyone called.

She hung up and leaned back in her chair. There was no doubt the situation had become dire in the last year. While her father was a whiz when it came to real estate transactions, retail had been her mother's gift, making for a good partnership at the time. But the retail arena was different now. To save the stores and the employees' jobs, not to mention the Sea Kiss home she loved, they needed to make changes in how the stores were operated. And they needed cash and lots of it. With the leak of the report, it would be difficult to get a loan from any of the banks, and worse, it was possible some of their vendors would start cutting off their lines of credit.

Opening her personal folder once again, she ran down the list of prospective white knights she had identified. After this morning, she could cross a number of names off the list. Only a few viable candidates remained, including Owen Pierce.

She didn't know why she had recently added him, except of course that she had no issue with him personally. If anything, she had long felt it was time to end the rift between the families. Maybe even explore her fascination with Owen in order to get past it.

Owen had been on her mind a lot since Tracy's wedding and their assorted meetings in the last few weeks: the late-night beach walk, their local gym, her favorite neighborhood Italian restaurant, and, last but not least, during her walk-through at the store the other day. That barely there kiss on her cheek had held the promise of so much more.

Or is that just wishful thinking on my part?

She shut her eyes tightly, picturing him in his tuxedo at the wedding and jeans afterward. Remembering him in his elegant suit as he stood in the store, thoughtfully looking for a gift for his assistant.

"Ignoring me?"

She jumped as she realized her father stood before her desk, a bemused look on his handsome face. Shaking her head, she rose and invited him to take a seat. "Sorry, Dad. I was lost in thought."

Guilt bit into her that she wasn't being completely truthful by omitting what she had been thinking about. Or rather, *who*.

"I know it won't be easy to handle the reporters or the other shareholders after this morning," her father said.

"I don't mind, except there's one question that is sure to keep popping up: What do we plan to do about the stores?"

Her father's features tightened, and his lips thinned into a disapproving slash.

"I don't want to discuss this again, Maggie. You know my position on it."

With frustration, she raked her fingers through her hair, pulling the shoulder-length strands away from her face. "It's been a very long time since Mom died, Dad. It's time to let go and honor her memory in another way," she urged.

"Really, Maggie? How do you propose we do that?" he challenged, ruddy color erupting on his cheeks. A nervous tic pulsed along his clenched jaw.

"We make the changes we need to so that the stores can be successful again. We make Mom proud of what we can do together."

"Maggie, I'm not sure—"

"Can you do that, Dad? Are you willing to take that risk with me?" she pressed, trying to make her father understand that they were almost out of options. As she met his shuttered gaze, however, she knew he was unconvinced, and that left her with few prospects for the future. As much as she wanted to honor her mother's memory and save the stores, she wouldn't do it by dishonoring her father by getting the other shareholders to give her their votes in order to have control of the board.

It was why she had mortgaged so many of her personal assets to provide loans to the company, but she was close to the end of her rope. She had to do something to convince her father to change his mind or risk losing everything.

Author's Note

Oftentimes I'm asked if there's anything of me in the characters that I've written. In this story, there's no doubt that there is a lot of me in Lara. I was the little girl hiding under the bed from soldiers and afraid to leave the car to go to school. *The Sound of Music* is one of my favorite movies, mainly because I remember sitting there with my mother and feeling that connection to the von Trapp family as they escaped Austria, just like my family and I escaped Cuba. Actually, with the exception of the threads about Carlos and a multimillion-dollar business, many of the stories in this book are my family's history. For years I tried to write that history and couldn't, but weaving those other fictional elements together with it somehow made it easier to share. Like Carmen and so many other exiles, I hope that my family will one day be able to see Cuba, but I have no doubt that America is my home now. A home that has given me so much and for which I am eternally grateful. I am blessed to be able to call the United States of America my country.